AGGIE SEES DOUBLE

Izzy Auld

iUniverse, Inc.
Bloomington

Aggie Sees Double

iUniverse books may be ordered through booksellers or by contacting:

iUniverse
1663 Liberty Drive
Bloomington, IN 47403
www.iuniverse.com
1-800-Authors (1-800-288-4677)

ISBN: 978-1-4620-1528-3 (pbk)
ISBN: 978-1-4620-1529-0 (ebk)

Printed in the United States of America

iUniverse rev. date: 5/2/2011

IZZY AULD's
mystery and suspense series with
Aggie Morissey and Adam Temple

THE FIRST IZZY AULD lost the single copy of her single novel when it blew away in a tornado! This **IZZY AULD** won the Herald House award for Best First Novel of the Year with *A Time of Rebellion*. She's been a management consultant, a professor and a secretary. Order her family-saga mysteries from Amazon.com for your Kindle reader: *Aggie Sees Double, Aggie's Broncs, Aggie's Double Crowns* and *Aggie's Double Dollies;* also travel with Adam Temple in Izzy's church-crime novels to peculiar cults in *Adam's Zoo, Adam's Yacht, Exhuming Adam's X-Ray* and *Adam's Wily Woman*.

THE VICENTE-AULD FAMILY CHART

George Washington and Rose Clark Vicente named their sons after U.S. Presidents, while Raymond Luther and Essie Auld named their daughters after flowers. Three Vicente brothers married three Auld sisters. Their children are *double cousins*—Nasty, Aggie, and Lisa (not shown are the boys). The just-plain first cousins descended from Teddy Roosevelt Vicente and his sister, Ruby Vicente. Of the older ladies, Nasturtium the First and Hepzibah are still alive, bur they play minor roles in the series that mostly features **Aggie, Joan,** and **Nicole**—three generations of lively, mischievous women.

George Washington VICENTE & Rose Clark	**Raymond Luther AULD & Essie**				
Thomas Jefferson VICENTE	Nasturtium "Nasty I" Auld	Nasty II	Nasty III	Ned Fleetfoot	
Grover Cleveland VICENTE	Violet Auld	**Agatha** Vicente Morissey & Randy	**Joan** (Jaquot) Vicente (& Jack Jaquot)	**Nicole** Jaquot Taylor & Cowboy Billy Taylor	Stevie Taylor
Abraham Lincoln VICENTE	Lily Auld	Lisa Vicente Schwartzkopf & Colonel Peter		Beth Schwartzkopf & Brad Gifford	Twins: Brianna Britanny
Teddy Roosevelt VICENTE & Hepzibah	Rudolph VICENTE & Isabelle			Teddi Vicente	
Ruby Vicente	Martha Washington				
	Betsy Ross				

PROLOGUE

"I'm going to make sure this time that we assassinate the President," said Harris. He stopped pulling his weight on the pink paddle to glower at his brother.

"Later. After you've practiced more. Prove you can do it. I told you before," said Howie. "You start with a mayor, move up to governor, then you take out the President." Howard, too, hated the President, but, of the two brothers, he was less likely to go off half-cocked. Plan, wait, work it out first, that was the way to get it right.

"Just because Diane shot Alberta, you've lost the faith."

The brothers, flush with funds, were vacationing in Vermont where they'd made their first fortune. Their pink canoe drifted lazily across the blue waters of Lake Bomoseen. After realizing a bundle with an Internet scam they called Ham instead of Spam, they'd grown restless. By that time Howie had wanted to make it in the religion game and Harris stumbled after. Howie called his new church the Salvationists but then added the prefix of Sin-Sick because he was sick, he said, of sin. Harris turned Sin-Sick into another big scam, raking in ever more dough.

When the pair first headed west to establish their faux church, nothing but a cult, really, Old lady Wallop, herding her cattle off the back of her palomino, and looking after her half-blind son, Wendell, was ready to sell out. "Taking my sonny boy to Mexico where doctorin', or so I've heard, is cheaper."

The Holloway brothers had picked up Wallop's ranch for a song, turning it into a retreat, attracting and converting their members from among the young and disillusioned rich. Which was where and when Harris Holloway perfected his method of hypnotism.

"Remember what they say, Harris," said big brother, by then the self-proclaimed head of the Sin-Sick Salvationists. "You can't command people, even though hypnotized, to do your will, if to do so goes against their personal moral fiber."

"Hah, sprinkle my special ingredients into their lemonade, they'll do anything."

His protégée, Diane, had killed all right. Except instead of Cheyenne's mayor, the hypnotized murderer had shot her best friend, Alberta. Who, before dying, shot Diane right back.

"Why'd you do that, Diane?" Howie wailed.

With her last gasp, Diane said she was mad because Alberta wore burgundy. "Blue's her color, burgundy's mine."

Now the Holloway brothers were back on Lake Bomoseen where their plans had first blossomed from seed to flower. "If only my best killer hadn't got away," complained Harris. "He was the best candidate I've ever had. With him on the trigger I could have skipped right over shooting the governor. Gone for the President straight off"

"Yeah, but his daddy rescued him and the girl. Then called in a deprogrammer."

"This time will be different," said Harris. "You'll see. When the President comes to visit his *Surrogate Mom* at this retreat, my puppet will shoot straight for the heart."

CHAPTER 1

DECIDING TO SURPRISE HER husband at home working on her stock market accounts that afternoon, Aggie had skipped out of the business meeting early. Mrs. Morissey loved her charity work, but not the nitty-gritty details of organizational administration. She left the country club to hop into her black Mercedes, and took off, on her way home. Their lovely old house, located on what was once called Millionaire's Row in Cheyenne, was hers, inherited from her grandmother.

Hershey, her chocolate Labrador retriever, was waiting at the door for her. Now why on earth hadn't Randy taken the dog for a walk? Aggie grabbed Hershey's leash from the coat rack, slipped it on him, and opened the door. Hershey was pure muscle, all one-hundred pounds of him, and he was just too strong for Aggie to hang on to. He began to bark at the skittering sound coming from the hole beneath the shed.

"No, Hershey, no!" Aggie commanded. In the next moment a skunk sprayed her dog all over. Aggie managed to grab Hershey's leash, and then she got sprayed too. While Hershey did his business, Aggie pulled out her cell phone and clicked on nine-one-one. "Yes, this is an emergency! I stink of skunk. Connect me with Animal Control."

Dammit, she couldn't count on Randy for anything. He was supposed to have run off the skunk or called the people to come take care of it.

Inside the house Aggie rummaged in the cupboards, searching for the tomato juice Clara had purchased earlier that week. Gathering the cans in her arms, Aggie dashed into the maid's suite behind the kitchen, peeled off her clothes, and jumped in the shower. Clara, a long-time family friend, was away visiting her sick sister. She wouldn't mind Aggie's using her bathroom; it was

1

closest to the back door, anyhow. Aggie hopped into the shower and spread tomato juice all over herself, then soaped with deodorant soap.

With the towel wrapped around her head, Aggie tiptoed up the stairs after the hairdryer. Meanwhile, she meant to sneak up on Randy, nuzzle his neck. Her husband was no doubt in his upstairs study, the one that adjoined their bedroom.

Instead, Aggie got the surprise of her life. First, the scent of mulberry candles burning. Then a rumpled bed. Aggie knew she'd made it that morning. A scuffling in the hall. Aggie spotted her cousin Lisa dash out of the room. Lisa wasn't wearing one stitch of clothing.

Aggie saw red. She trembled. Her husband had been making love to Lisa, her double cousin. If she'd had a gun, she would've shot them both!

Hershey came running up the front stairs and jumped on Randy, who emerged from his own bathroom wearing only trousers. "This dog's been skunked!" shouted Aggie's husband. "Get him off me!"

Aggie glimpsed the top of Lisa's blond curls as she hurried down the back staircase.

"Omigod, Agatha. You shouldn't have let Hershey near the shed while that skunk was hanging around." Randy shook his head in disbelief. "You got sprayed, too, right? Agatha Ann Morissey, you are the queen of chaos!"

"Why didn't you call the county's Animal Control like you promised? I have to do everything around here." Aggie stamped her foot, but Randy ignored her. He turned back toward his bathroom.

Aggie was furious. Rummaging in her dressing room for fresh clothes, she fantasized about throwing all of Randy's stuff out onto the front lawn as punishment for his screwing around on her. Three-plus decades of togetherness, from age fifteen. How dare he make love to another woman, and her double cousin at that! Aggie was livid.

She and Lisa were double cousins because they were related on both sides; their fathers were brothers and their mothers were sisters. The women were best friends, too. Born in the same hospital, on the same cold night. They'd been bosom buddies all their lives. Now, this—the bitter pill of betrayal.

"You can't go," Randy said. With a scowl wrinkling his face and his arms crossed like a forbidding Buddha, he slammed shut her suitcase. "Agatha, you can't even keep track of your engagement ring, how can I trust you to take care of yourself?"

Aggie didn't look at him. Nearly a week had passed since she had caught her hubby and cousin together in this very room, on this very bed, and she still couldn't meet his eyes. As for the ring, true, she had lost it, but what did that have to do with anything?

Agatha pretended to ignore her husband. "Why not? You think I'm a baby who can't make her own decisions? For cryin' out loud, Randy, we've traveled the world."

"That's the point, my dear. *We've* traveled. Not you, all by yourself."

"I'm going to Vermont with Joan, and that's that. Besides," Aggie added lamely, thus diluting her statement of independence, like adding water to his cereal cream, "Our daughter will be with me. Joan's counting on me to go with her."

"I don't know why. She never has before."

Tucking away the see-through black lace nightgown she had bought as a romantic surprise, Aggie reached for her old flannel robe and left the room. Alone in the bathroom she splashed cold water on her face. She was definitely going to Vermont with Joan.

A geologist in search of oil the world over, Randy expected his wife to stick to his side; serve as unpaid secretary, sex slave, gofer. Whatever he needed, he had but to beckon. Damn it all, she invariably obeyed him, at home and away. Having taken early retirement, he was constantly underfoot these days. With nobody and nothing to manage except her, he was determined to take over the household, tell her what to do.

The phone rang. Through the bathroom door, she heard Randy pick up.

When she finally emerged, pulling the cord of the old robe tight around her narrow waist, her husband was scowling. He picked up a pen and scribbled. His forehead a map of deep wrinkles, his brow could have been a furrowed field, ready for planting. The conversation was short and businesslike. Hanging up, he turned to Aggie.

"I agreed to a consulting job with AmRan Oil," he said. "Gotta leave in a couple of days. Won't be gone long, Agatha, so you better not get in mischief behind my back."

Aha, Randy too was leaving town, so what did he have to complain about? She kept the freezer and refrigerator perpetually stocked with food to please his finicky palette. This time was no exception. In case he returned before she did.

Suddenly Agatha had a fantastic thought. Why not retrieve that moldy food she'd discarded. Repackage and relabel it as his favorite dish. Kill him in her absence. With any luck, Lisa would be sharing a meal with Randy and they'd both drop dead.

Aggie held her breath. Would Randy expect her to accompany him as usual?

"You can't come with me this time. Hate to see you kidnapped, sold into white slavery." He smirked, as if in jest, as if suggesting who'd want to steal her? "I gotta hit several of those little *stan* countries--Kazakhstan, Uzbekistan, Turkmenistan..."

"Which one, dear?"

"Ashgabat. That's a city. Pack my bag and get me on a flight."

Aggie nodded. She must check the weather in Eurasia at this time of year so she could decide what to pack for him. As usual she would use the Internet to develop his itinerary and book flights. She had never heard of Ashgabat, didn't know whether the city had an airport. Aggie shrugged. She knew what to do and how to do it.

From her point of view, the best part—get rid of him for awhile. Thinking she could poison him by long distance was absurd. She wasn't the type to commit murder, in front of his face or in absentia. As for Lisa, Aggie hadn't spoken to her beloved cousin since discovering the pair's betrayal. If faced with the adorable little blonde, Aggie thought she might scratch out the eyes of the city's most influential social butterfly.

In the meantime, she must get her own eyes checked. This fuzzy vision had hit abruptly, as if her body as well as her heart were rebelling against the truth of Randy's adultery. The problem intermittent, she'd see fine for awhile before seeing two of everything. Pray it would clear before she and Joan left for Vermont.

Leaving her own packing by sticking the closed suitcase beneath the bed, Aggie left their bedroom to take up residence in Randy's study next door, where she switched on the computer to commence serving hubby. She could hear his voice on the phone but not well enough to know who was on the other end. Lisa, I'll bet, Aggie fumed. Or some other floozy. The murderous feelings returned to make her feel all hot and sweaty.

Forty-five minutes later, with flights confirmed and his bag packed for him, Aggie ran downstairs in stocking feet to find Randy in his den. He needed both a den and a study, he claimed. "For all my business. And for privacy." Truth was, he lounged and watched television in both upstairs and downstairs sanctuaries, which she wasn't allowed to enter while he was busy doing his thing.

Now she wore her going-to-town clothes, as Randy called them. He didn't bother to look up when she turned over the sheaf of computer printouts to him.

"You can pick up your e-tickets at the airport whenever you leave." Aggie felt like a puppy groveling at his feet, awaiting a pat on the head. Why oh why couldn't they be enjoying his retirement the way they had always planned—in romantic bliss, traveling, or at the very least being sweet and nice to each other.

When Randy neither nodded nor reached for the pages of itinerary and instructions, she laid them on the table beside him. He didn't notice her at all. She could have headed downtown for her doctor's appointment wearing the same faded old flannel bathrobe, for all the difference it would make to her beloved sweetheart. Make that *former* beloved darling. Now he might as well have been a total stranger to her.

"Back, later," she called, closing the front door softly behind her.

Joan was sitting in her car at the curb. "Where to, mom?" she asked, as Aggie crawled into the passenger seat.

Petite, five-feet-period, Aggie wore her thick hair styled after the manner of Geraldine Ferraro, one-time vice-presidential candidate. For her visit to the ophthalmologist, a some-time golfing partner, she wore a proper gray flannel business suit with ruffled lavender silk blouse and carried a leather handbag, also in gray.

"I can't go to Vermont with you while I'm seeing double," Aggie protested.

"Hie thee to Dr. Potts and get the problem fixed, then," Joan said irritably and without sympathy. "I'm counting on you to join me, mom."

"Yes, dear, I know. I've nearly finished packing."

"How did you talk Dad into letting you go?"

Aggie looked sheepish. Should she admit he forbade her? Naw, forget that. She'd turned a new leaf. If not to murder, at least to assert herself. "He's leaving town himself, dear. Off to Eurasia. Without me, this time."

Joan heaved a sigh of relief. "I expected a big battle."

"Hardly." Hey, telling fibs wasn't nearly as difficult as she'd imagined.

Joan dropped off her mother in front of Dr. Potts' office in downtown Cheyenne. She had errands and would return later, she said.

Oblivious to passersby, Aggie paused in the middle of the sidewalk near the gun shop to rub her eyes. Her ailment, temporary she hoped, was back. She was seeing doubles again; or else it was twins pushing through the doors of the store. They carried rifles, or perhaps shotguns. The pair walked directly into the bank next door, which made Aggie wonder. People didn't walk around manhandling rifles and shotguns in broad daylight, did they? She edged up to the big plate glass window, cupping her hands around her eyes to peer through the tinted glass and see what was happening.

Not much going on, everybody standing around doing nothing, as if in tableau. She stepped away from the window, her mind elsewhere.

Staring unfocused as she ambled along the sidewalk, Aggie spotted the twins again, this time rushing out of the double bank doors to run straight toward her; no, not her, rather their pickup parked just past her down the street. Shots rang out, as one of the pair stopped to point and shoot. Aggie ducked behind the fender of the Ford Focus next to the curb, in front of their brightly polished truck. She looked over her shoulder to see what the chap was shooting at. Ahah, the baker, standing in his open doorway.

Suddenly he dashed toward the curb, stained apron tied around his middle and waving his rolling pin. Aggie understood the use of kitchen weaponry. She'd welded one herself from time to time, like a month or so earlier, when she'd taken off after a bandit; run him straight out of her kitchen and across the back yard.

This time it felt like—same song, second verse. As if Lisa's mockery at her typical bumbling echoed in her ears, Aggie fumbled with her handbag, tripped over a pebble, and went sprawling on the sidewalk. The baker fell across her with an oomph. And one of the two thugs on top of him. His twin bent to help, cussing his head off.

The two thieves, still with those long menacing looking guns, but now hoisting huge money bags as well, tried to push themselves up, off and away. But Aggie stuck out a foot to trip the one closest. He bonked her on the head and she promptly passed out.

CHAPTER 2

RANDY SHOOK HIS FINGER at her. Aggie cowered. "The police said you tried to stop the thieves. I demand to know what the hell's wrong with you. You're no cop, Agatha. Certainly not a private dick."

A nervous giggle bubbled up from her belly, erupting like Vesuvius. Aggie tried thinking of a good excuse. Why hadn't she already devised a potential reply? Randy, if not Lisa, was bound to have found out she had thrown herself at the bad guys. She should have anticipated a full dose of ridicule.

Aggie opened her mouth and out came a stammer. "I, uh, expec-pected to foil the bad guys." She asked whether the look-alike robbers had got away.

"No," said Randy, admitting that Detective Walt Fletcher had praised her for stepping up like the good citizen she was, to try making a difference. Grudgingly, Randy said the mayor and police chief expected to give her a commendation the next day on the steps in front of City Hall.

One half of her brain wanted to gloat, while the other was embarrassed. Aggie didn't think she ought to be getting a medal when it was actually their friend and neighbor, Walt Fletcher, who had made the collar.

This wouldn't be the first time Walt had seen she'd gotten the honor. Just that spring she had managed to get the best of an escaped convict who thought he'd make her lovely old mansion his hideaway. After striking him in the back of the head with her rolling pin, and chasing him out the door, she had calmly washed and dried the rolling pin before continuing to roll out the dough to make her homemade cinnamon rolls. Randy had had a fit over that escapade, too, of course, though she'd had the presence of mind to wrap up the bad guy with duct tape—front, back, mouth, hands, feet. Trussed up like a Christmas ham, he'd lain helpless, out back by the shed, suffering total humiliation while awaiting Detective Fletcher's arrival.

Back then Randy had called her dumb to try such a thing, as the ending could easily have been reversed. "What if he'd killed you, Agatha? Who would make my bakees?"

Randy called cookies *bakees,* because, he said, you didn't cook the cookie dough, you baked it. Along with two or three favorite recipes for GORP— "good old raisins and peanuts"—Aggie kept her husband's tummy happy with an entire repertoire of goodies.

Now her thoughts ran rampant, from the husband who had once appreciated her performance in both the kitchen and the bedroom, not to mention at the computer, to the cantankerous old coot she lived with now. Abruptly it occurred to her that without his former full-time job with AmRan Oil, Randy might feel lost and floundering, like a fish flopped from its familiar aquarium to fall at her feet, where she was in charge of the roost. She must learn patience, try to be more understanding.

From over her antique oak table, Aggie felt several pairs of eyes accusing her. Even from her daughter. Apparently she had missed something.

Joan repeated herself. "Mom, I told dad he should enroll in the Vermont seminar, too, because it's about relationships. The two of you could learn a thing or two about how to get along during the golden years of retirement."

Good grief, just because Randy had taken early retirement didn't mean she had. Aggie had a full schedule of charity events coming up, volunteer work that included plenty of organization and management, along with the requirements of hosting a number of different social functions. She might once have found employment as a paid event planner. Plus she was involved in the very demanding business of spearheading various political fundraisers across the state for the President.

"Oh, for cryin' out loud, Joan. That's not what you told me," said Aggie.

Joan looked like she'd been caught stealing paper clips from her dad's office. "Uh, what was that, mom?"

"You said this conference was funded by a special grant, directed by a really special guy; that you wanted to learn from him, pick up some presentation strategies. And that you couldn't attend if I didn't accompany you." Aggie scratched her head. "Why was that, dear? I'm not at all sure I understand."

"I'm not sure I do, either," said Joan. "Something about the conference being short on mother-daughter pairs. Since the seminar addresses familial relationships, the grant's provisions require that every sort be represented."

"I'm not sure I understand, dear."

Joan rolled her eyes, a clear indication she'd spelled this all out before.

"Fathers and sons, uncles and nieces, brothers and sisters, cousins, different kin connections, see. For some reason, you were specifically named as an invitee. Don't ask me why."

Suddenly Aggie thought she knew. The media had labeled her Dom's *Surrogate Mom,* when in fact she was a mere decade older than the President. All because he had boarded with her while in college, long before he was elected to the most powerful position in the world. They had stayed close thereafter. And now, she'd bet an eye tooth, somebody else wanted to get close to the President. Through her. It wouldn't be the first time people had tried to use her as a stepping stone. Dom had made sure the secret service and FBI had briefed her thoroughly in how to thwart opportunists.

"Sounds pretty damn lame to me," said Randy. He turned to Joan. "Your mother was just looking for an excuse to get away from me, and you came up with this silly business."

Disgusted with them all, including Lisa, who sat across the table with her arms folded across her chest and a look of smugness spreading across her face, Agatha rose to check on the tea, brewing in its antique flowered teapot on the granite counter of her sunny kitchen. She poured cinnamon-apple tea for everybody--Randy, Joan, Lisa, and herself. Recalling Cousin Lisa's betrayal in her and Randy's very own bedroom, Aggie found it hard to look at Lisa without shooting daggers. So Aggie kept her glance stuck on the shelf overhead. The fragrance of lilacs permeated the air from the vase of flowers sitting there. Staring at the petals, she missed Lisa's cup and splashed tea all about.

Ignoring his tea, Randy stood to pace. Leaving Lisa and Joan to stare up at him, he again shook his finger at his wife, now clear across the room..

"See what I mean, Agatha?" Randy demanded, scratching his head in wonderment. "I have to watch you every minute or look what happens. Turn my back and you get in trouble. You told me you were going to the eye doctor. Instead, you fall on the ground beneath the baker," he snarled. "Then you stick out your foot and trip the robbers. I don't understand you at all; why you think you've got to take the whole world on your shoulders, solve everybody else's problems. Your duty as a wife is to me."

At five-six, and half bald, Randy had to poke out his chest and roar to make his intimidation convincing. Amazing that she had never realized he was mostly huff and puff, like a dead dandelion fluff. Not that he couldn't make her suffer emotional turmoil. He and Lisa both. Aggie felt all this brand-new hate for the pair bubbling up like gas.

As if Lisa had read her mind, Aggie's double cousin pushed back her chair to enter Aggie's inner sanctum—her cooking and baking laboratory. Lisa jerked open the door beneath the sink, grabbed a sponge and a bottle of

Lysol spray, and commenced to scrub Aggie's gleaming granite counter tops. As if to say Aggie's methods left something to be desired, and the result was pure filth if somebody didn't trail along behind her, fixing everything. Aggie gently removed the bottle from Lisa's hand.

"Don't harm my granite counter. I clean with pure soap and very hot water."

Lisa looked surprised. Shocked, actually, at the reprimand.

Aggie bit her lip and backed off. Otherwise, she might start snatching clumps of pretty blonde curls right off the top of Lisa's head. Aggie returned to the table where Joan was now doing battle with her father, who'd returned to his seat.

Aggie wasn't the only one Randy criticized; their daughter Joan, too. He had never gotten over Joan's divorce. He argued, ad nauseum, that a woman's place was beside her man, not gallivanting all over the country after first one and then another college degree. Now Joan was a university professor who also traveled, in this country and abroad, on the international lecture circuit.

A quick glance at the two of them suggested that Randy had come full circle. He used Joan's lifestyle as cause for why he kept a tight rein on Agatha. She slipped away.

At the door, Aggie called out, "I've got a meeting and need to shower and change. You guys don't need me for your debate."

"Mother!" Joan protested, grabbing her mom's sleeve. "You tell daddy. You're going to Vermont with me, right? Tell him, mom, tell him."

Just then Aggie's cell phone buzzed, making her jump. She reached in her apron pocket, clasped the phone and jerked it open, even while turning her back.

"Who's that?" Randy called out authoritatively, as if anybody calling his wife was as much her husband's business as her own.

Ignoring her husband, Aggie chirped into the mouthpiece like she was flirting.

"I demand to know who you're talking to."

"Oh, daddy, leave her alone."

"Sounds to me like your mother's on the phone with Dom again."

"Why are you surprised? This is her birthday week. Hers and Dom's."

"Mine, too," said Lisa, having returned to the kitchen island. "Except that Agatha regularly ignores my birthday whenever the President calls her." She meant the President of the United States, of course. Lisa could put as much disdain in her voice as Randy.

As for Joan, she was proud of her mom, Aggie felt sure, though daughter-dear seldom mentioned it.

Randy left the country for Eurasia and his petroleum consultation assignment in several of those little *stan* countries. Unknown to him and despite his orders to the contrary, Agatha accompanied her daughter to the New England seminar.

In Vermont with Joan, Aggie began to fantasize about divorcing Randy. Of course, then Lisa would have him all to herself, but Aggie no longer cared. What had once been magic between the long-married couple had now turned to dust.

Now she was excited about meeting new people. Dr. Petroski, Joan had said, was not only the head of the Center for Cautious Change, but also the man who had made this conference possible. Only eight people were honest-to-God paying participants. All the others, Joan and Aggie included, had come on a grant that covered expenses, including their flights, which also paid them an honorarium. So Aggie was actually earning money. With Randy out of the country, how could he complain?

"Where did the funding for this grant come from?" Aggie asked idly.

Joan's glance was indifferent. "From some odd-ball church group out in our home state. They call themselves the Sin-Sick Salvationists.

CHAPTER 3

JOAN'S APPLICATION TO JOIN the relationship group had been accepted, and here they were, in the Vermont dormitory, settled in like two ova in a fallopian tube. Beige spreads covered the twin beds and matching drapes hung lopsidedly from the windows. With bookcase, desk, two chairs, and a TV set, the place was serviceable, though hardly memorable.

The three-story dormitory building stood among tall evergreens growing so thickly the mother-daughter pair could hardly see the sky above. They discovered the learning center next door to the dorm by strolling along the twisting path through the dense forest. The fragrance of fresh green growing things, though familiar from their own mountain state, was delightful and refreshing. Outdoors, Agatha and Joan took deep breaths and grinned at each other under the pleasure of this shared experience.

Dr. Petroski's Corner for Cautious Change, or the CCC, was situated offshore maybe a hundred yards from Lake Bomoseen, in what was otherwise known as the learning center. Thus the small campus was interchangeably called the center, the corner, the complex, or the CCC camp, for short. Each building comprising the complex was designed with six sides, representing the six states of New England. Disconcerting really, Aggie said, with all those odd angles in dorm rooms, dining hall, lounge, and large and small seminar rooms.

"Okay, now we've got the lay of the land," said Joan, turning back to the dorm, "let's bathe and change and then return to the lounge to start getting acquainted."

While her daughter splashed through the shower, Aggie leaned her elbows on the windowsill to stare down at the forest floor. She spotted a pair of squirrels playing grab-ass up and down a tree and then a mama rabbit leading her baby bunnies.

"Babies, plural. That must be nice," she said aloud. Randy had contracted mumps as an adult and that was the end of her dream to populate the big house.

With the women in her family making babies while practically children themselves, grandmotherhood had come early--for her that was age thirty-two. She was sixteen when Joan came, and Joan was sixteen with the birth of Nicole. Nickee waited until she was seventeen. It was still hard to believe that Aggie could be a great-grandmother well before she'd turned fifty!

Lisa's smart-aleck crack in her kitchen about Agatha modeling herself after the cousin with the "perfect figure" was absurd. Aggie's weight topped out at a hundred-five. Maybe she could lose those extra five pounds while occupied with this seminar. Then Lisa would have nothing to crow about. Scratch that; Lisa, like Randy, would always pick on her about something. That's why the two of them deserved each other.

Aggie couldn't think through and plan everything. Let things unfold on their own, naturally. Now Randy thought she was home out west, but she intended to have fun back here in New England.

Aggie took her turn in the shower while Joan blow-dried her hair and got dressed. Daughter was quick, Mom was slow. Standing in front of the closet in lavender bikini panties with lacy matching bra, Aggie said she couldn't decide what to wear.

"What's to decide? You always wear purple, lilac, or burgundy."

"Do not."

"Do, too."

"Also black and gray. I can't wear pink. That's Lisa's color. The Nasties all wear blue." Aggie referred to another set of cousins, all with the same name, Nasturtium. All three of them, including Wyoming's Secretary of State, were nicknamed Nasty. The family and everybody who knew them well, differentiated between and among that set of double cousins by using numbers: Nasty One, Two, and Three.

Settling on a lavender print shirtwaist, Aggie got dressed before asking Joan to fix her hair. Fussing at each other like pals, they bantered back and forth. With a mere sixteen years separating them, they were closer, probably, than many a mom-kid pair.

"I meant to go around and visit the family before I left. Say goodbye."

Brush in one hand and blow dryer in the other, Joan's motions paused in mid-air. "What's with you, mom? We didn't take off for Mars, just Vermont. This isn't death."

Aggie was thinking she might never return to Wyoming. Vermont was a nice state. Why not live here instead?

"Who did you want to see?" Joan demanded.

"Hmm? Oh, everybody, I guess. Especially old Hepzibah and Aunty Nasturtium. They can't live forever, and I'd like to find out before Hepzibah dies what the heck she's been knitting all these years. Twenty-six feet long, she told me once. That's the stopping point before she makes her daughter-in-law Isabelle unravel the yarn so she can start anew."

"You couldn't see old Nasturtium, anyhow, mom. Nasty One is still down at her villa in San Miguel de Allende. She e-mailed me that she's enrolled in First-year Spanish for the third time." Obviously humoring her mother, Joan smirked.

Aggie shook her head in amazement at the courageous adventures of the oldest living sister in her mother's generation. She doubted she would ever live to be ninety, like Nasturtium, much less a hundred, like Hepzibah. Joan grabbed her mom's head to hold it still. "Be still, or we'll never get out of here. We're going to go meet people, remember. That's what you said you wanted to do."

Their trip had taken them on a circuitous route. Flying out of Cheyenne, they had changed planes at Denver International to fly nonstop to JFK, where they'd caught an Albany-bound plane out of LaGuardia, where they had taken a bus to the wee village of Castleton, where they were met, finally, by their Vermont hosts. Both Wyomingites plus a number of other pairs and groups arrived dusty and disheveled at the close of Vermont's "fifth season": summer, autumn, winter, spring, and "mud."

At the seminar every combination of family relationship was to be represented: father with son or daughter, mother with daughter or son, grandparents, siblings, aunts, uncles, and cousins; only one partnership per each of fifteen states. Joan and her never-employed mom were selected from Wyoming. The project design addressed the "stick states" and the selectees, Joan surmised wryly, were perhaps considered country bumpkins, sticks-in-the-mud ignoramuses, despite the fact that most of the conference participants hailed from university campuses and state government bureaus. The Joan-Agatha pair was the single exception. The roster was short on mother-daughter partnerships, except for her and Joan. So it didn't really matter, Joan said, that Aggie wasn't currently employed in some prestigious state office, nor ever had been.

Aggie forgot her suspicions about why she was invited. If somebody wanted to get the President's attention through friendship with her, Aggie didn't see how that would work, or why. This workshop or retreat, whatever they called it, was situated in the back of beyond. The United States President was hardly likely to drop in on them.

Before they could join the others for the orientation session, Aggie's cell phone buzzed. She would rather have a chirp or a little song, but Randy had downloaded the sound that made her think of bees buzzing.

"It's more likely to catch your attention than the peaceful sound of birds singing," said her husband. "I don't want you to miss any of my calls."

Which was probably why she jumped every time the darn thing buzzed at her. Aggie wasn't exactly allergic to bee stings, but she hated all that itching, scratching, and especially the stinging pain. Bees stinging made her think of Randy. The number showing on her phone now didn't look familiar, but it was foreign.

"Yes?" Aggie said diffidently.

"Stop sounding so timid, like you don't want to talk to me."

"Wh-who is this?"

"Your husband. Who the hell you think it is?"

"Oh, Randy, it's you." Aggie felt both relieved and anxious. She should have laid out a whole list of potential lies, ready to spiel off at him quite nonchalantly whenever he asked her one of his dang-fool personal questions. She sometimes thought he expected her to confess every time she blew her nose, or had a mean thought. Right now, however, she had to be prepared to tell him some whoppers. She wasn't anywhere near home, and wouldn't be for a whole week. Randy wasn't supposed to know she'd taken off for Vermont with Joan. "How are you, dear?"

"Fine, but I need you to take a letter. Get a pen."

At first confused, Aggie couldn't think straight. Then, remembering she was supposed to be standing around somewhere in her big house, she imagined herself in their sunny kitchen with the sun-yellow cotton and white eyelet café curtains she had sewed herself. She could be pouring a cup of tea from the flowered pot left to her by Great-Great-Grandmother Rose. Mmm, the aroma of herbal tea scented with apples and cinnamon almost seemed real.

"Yes, of course, dear. I'm having tea."

"I asked you if you had a pen at hand. I need you to take a letter."

"Of course, dear." Frantic, Aggie motioned to Joan, who unzipped her day planner to fetch notepad and pen for her mom.

In due order, with only occasionally asking for clarification, such as the spelling of a foreign name or the repetition of an unusual phrase, Aggie completed her husband's assignment. "Now what, dear?"

"What do you mean, 'Now what?' You know what. Transcribe the damn thing and get it in the mail, priority mail, overnight delivery. You know what I mean, Agatha, FedEx it."

Oh dear, Aggie didn't know whether they even had a Federal Express facility or pick-up station way out here in the Vermont woods, but she could hardly admit her quandary. She did have her laptop with her, however.

"How about if I transmit your correspondence by e-mail, dear?"

"Sure, if you can find their address. It's a Washington agency, you know."

She didn't know, because Aggie often operated on automatic pilot when handling her husband's administrative tasks and various other clerical or electronic assignments.

"Yes, dear, I'll check it out."

To her daughter after closing the phone, Aggie directed Joan to go on ahead. "I'd better take care of your father's needs right now or I'll forget all about it."

Joan's eyebrows arched toward the heavens. "Mom, tell me something."

"Oh dear, I hope this isn't personal."

"It's personal, though not intimate. I want to know whether you depend on dad as much as he does on you. He takes you for granted."

"What husband doesn't? That's marriage, dear."

"It doesn't have to be that way. Mom, pay attention to me. This seminar is important. It might actually make the difference between your saving your marriage and making it better. Versus throwing in the towel."

Startled, Aggie looked up from opening and setting up her laptop computer and arranging her shorthand notes ready to transcribe. "You're thinking your dad and I are on the brink of divorce? Whatever makes you think that, dear?"

"The way you've been talking lately. The way dad has turned into a crotchety old coot since he retired. He doesn't appreciate you one bit. Not that he ever did."

Aggie sat down in front of the laptop, merely glancing at her daughter. She wasn't ready to make eye contact. Not on this topic anyhow, and doing chores for Randy was a good excuse to keep herself occupied.

"Your father's hardly old, Joan. He won't be fifty-six until his next birthday, for cryin' out loud."

Joan threw up her arms in despair. Then she flopped on the bed and picked up a book, the third in the Stieg Larsson trilogy. "I'll wait for you, mom. Don't take all day."

Agatha smiled to herself. These young people, thinking they were so modern and advanced, yet Joan still carried around actual books. Aggie decided to show off her digital reader, and to explain that the thin, nearly weightless little thing contained several hundred novels she had downloaded, among them the translations of the same Swedish author, now deceased. Oh well, plenty of time later for things like reading novels for pure enjoyment. Right now they were headed to the common rooms to meet people and get acquainted. Agatha shivered, thinking of the nice friends they would soon be making.

Mother and daughter strolled into the seminar room with its six sides and tall windows and the drapes that matched those in the dormitory. The institutional room, much like one of those hotel rooms set aside for meetings, was arranged with four round tables and eight chairs to a table. The women were handed their seating assignments and a bundle of materials.

Excited, Aggie glanced at the other six members seated around them and wondered how well they would get to know one another. A great babble arose in the room as people at every table began introducing themselves and sharing personal data. The fun part of any conference, Aggie suspected, was interacting with the people involved. Invite a bunch of duds and you could expect a duddy session. Joan said she could testify to that, for she not only attended a lot of conventions but she ran seminars of her own, in both the corporate and private sectors.

Two members of the center staff sat at their table. The boy-girl pair introduced themselves, but Agatha, hearing impaired since birth, didn't catch their names. Next came two redheaded guys with matching red mustaches from Tennessee, and then an uncle-niece pair from Arkansas. Joan and Aggie completed this table of eight, or four sets of doubles. Couldn't call them couples, as the redheads were cousins, the big man and slender little lady were uncle and niece, and Aggie and Joan were mother-daughter.

Donald Delano, whose red mustache was by far the bushier, pulled out his wallet and extracted a business card. "I'm a professor of education," he said; expectantly, as if inviting particulars from everybody else.

Tom Carson, the uncle, promptly responded with his own card and handle. "I'm an assistant professor of technical education at Arkansas State U. And my niece is Penny, the director of computers in the state department of education."

Kristi's eyes lit up. She suggested from across the table that she and Penny had something in common. "I'm the computer operator on staff here, Penny."

"I prefer to be called Penelope," said Penny primly, dropping her head and scowling, as if in reprimand.

In the embarrassed silence that followed, Aggie reached for the pitcher of ice water to fill her glass, readying herself to speak. She hoped her daughter wouldn't tell embarrassing stuff about her, like her getting sprayed with skunk perfume, or how she'd helped to capture the twin thieves. But if Joan did, Aggie wasn't about to scold her daughter in public, like Penelope's uncle.

Soon they were interrupted with the arrival of their leaders. Dr. Petroski and Sam Jones represented the team of management consultants calling their organization the Corner for Cautious Change. The blind man, Dr. P., tall, bearded, and slightly bent, although apparently once virile and sturdy, hardly acknowledged Jones' introduction before jumping right into what would soon become obvious as one of his pet themes.

"Every human change is traumatic, even the positive ones," Dr. Petroski said in his opening address. "Marriage, birth, leaving home for college, getting promoted in the work place--all these are based on personal choice, yet these changes, too, can temporarily unbalance one's physical, emotional, and mental equilibrium. Naturally the negative and involuntary changes shake people to their roots, like getting hit with tornadoes, hurricanes, earthquakes, and other victimizing situations such as auto wrecks, or, as innocent passersby, getting in the way of bullets..."

Joan arched an eyebrow at her mom, who, by then, was wondering about the post-robbery and whether the baker was experiencing traumatic stress over his harrowing experiencing of facing down a couple of thugs. Little wonder people needed grief counselors, Aggie mused. Perhaps she, too, was under stress and should see somebody. If not because of the burglary and losing her dignity to fall splat, flat out on the sidewalk with her underwear showing, but rather because of stumbling onto the naked scene between hubby and cousin. Never mind the dramatic changes in Randy's behavior lately. She had her own set of changes to deal with, especially how hubby's new retirement attitudes, sharply different from days gone by, had sent her into a tailspin of mixed emotions.

In the midst of the session, while Joan, who had explained in a whisper, was taking time out from listening to assess their leaders and peers, Aggie's mind wandered. Was there some way she could change her life without resorting to divorce? Perhaps she could start her own business so that she would not wind up homeless in the streets. Now there was a thought. She wondered what type of business she might be good at. Maybe it would be easier to change her husband. Still, it was hard to imagine finding some way to change Randy. He had always been one-of-a-kind and stubborn. She thought back to the time they'd been in Florence and Randy had insisted on buying her an eighteen karat gold necklace on the Ponte Vecchio. Surely, he had loved her then. The next day he had embarrassed her by insisting that she wear a garbage bag on her head in the rain. With Randy, it had always been give and take.

"Most people realize that bad things will affect them, thus producing the trauma of change," Dr. P. was saying, thereby drawing Aggie's attention back to the seminar. "What we don't generally understand is that even small changes are upsetting to one's system. Whenever you propose to make a change in your life, our recommendation is to do so with caution, step by step. Thus the name of our organization, the Corner for Cautious Change." Dr. Petroski said a lot more. When his enraptured audience of two-and-a-half dozen was not scribbling furiously in their open notebooks, they were gazing enthralled at their world-famous leader. An industrial psychologist, many of Dr. Petroski's explanatory anecdotes came from his experiences in the corporate sector.

"You folks representing universities and state governments operate in the non-profit arenas of bureaucracies. Yet, you people here today hold key positions of leadership in education. Upon completion of this conference and your acquisition of new insights, we trust you'll spread our message back in your home states."

He certainly knew how to make people feel important and good about themselves, Aggie noticed. She'd marked the attentiveness of Dr. Petroski's audience, how most people sat up straighter, smiling at themselves and each other.

"Each of us brings to the workplace a lot of baggage," said Dr. P, "not the least of which is how we view ourselves as a result of the influences--both positive and negative--upon us from our familial relationships. Between wives and husbands, of course, but also those in the extended family."

Aggie shuddered. She and Randy should have enrolled in this seminar together. Better this kind of thing than their honeymoon in Saudi Arabia, where she as the bride had sat sweating on a broken-down chair in a sweltering, un-air-conditioned room, and the groom had spent the majority of his time glued to the phone.

Back in their room that evening, Joan paced the floor before sputtering, "I hate him already!"

"Hate's a pretty strong word, dear." Hah, Aggie was one to talk. "What, or rather who, is bothering you?" mama asked daughter.

Joan said it was Sam Jones, the assistant director, a cold man with steely black eyes and black hair combed straight back and slicked down with some atrocious smelling hair oil. Apple shaped with big belly, short-tempered, Sam Jones seemed eager to wrest control from the blind director.

"People make impressions in the first seventeen seconds, based on the five senses. I've told you that before, mom." Joan's major field was communications.

"'Yes, I know, dear."

Joan mumbled on before pausing. "Mom, you aren't listening to me."

"Yes, dear." Ahh, ADD, Attention Deficit Disorder plaguing her again. That's what Randy called one of her *problems*, when she invariably tuned out his criticisms.

"I was talking about Sam Jones," Joan said, drawing her mom back from the distant shore of mental meandering. "Innocuous name to match his obstreperous personality. How does Dr. Petroski tolerate Jones? He ought to fire the S.O.B."

"Now, Joan. That's a bit harsh. We don't even know Jones very well yet."

They had returned to their room following the orientation session, dinner, and Director Petroski's key address that evening. Obviously Joan had studied Jones the whole time, marking his patronizing attitude toward the director. She had resented, along with the others, his annoyance at their questions that addressed the small but necessary details comprising their settling in and learning the routine. "Body language, mom," Joan said now. "I spent the entire evening's presentation in studying Jones as much as Dr. P. Moreover, the assistant director is totally patronizing, especially to young Penny. She appears insecure enough as it is, she doesn't need him pointing out her inadequacies."

"*It's quite easy locating the facilities,*" Sam had snapped at poor Penny, which is what Joan described to her mom next. "*You'll find them marked with skirts for females and long pants for males.*" Joan continued with repeating the exchange.

"We're supposed to notice drawings in the dark of night?" Penny had muttered to Joan. Before the communications professor had a chance to reply, the girl's uncle had commenced growling at her.

"Hush, child! Don't you have the least little bit of sense to talk like that in public? Keep your mouth shut, and don't embarrass me."

Joan said to her mom that furthermore she was thoroughly disgusted with Jones' fawning, his patting and pawing of several of the younger women. "I predict he's headed for trouble," Joan said. "He's mistreating professionals." Aggie sympathized, but had no recommendations. "After humiliating Penny in public," Joan continued, "Jones pats her head, then rubs her back, right down to her bra. I swear he was pawing around trying to unfasten it."

"Good grief."

"Yes, indeed, mom. I'm sure you'll see what I mean if you watch and listen to Jones more carefully."

"I thought we were here to listen to Petroski." Aggie smiled to temper her tone.

Their first assignment as seminar "students" was issued at the close of the evening: they were expected to return to their rooms to preview the week's program.

Aggie made coffee in the Mr. Coffee machine she'd packed in her luggage and Joan set out cups. They were expected to tune to the closed-circuit television program. The conference presenters had each prepared a five-minute promo describing their topics. From these brief summaries, the participants were to sign up for their first five choices out of a possible eight, taken from the following topics:

- family relations and health
- identifying relationship traumas
- socio-psychological influences on family relationships
- using positive paralanguage and body language to improve familial communications
- intra-family dynamics
- conflict resolution
- carrying familial pressures and traumas into the workplace
- identifying psychopaths and sociopaths within the extended family.

Aggie knew she'd have trouble eliminating topics. Every single title had caught her fancy. Well, except, perhaps, for the subject of workplace relationships. Having never worked an actual wage-paying job in her life, she'd have trouble relating to some of the issues to be addressed. When she discovered, off the television screen's further information dialogue, that it was Sam Jones who would handle the condensed version of a semester-long course, Agatha was just as glad she'd bypassed the workplace topic, dismissing it out of hand.

"You know what, Joan?" Aggie said, with a playful snicker. "They forgot a very important topic."

Absentmindedly replying with a mumbled "Huh?" Joan's attention was captured, as always of late, by Jones, who couldn't keep his hand off his balding head, nor his glance off the more shapely girls. Unlike his colleagues who spoke individually in front of the camera lens in an empty room, Sam's formal promo presentation was conducted with a full audience present, as if this was a repeat performance for him.

"Sex," said Aggie in her huskiest voice, as if yearning for the real thing, not just talk. She was well aware of Joan's interest in Jones, and it wasn't a positive reaction, either. She stared at the man, not like she could eat him up, but rather beat him up!

At last Joan gave her mom a cursory glance. "I suppose. But frankly, I couldn't care less." She voice sounded as flippant as the hand that tossed a few fingers in the air.

Aggie wondered when, or rather, whether, Joan would ever get interested in men again. Frankly, she figured not ever, not unless she got back together with her ex-. Those two were meant for each other and should never have broken up.

Aggie sighed, turning her attention to a new topic, specifically, the last one on the list, the one about identifying bad guys in the work place. Or in any family, group, or organized setting, for that matter.

Like, for example, what if or whether, there was a single psychopath or sociopath walking among them, here at the Vermont seminar? Although she had majored in psych-soc, that was a good many years earlier, and she was no longer sure she could differentiate between the two deviants. One hated society and the other himself? Or herself? Or perhaps people in general. Agatha thought she remembered one thing correctly--they might inflict untold torture on others, but simultaneously they could hardly bear a splinter's worth of pain delivered to themselves. Meaning those creeps in the horror movies who could produce a belly laugh bubbling up from their own insides with every fingernail they jerked out by pliers or every gash to the flesh from a serrated knife, ax, or chain saw, they couldn't bear it if you tapped them on a knuckle. Seemed like a strange concept, yet what of all those psychopaths who shot up a school, store, or church, killing a half-dozen at a time with the sweep of their UZIs? They must take delight in their murderous sprees. And yet, as it often turned out during the aftermath that included in-depth analyses, for the prior duration of their whole lives there were few who identified them as worse than unusual, perhaps just looking or acting nerdy.

Agatha vowed to study the whole group when they reconvened the next day. What if a sociopath walked among them? Might Sam Jones, or whoever had chosen the participants, specifically and purposely have tagged a really bad person to join them? What for, just for the heck of it? He, himself could be one, and wasn't there a saying that *It takes one to know one?* Joan might be right. Sam Jones, assistant director, might bear watching.

Getting serious about her purpose tonight, Aggie started paying attention. Joan was already finished! After reviewing the speakers' promotional segments, for the third time, Aggie concluded she'd probably try to sign up for just about everything. This was fun. She hadn't taken classes of any kind for an age. Joan finally suggested that they choose different presentations. They promised to share notes and impressions, to get all-round exposure to the whole conference. They signed their sheets and returned to the crowd. Time for the next activity.

Later that night a number of them, young and old, broke away to go into Rutland, sixteen miles beyond Castleton, to find a bar and party--dance, drink, laugh, start breaking down the barriers of strangership. Joan left with them but Aggie opted for the small group gathering like chicks in a henhouse to hear more from Dr. Petroski.

Sitting around in his sumptuous suite on cushions, while others leaned against the walls, they sat, enraptured, like the twelve disciples at the feet of Jesus; or Mohammed; or Confucius, maybe; or Socrates.

Paul Petroski had lost his sight in Vietnam, he said. Returning to the States he'd learned Braille, studied for his bachelor's in business and technology, his master's in education and history, and a couple of Ph.D.s in philosophy and industrial psychology. What a conglomeration; he'd certainly run the gamut. All without benefit of private tutors, he said. A consultant now, Petroski regaled his entranced audience for what seemed minutes but was actually hours, taking them into the post-midnight period of relaxed contemplation. From memory he quoted facts and statistics peppered with amusing anecdotes to convey his knowledge, experiences, and theories. Aggie felt the thrill of intellectual and emotional stimulation. No matter what questions anyone posed, Dr. P answered--calmly, knowledgeably, and with care, compassion, and precision.

The session was interrupted, at last, when Jones burst into their quiet and by now cohesive unit to berate them for keeping the director awake. "Get outta here. Go to bed. Paul's not a well man, you know."

They didn't know. How could they have? He seemed fit, mentally.

Back in the room they shared, Joan was fast asleep. Just then her cell phone sang to her and she bolted straight up, immediately wide awake. She reached for the instrument off her bedside and popped it open.

A few moments and a number of questions and pauses later: "It was Cherri Chavez, one of my chickadees, or will be with me the fall semester, I trust," Joan said. "Cherri apologized for calling so late, forgot about the time difference, she said. Trouble with her application, getting into my graduate program. Minor problem, no doubt. I'll make some calls tomorrow, straighten this all out." Joan flopped back down, returning to sleep almost at once.

Aggie glanced down at her daughter, amazed that Joan could come awake so fast, tend to people she cared about, then fall back asleep. Some professors, like Joan, must be like firefighters, medical doctors or homicide investigators on duty.

Clad in robe and slippers over a long nightgown covered with tiny lavender flowers and trimmed in lace and ribbons, Aggie left their dormitory room to tiptoe down the corridor. She wanted to breathe the cool night air off the lake. Tucked in among the evergreens and deciduous trees surrounding Lake

Bomoseen were a number of large houses and smaller cabins--all of which the natives referred to as "camps."

En route to the front door of the dorm, Aggie rounded one of those odd angles in the hall to nearly run smack into Assistant Director Sam Jones. She backed away silently. What was this creep doing prowling the place in the wee hours? Had he just emerged from some lady's room, a naïve lass who had readily succumbed to his wily ways? Apparently Sam could project an appealing façade when he chose; turn on and off the charm like pinching tight a water hose to stem the flow or release it in a big spurt when desired. Like daughter Joan, Aggie had watched the predator closely all that afternoon and evening even while getting her intellectual thrills from by Dr. Petroski.

Peeking around the angled corner, Aggie saw Jones glance slyly right and left. Satisfied possibly that he was alone and his actions unnoticed, he stealthily twisted the doorknob of the big suite. One hand over her mouth as if to capture an unruly gasp, thereby revealing her presence, Aggie pushed herself tight against the wall to remain still as a corpse. Jones disappeared into Dr. Petroski's suite, closing the door as quietly as he'd opened it.

Perhaps the two men were gay. That would explain a lot, Aggie concluded; Jones' protective stance toward Petroski, in particular. As for the manner he adopted toward the conferees, that could be jealousy, resentment of the boss. Their sexual preferences were no business of hers, of course.

CHAPTER 4

BETWEEN FATIGUE AND STUDYING Jones, Aggie struggled to concentrate on the morning session. For one thing, she had to strain to hear. Hearing-impaired from birth, Aggie had once begged her double cousin Lisa, who was also hard of hearing, to enroll with her in a lip-reading class. It was disappointing to discover they would never be able to decipher every word. Lisa forgot most of the skill, opting for hearing aids.

Now Aggie had to keep her eyes pinned to the speaker's face if she were to combine both skills--hearing and reading lips. That plan increased the number of words coming through.

Meanwhile, she had begun developing a secret section in the back of her notebook--an account of Sam Jones, his activities, and the impressions he generated among the others. Whenever he spoke to them in that harsh, grating voice, people responded with negative body language: squirming, shuffling their feet, staring at the walls, and lowering their eyes or frowning. Flipping back and forth between this sleuthing diary and her class notes proved distracting.

Also disturbing was the man seated at table four behind her. Introducing himself as "One of the Houstons from Idaho—not Houston, Texas, hee haw," his name was either Mick or Max. Aggie hadn't differentiated between father and son, or which first name belonged to whom. But one of them had that annoying habit of jiggling his leg and foot up and down. Except that Max, or Mick, whichever, thumped when he pumped, so she mainly heard a thump thump thump, pause, thump thump thump in her good ear.

Aggie wondered whether a hard stare might make Houston aware of himself and his annoying habit. Probably not. Besides, to be rude in kind wasn't her style. Tom Carson, at her own table, picked up the beat and tore into Houston with a steely look, glowering from leg to foot and back again. Houston merely smiled, continuing to pump and thump.

Meanwhile, up front Sam struggled with overhead transparencies in one hand and a stack of handouts in the other. Reggie, from her own table, leaped up to go help the assistant director. Enlisting Kristi to cover the opposite side of the room, the two young people, staff members, quickly distributed papers among the conferees. Dr. Petroski, as the morning's single presenter, used the diversion to sip from his water glass and to clear his throat with a loud harumph.

Aggie continued to observe her fellow table mates. Reggie and Kristi belonged to their group. As members of the center staff, they would be coming and going, they said. Kristi, the seminar's computer operator, was young and cute. Reggie, the food manager, was young and gangly.

Next to Joan sat the Arkansas pair, Penelope and her Uncle Tom Carson. Penny's pale, thin hair fell across her face like a gauze curtain fluttering in the breeze. Her skinny body looked anorexic. Finger and wrist bones appeared so fragile, Aggie was reminded of a skeleton. The physical impression the girl projected combined with downcast eyes and whispery voice left Aggie thinking a ghost had joined their circle. Aggie recalled that Penelope served the state of Arkansas as a computer director. The back-room job made sense to Aggie, given Penny's self-effacing, introspective manner.

By contrast, the young woman's Uncle Tom was big and loud and blustery with a shaggy beard. His was the typical football player's physique, huge with a neck as thick as the mighty oak. However, his chest didn't sprawl across the landscape or expand, like her Randy's, when he huffed and puffed. Concave, in fact; symptom of heart disease, maybe.

Returning to the table, Reggie played host, pouring water for everybody before resuming his place. Kristi and Joan exchanged smiles. Tom stared at his niece. To be more accurate, he frowned down on the top of his niece's head. Eyes on her fingers, Penny seemed oblivious to Tom's scowl.

Aggie couldn't recall much about the other two guys seated at their table, even though she had pocketed their business cards. Their backs were turned, as they faced the speaker. Plenty of time to get acquainted later.

People had already nicknamed their director; calling him, even to his face, the abbreviated "Dr. P." His voice resonated. When he said we should *Accentuate the positive, eliminate the negative* as a means of improving relationships, he smiled and looked right at her, one hand stroking his beard, barbered into a Van Dyke shape. Aggie smiled back, a natural transaction-- get one, give one--hardly aware he couldn't see her; Poor Dr. P couldn't see anybody or anything.

Aggie had read or heard his philosophy before. When you're mad at somebody all the bad feelings come out. To feel better about him or her, you're supposed to recall the good times. Okay, she could do that. What was good about Randolph Morissey? Thanks to his prodding, she'd taken a degree. He didn't want an uneducated wife, he'd said. That was a good thing, surely. Not that she could ever think how to make a living from her psych-soc studies.

Dr. P. spoke articulately and succinctly, moving smoothly from one topic to the next, like sailing across Lake Bomoseen. Or smoothly, like a baby's bottom. Smooth as butter or cream? Typically, Aggie's mind meandered down several paths simultaneously. She could have been Hansel leading Gretel through the woods.

One nice thing about this seminar was the opportunity to spend time with her daughter. The next best thing was getting away from both Randy and Lisa. A whole week without pretense or hate. If she could push their affair to the back row, she could free herself awhile from the debilitating feelings of hate. Then, too, she might actually learn something. Okay, she promised herself, for this one week, don't hate or resent or even get mad at either Randy or Lisa. Easier to do when they were half-way across the country, as with Lisa, or half-way around the world, like Randolph.

Dr. Petroski had said an upcoming topic was assertiveness training. She could use a big dose of that. Nearly everybody in Dr. P.'s audience sat mesmerized. Like Aggie's daughter beside her, people appeared to move only when scribbling in journals.

Everybody sat in awe of this man, except one. Sam Jones, Aggie noted, stood off to the side, leaning against the wall and darting his squinty-eyed glance from the director to the participants and back again. A disdainful sneer played across his lips, coming and going like a stage actor responding to cue. She couldn't imagine what cues stimulated the changes in this despicable man; changes from positive to negative, and back again.

Aggie whispered in Joan's ear that between travel and her late night out, she was too tired to concentrate. "After lunch I'll grab a nap. Take notes for me."

At the mid-morning break while Reggie rolled in a big urn of steaming coffee, its aroma enticing, Aggie hurried away to use the facilities. In the ladies room she tried to initiate a conversation with Penny. The pitiful looking waif barely glanced up. Irritable, she seemed deeply depressed. Thinking the girl might warm to an older woman, Aggie stuck with the Arkansas computer director as they passed down the hall.

On the way back to the conference chamber, the pair passed a small room designed as a worship center. Aggie clutched Penny's arm. "Wait, dear, shall we visit the chapel and light a candle for someone?" Ordinarily her choice would have been Randy, first; followed by various family members in pain or trouble.

Without a word Penny pulled away. As if seeing a ghost she stared into the dim and silent room. Aggie shuddered, for she had sensed not the calming Spirit of the Lord, but a cloud of evil, descending upon them as if it were a fog.

Penny fled down the hall—perhaps she had a thing about organized religion. Aggie found herself entering the little chapel and kneeling down before the altar.

"O Lord," she prayed. "Help me to forgive Randy and Lisa and move on with my life. Help me to understand them and to understand you better. Right now, I feel lost inside without the love of my husband and I need your guidance, Lord."

Aggie felt suddenly lighter, as if a weight had been lifted from her shoulders. She left the chapel and returned to the conference.

The rest of the morning passed with more enlightening ideas dropped like raindrops into the mouths of thirsty babes. Aggie wished she could pay closer attention to the meat of this meal, but she was so tired. When the noon break arrived, she looked around for somebody who might need comfort or companionship. They could help each other, as she needed something interesting enough to keep herself awake.

All her adult life Aggie had been as concerned with the needs of others as with her own petty problems. She was the typical caregiver, meaning a nurturer. Despite her recent change of purpose, her loving character burst from the depths of her soul to emerge in the light of day. Once more she felt like her old self.

"I must go see about Penelope," she told Joan, as her daughter came up beside her. "She seems to be in some sort of trouble."

With her hands full of notebook, handouts, and additional materials she'd talked Dr. P. out of sharing with her, Joan was preoccupied. She briefly rolled her eyes, much in the manner of her daddy, while muttering resignedly: "You found another lost duckling to mother? I could have guessed."

Once upon a time it was Dominic Alexander Davidson Aggie had befriended. Now Dom was President of the United States and the two had remained close friends. He regularly called her just to chat, he said. When her cell phone buzzed and she glanced down at caller ID, the "restricted" notice caught her attention. She smiled, thinking of Dominic.

Aggie suspected that Dom, like Randy, was checking up on her. Her diminutive size seemed to affect some people, especially men, like that. They wanted to take care of her, like she was incapable of managing on her own. "How are you, Dom?"

The President suggested they celebrate their birthdays together.

"If you're inviting me to the White House this week, Dom, I can't come."

"Randy giving you a hard time again?" The President chuckled, although he had not always been so accepting of her husband's attitude.

Randolph Morissey and the President never had gotten along, not even back when Dom was enrolled at the U and making a name for himself on the western rodeo college circuit and bringing home trophies to the University of Wyoming. Not even when Dominic was elected student body president. Randy could have been jealous of the attention his wife gave to the promising young man. Because Randy also ignored Dom when Aggie chaired the Presidential candidate's political campaign in Wyoming. By then Randy was voting the opposite ticket and demanding that his wife share his political inclinations.

"I vote for the man—or woman; not for the party, Randy. Besides, I must vote my own conscience."

With that, the battle lines were drawn and no matter what Aggie said or did (or the President, for that matter), thereafter, Randy was not about to come over to their side. Frozen fast, his feelings for the President might as well have been set in cement.

Now Dom suggested he might come to Lake Bomoseen so they could celebrate their birthdays together. "The first lady and the first miss, too, of course."

Aggie knew and loved both Julia and Jerica, so she might have agreed, except for the uneasy feeling that swept over her like a wave of ominous premonition. "I don't think it's a good idea, Dom. Do you suppose it's safe for you to come to Vermont?"

"Lordy, Luv," Dom said, the down-home language of his home state of North Dakota slipping through the crack. "I don't know why not. Surely Lake Bomoseen is as safe as Camp David. We take off for the Presidential retreat every now and then."

Both of them chuckled at the absurdity of a bomb going off at the CCC Camp, with or without the President's physical presence. "You be careful now," Dom said, breaking the connection.

Again on the lookout for Penelope, Aggie headed down the hallway. Rounding one of those odd-angle corners, she discovered Penny caught in the middle of an altercation, a verbal exchange that threatened to go physical.

Shivering frightfully, Penelope hovered a few feet behind her uncle as Tom shook his fist in the face of Sam Jones. "You don't fool me. You're nothing but a dirty old man, hitting on women. I saw you at mid-morning break. You had Penelope cornered behind the potted palm. Think you can fondle an innocent, frightened girl, eh? I'll show you a thing or two!"

Tom let fly. Sam dodged. Tom's fist smacked into the wall behind the assistant director's head. Penny's uncle briefly paused in his tirade to rub his knuckles.

Quickly Aggie retreated to hide behind a potted palm. She didn't know whether to step forward, embarrass the men into civility, or stay hidden.

Switching tactics, Carson grabbed Jones by the shoulders. He snarled menacingly, "Keep your hands off my niece or I'll turn you into Shredded Wheat!" Trembling, Tom then snatched at the shirt Sam wore, gathering it up in his hand to give it a hard shake. Sam cowered but said nothing.

Penny tugged at her uncle's sleeve. "Please, Tom, leave him alone. You'll get us both in trouble." Her uncle ignored Penelope.

"Stay out of it, Penny. I'll tend to the S.O.B., this damn tub of blubber!"

"No, no. Let's don't make waves, Tom. Please."

Aggie peered between a couple of palm fronds to see better. She had no problem hearing this close up. Despite Penelope's efforts to shush her uncle, Tom bellowed a few more expletives at Jones. Releasing Jones' shirt, Carson finally stalked off, Penny timidly following.

The whole time, Aggie realized, Jones had neither said a word nor changed expression; not a flutter of eyebrow nor a twitch of muscle. Other than jerking his head away from Tom's flying fist, Sam had stood as still as an ice sculpture. When the Arkansas pair departed, though, Jones' ice rapidly went into melt mode. First there was the squinty-eyed, pursed-lips sneer, followed by drop of jaw; then the collapsing of belly over buckle and slump of shoulders. Finally, he seemed to collect himself, as if he were his own sculptor gathering up the ice shards that had been whacked away.

Aggie resumed breathing. Another trip to the ladies room was essential. The terrible encounter she'd witnessed sent her bladder into overdrive.

She joined Joan at their luncheon table, hesitating whether to share the stomach-churning scene just witnessed. No, she changed her mind. Aggie knew how to keep secrets, and this one was Penny's, not hers, to share.

Two more pairs of seminar participants joined Aggie and Joan. Lucille and Maude were sisters from West Virginia, but not members of Agatha's table. The men introduced themselves as father and son from Idaho, but Aggie didn't catch their names.

Beside her mom Joan nibbled at her salad, while Aggie listened to the chatter of these people—every one of whom was assigned to table four. Their gossip addressed fellow group members. Aggie didn't know any of them and wasn't attracted by the backstabbing.

Mentally she reviewed her secret notes. By lunchtime she had actually recorded more scribbles about Jones than from Dr. Petroski's lecture.

Sam Jones soon interrupted the idle chatter. Striding to the front of the room, the assistant director was, as Joan put it, a *picture of pompous portly pretentiousness.* He immediately proceeded to alienate most of the diners with his long list of do's and don'ts. *Don't play loud music or make any disgusting noises after ten, do take showers, don't litter, do clean your rooms, don't disturb the staff, do study your notes,* and on and on.

"Great jumpin Jehosephat," grumbled the Wisconsin grandpa and professor from the table three group now clustered behind Aggie and Joan. "You'd think we were kids at summer camp."

Dr. P didn't join them for lunch. Perhaps he really wasn't well and Jones therefore assumed the role of protector, to stand as buffer between the great man and his adoring fans. Aggie added this supposition to her notes.

Following lunch Joan went off to join a group singing around the piano, some of whom she'd partied with the night before. Aggie preferred to nap.

Presently Joan burst in, slamming the dormitory door. "I could kill him!" she muttered. "Jones changed my schedule, for no reason. Just glared and growled at me. And all because I wouldn't submit to his advances."

Aggie sat straight up in bed. "What!? He came on to you?"

"Started feeling me up. Right there in the hall. Quick as a pickpocket, Sam plunked one hand on my breast and the other darted for my crotch. Before I could bat an eye, he goes squeeze, squeeze, in both places. Me, a professional colleague he's attacking. Me? I'm dropping my jaw, don't know whether to spit or go blind."

"Joan, that's terrible! What are you going to do? Report him to Dr. P?"

"Of course I am." Joan stalked off, slamming the door behind her.

With her quiet nap forgotten, Aggie donned her aerobic-workout clothes to quickly follow. Not fast enough, though. Instead of going to the director's suite, Joan slipped away, out the front door and down the path into the heavily wooded area surrounding the complex of buildings.

Losing sight of her daughter, Aggie nearly panicked. She knew now how Tom Carson had felt when he attacked Sam over his niece Penny.

What if this abuser had caught Joan out here alone? Less fit than her mother, the slender professor would be no match for her molester. Sam could knock down Aggie's darling child and have his way with her in no time.

Wearing sneakers and purple sweatsuit, Aggie thought she had the advantage over puffing, potbelly Jones. She could easily run, kick, or grab a fallen limb to beat the spit out of him, if it came to that. She caught her breath, pausing a moment to reconnoiter. Should she continue on the left path or return to the fork and take the other one? She couldn't imagine how Joan had managed to disappear so quickly.

Rather than dash about like Bambi after his mother was shot, she'd best collect her wits. After no more than another couple of dozen yards, Aggie paused, this time to stand perfectly still and listen.

And <u>then</u> she fell apart. For what she heard made her flesh crawl as if her clothing had been suddenly invaded by small fuzzy creepy critters.

What she'd heard was muffled crying followed by the thrashing of a wild animal. If not a wild creature, it could well be a human predator.

CHAPTER 5

AGGIE ARRIVED AT THE foot of the big tree surrounded by bushes in time to see a man bend low over a crumpled figure. It had to be Joan lying on the ground, sobbing, her hands clasped over her face. Short wavy red hair and a stricken figure were all that registered.

"Joan, Joan!" Aggie screamed, raising the limb she'd grabbed from beside the path to swing it in a wide arc over her head.

"Wait, wait!" hollered the hovering figure, backing off from his thunderous-faced attacker. He threw up his hands to shield himself.

Though the message her eyes sent to her brain was swifter than the speed of sound, it did not close connections fast enough to squelch her ongoing thrust with the limb. The defendant ducked and her weapon crashed and splintered against a tree.

"What are you doing to my child?" Aggie shouted. She didn't wait for an answer but spun back to help Joan.

The mustached redhead stood on his own. It wasn't Joan but Kurt! This pair belonged to her own table. "What on earth?" she gasped.

"That's what I say," said the redhead's partner, who wore an identical red mustache. "Have you gone mad, woman?"

Aggie apologized profusely. She couldn't be sorry enough, she said; she had no excuse save fear. She had no intention of revealing to these strangers that what had prompted her bizarre behavior was the despicable assistant director. She had sincerely believed it was Sam molesting her daughter!

After witnessing the altercation between Carson and Jones, she had come to suspect that Sam was a pervert. Maybe the kind of guy who swings both ways. Neither Joan nor Penny was safe from him. Or even Dr. P.

Donald reintroduced himself and his cousin Kurt, as they had done the previous day. "We're the Delanos from Tennessee, ma'am," Don said slowly, his agitation making his Southern accent more pronounced.

Aggie explained to the two redheads that she thought somebody had attacked her daughter. "Joan, too, is a redhead. Well, almost."

"Yeah, I noticed," Kurt said, grinning.

"And then what?" Donald barked. "You mistook me for a grizzly? Or perhaps an elephant tromping on your daughter? You could use a dose of common sense, plus a little courage."

Hell revisited. Don's words echoed Randy's recent hurtful insults.

Kurt continued to grin at her. In fact, he giggled right out loud.

"No, wait; wait for me," she called as Donald headed out, hauling Kurt with him. "I said I was sorry, that I was just trying to protect my daughter." They marched on. "At least you can tell me what was happening back there in the woods. I deserve to know that much."

"You don't deserve to know anything," said Don.

"Sure, she does," argued Kurt. "Hold on, Donny."

The cousin pair, also wearing sweats and who also had obviously skipped an afternoon session, paused at last. Don stared straight ahead, but Kurt turned back to await Aggie. Sympathy written across his pretty features, he smiled tentatively, as if making a decision. They had stopped beneath the overhanging branches of a towering pine tree. She watched as they whispered and argued. Then they returned to her.

"I've been watching you, Mrs. Morissey," said Kurt.

"Who, me? Why is that?"

"Yes, you remind me of a favorite aunt. You're a comforter, aren't you? Looking after Penny, that kind of thing. Well, Mrs. M., I'd like your advice."

"I'm not very good in the advice department. But of course I'll listen."

"Okay, I'll tell you. But you've got to promise to keep my secret, okay?" Aggie nodded. "Down in Tennessee, ma'am, I'm an educational consultant in the state department of education. See, ma'am, it wouldn't do for the administration to learn the truth about me. I'd be fired on the spot. Never again get to work with teenage boys in the public schools. I'm gay, you see."

"Jones suspected the truth, and accused him of it," Don added, grabbing Aggie's other arm. Donald, too, seemed willing to talk, now that Kurt had broken the secrecy barrier, like Cousin Peter's supersonic Blackbird flying at Mach 3. "Jones called Kurt a damn fairy and said he'd report my cousin--and me, for hiding the truth--to our state superintendent of schools..."

"And I'd be found out and fired. Don, too, for complicity..."

"I'm a professor of education and Kurt and I often work together in the public schools, both of us with kids. So I'd be fired, too. Both of us would be. Probably black-balled for life; couldn't get jobs of similar caliber anywhere."

"Good grief, in this day and age? Now who's being silly?"

"You don't understand the climate down where we live, ma'am. Real Bible belt country. I tried coming out of the closet a few months ago and it was purely disastrous. Got a preachin' to, like you wouldn't believe; told to go and sin no more. To seek help and guidance from my preacher and the Lord. So, now you know, ma'am. You won't tell, will you? Ma'am?"

"Of course I won't. Your secret is safe with me; it's your own business." Out of the woods now, they walked three abreast. "What I still don't understand is what your confrontation with Jones had to do with your accident out in the woods."

"Kurt ran out the door, with me close on his heels," Don admitted. "Right after Jones accused him of being gay, and then said he would report it to the Tennessee state superintendent of schools and perhaps also the university where I'm employed. He said he hadn't made up his mind, yet, exactly what else he might do." Don's voice quivered with anger. Then he lowered his voice as the trio drew close to the central building. Others were now within earshot. "In the woods Kurt stumbled, twisted his weak ankle, and fell. He was crying from the pain when you burst onto the scene."

Aggie said goodbye, again reassuring the men that her lips were sealed. She felt like employing the childish gestures of zipping her lips and crossing her heart, but they could find that insulting.

Imagine their fright over Kurt's homosexuality being discovered. She shook her head. Hard to believe.

Then she recalled what had happened in Wyoming to Matt Shepard, the small gay university student. A couple of rednecks had lured Matt from a bar to beat and torture the poor lad. Next they crucified Matt by tying him to a fence, where they left him to die a lingering and terrifying death. The media had promptly arrived to make of Shepard's murder the national focus on gay and lesbian discrimination. Various minority groups showed up to demonstrate and protest, followed by a bunch of Bible beaters who took the opposite view, accusing gays of sinning against God's word. Soon Wyoming was projected as a place full of rednecks. And if all that wasn't bad enough, two movies and a Broadway play had been made of this horror story.

Oh, yes, Aggie could believe that some people still gave gays a bad time.

It wasn't until later that she wondered whether they were putting her on. It didn't make a whole lot of sense why Sam would threaten the Delanos with his knowledge, unless he intended to capitalize on it by blackmailing them. They hadn't mentioned that, and she hadn't thought to ask.

Aggie found Joan in the lounge blithely engaged with her new friends in chatting happily and laughing gaily, seemingly without a care in the universe. And all the while Aggie had been running about in the woods, going without her nap, and winding up confronting and attacking strange men. She must collect her wits, and stop imagining she was seeing bad guys around every corner, where none existed.

As for Joan, when confronted she said she'd changed her mind about reporting Sam to Dr. P. "I ought to be able to handle one dim-witted old fool," Joan said.

Before dinner, while they exchanged places between shower and the desk that served as makeup table, the room's landline phone rang. When Aggie emerged from the bathroom, hair wrapped in a towel and another tied modestly across her ample bosom, Joan was tossing clothes and cosmetics pell-mell into her luggage.

"I have to return to campus, mom. Cherri Chavez called again. She needs me. Despite all the calls I made this morning, the graduate school won't admit her to my program. The dean refuses to believe that Cherri's qualified, even though she passed the entrance exams. Now what do you think of that? Racial or gender discrimination? The graduate dean's got it in for Cherri? The old battle-ax dean won't budge. I'm returning to Laramie to face her. She hasn't seen battle until she's taken me on."

Mother and daughter hugged and Aggie sniffled as Joan rushed to leave. "Please take notes for me, too. While you're at it, keep an eye on Jones."

Oh, dear, who was going to look after her? Suddenly Aggie felt so alone. She didn't think Sam would come on to her. But he could target somebody else now that Joan was out of his way and he'd been warned off Penny.

CHAPTER 6

ACROSS THE NEAR END of Lake Bomoseen Howie insisted that Harris paint their pink canoe and paddles. "We don't want to stand out. Paint it green."

"I hate green."

"Who cares?"

Careless, Harris gouged a hole in the front bottom of the canoe. After glancing over his shoulder to make sure Howie wasn't watching, little brother unwrapped a whole package of pink bubblegum, chewed it fast, and smashed the wad over the tiny hole. Next he covered the tell-tale spot with duct tape, and finally with green paint. He repeated the procedure on the inside of the canoe. Standing back to survey his handiwork, Harris beamed with delight. Nobody could tell. He turned the dry boat over to Howie to try out, but Harris didn't explain what he meant. "Just watch if anybody notices you in a pink and green canoe."

"I meant for you to paint the whole damn thing, not just the insides, dammit."

Later, when it was his turn to float in the boat, Harris had forgotten the hole. Seated in the canoe off-shore, Harris raised his binoculars to peer across the lake at the conference site, where a few participants strolled around the grounds. Drat, he couldn't distinguish folk from here. Not that he needed to resort to long-distance hypnosis. His method was good for the long haul.

When Harris returned to the Holloways' luxury cabin, Howie was strumming guitar on the porch swing. "Go fix us some supper, Harris, while I sing my hymns and pray my prayers. How about *Nearer My God to Thee?* You like that one, right?"

Harris slammed the screen door behind himself. Fetching bacon, eggs, and a six-pack of Coors, he smirked. Somebody was about to find out what getting close to God was all about.

Despite missing Joan, Aggie ate heartily the next morning, the sizzling of bacon and the aromas of fresh-brewed coffee and pancakes making her mouth water. She joined Donald and Kurt, the latter accepting her readily, Don tolerating her.

Kurt was very entertaining. His analysis of power plays in the workplace was funny. He could have been Scott Adams drawing the *Dilbert* comic strip.

In the Arkansas government bureau where Kurt worked, his immediate boss loved to chair meetings, he said. His boss's boss, not to be outdone, began scheduling impromptu meetings to meet earlier or last longer. "The competition got so bad, we were meeting more than working. Then my boss's boss's boss got wind of it and fired my boss's boss."

Aggie excused herself to stop in the ladies room before the first session. Unexpectedly, as she approached the chapel she felt the tears gathering. That was when she recalled the previous day's experience, when a sense of evil had emanated through her whole being. Strange, as the small chapel seemed perfectly harmless today.

She was about to enter, kneel at the altar and say a quick prayer for family members, when the Bailey sisters emerged. Maude, the elder and shorter, had this enormous wart on her nose. If Aggie remembered right, they hailed from West Virginia. They were arguing in low voices, too quietly for Aggie to hear. She smiled and nodded but they ignored her.

She progressed through the ladies room, completing her ablutions, and turned to walk down the corridor to the classroom where her group was scheduled. Coming up on the outside, like Secretariat at the finish line, was the Wisconsin grandpa. Everybody called him that. Aggie would bet a buck he was the oldest participant, even though it was she who had a great-grandchild.

"Let's sit together," he leered, drool collecting at the corner of his lips.

She agreed, but only because she couldn't think how to get out of it. He held her chair, poured a glass of water for her, added ice cubes, and pulled up a chair for himself. He plumped down; close, way too close.

If she didn't scoot away, their knees would be touching. Eek. He'd think she'd done it on purpose, that she was coming on to him.

She'd forgotten the nuisance of dating, the troubles associated with being single. If Randy were to die, she would be all alone and prey to old geezers like this one. With no clue how to get away from him, she spread out her materials, uncapped a pen, and tried to look absorbed.

Presently he took the hint, or it was his bladder that signaled for attention. "Jumpin' Jehosaphat, got to go pee pee. See ya later, doll."

Aggie shuddered. When he didn't return, she tried even harder to get interested in the speaker. She didn't know why she'd signed up for the small-group session addressing communications. She got enough of that topic out of Joan--from paralanguage to body language, from color coding to power games. She smiled at Kristi, thanked Reggie for the coffee refill, glanced nervously over her shoulder again, and opened her notebook. Not to take notes; rather, to reread what was becoming a journal within a journal.

She had agreed to take notes for Joan, but this was ridiculous. Her daughter could have done a better job with this presentation. Ignoring the speaker, Aggie turned to the Sam Jones section of her notebook. Here she was keeping note of the unkind words and cruel behavior of the assistant director and the reactions of those with whom he came in conflict, which was just about everybody he came in contact with. Made her think of mice cowering from the rats in their crowded cage.

Nobody liked Jones, that was clear. Well, save for their conference director, who might simply tolerate the belligerent rat. If it were true that people who lose one sense develop their remaining senses more keenly, then why didn't Dr. P pick up on the non-sighted clues? Surely he was aware of the tension, the paralanguage of emotional nuance given to the spoken word whenever Jones spoke to or interacted with others, staff along with participants.

Perhaps Petroski didn't care; or, with compassion for the ugly Sam and the personal problems unknown to others that Jones might be shouldering, Paul was willing to overlook the obvious. Or, how about this? Paul Petroski depended on Jones more than was apparent to outsiders. Paul was perhaps a babe tossed into Lake Bomoseen and left to flounder without his keeper? With Dr. P's record of independence? Made no sense.

The session was over at last, whatever it was about. Aggie had taken not one single note for Joan. To avoid Grandpa, who could be lurking just outside the door, she slipped out the back way.

At lunch Aggie joined the Bailey women. Arguing again, neither Lucille nor Maude paid her any mind. Nor did Max and Mick Houston, who took chairs on either side of her, immediately addressing their remarks to the Baileys. Aggie felt invisible. Munching green salad with cucumbers and celery, crunching crackers, she considered the rendering of a series of little burps. That might get their attention. She missed Joan.

Across the busy, noisy dining room, Aggie spotted Grandpa again. Good grief. She didn't even know his name, and was afraid to ask. He could take her question as genuine interest. She wasn't, that was certain.

Jones intervened by drawing the Wisconsin professor out of the room. A sigh of relief escaping from between her lips, Aggie couldn't help grinning. Joan wouldn't believe that her mom was actually glad to see Sam.

Again she'd misjudged the potential interest of a topic. The afternoon was equally boring and Aggie didn't know anybody who'd signed up, until Penelope arrived late and sat down beside her. "What's hap'nin'?" Penny whispered, tugging on her tight, black leather skirt that hit her at mid-thigh. Aggie shrugged.

She looked forward to another late-night session sitting informally on the floor around *The Great One*, listening to him pontificate. No way, said Jones, following dinner. Standing at the head table, in Dr. Petroski's place, Sam smirked, as if he were responsible for chaining Dr. P to his bed. "He's ill."

Which set Agatha off, pondering the difference between sick and ill. Sick sounded like a cold or a tummy ache, while ill sounded painful, like recovering from going under the knife. The only time Aggie had ever had to endure going under the knife was when she had her tonsils removed, at age four, and who could recall that.

Aggie went to bed, to rest but not to drop off. Putting herself to sleep by counting sheep never had worked for her. Counting something else might do the trick. She began to count all the times Randy had said, "I love you." During the course of their entire marriage it seemed to boil down to a dozen, but she remembered each and every one, savoring those precious few moments. Had Randy meant those words? Then why had he betrayed her?

Nonsensically, her mind turned to what she would need on a desert island. Chapstick, she couldn't do without that, or her orange tic tacs,™ or handlotion. Toothbrush and toothpaste, of course, and deodorant; warm socks, and a couple of poncho shawls crocheted by old Aunt Hepzibah's daughter-in-law, Isabelle. Aggie and Lisa never thought of Isabelle as a cousin. She wasn't even a first cousin, much less a double cousin.

Lisa was biased in favor of the *double cousins,* as opposed to the just-plain-first cousins, and as for in-laws, they were less than nothing. To Lisa. Agatha knew nothing about the Nasties on this topic. The girls' paternal uncles, Italians, were named for U.S. Presidents—beginning with George Washington Vicente. While their maternal aunts were named after flowers: nasturtium, lily, violet, and daisy.

Thinking of Lisa's disdain for plain cousins and in-laws made Aggie giggle. Then she sobered. She'd forgotten she was mad at her favorite cousin.

Just then there was a commotion down the hall and Aggie ran out of her room wearing Isabelle's purple and lavender crocheted poncho shawl over her ribbon and lace trimmed nightgown. Aggie ran barefoot along the cold floor to race down the corridor with the other conferees, many of whom were also bursting half dressed from their own dormitory rooms.

"What's up? What happened?" Aggie called, approaching the Delanos.

"Beats me," Kurt said. This trio was joined by bearded Tom Carson, the Bailey sisters, and the father-son team of Mick and Max Houston.

"It was my niece Penny I heard screaming, I'm sure of it," said Tom. "Wait a minute, maybe she's around the corner here."

The whole bunch pushed forward to round one of those odd-angle corners in the corridor. Here they found both Penny and the assistant director.

"He's dead, he's dead!" sobbed Penelope, kneeling in the pool of blood spreading from beneath Sam Jones. He lay sprawled face down near the potted palm. Right in front of Dr. Petroski's suite.

Don bent to examine him, feeling for a pulse in wrist and carotid artery. "Penny's right. Sam's dead."

People reacted differently. Some gasped while others turned away.

"Looks like murder," Don added, calmly and with no emotion at all.

Aggie thought she might vomit. So much blood. Jones looked ghastly.

Aggie tiptoed back to her room. She tried to throw up, but couldn't. The dry heaves made her ribs ache. She felt dirty, so she washed her hands. She still felt unclean, so she showered and shampooed. At last she climbed into bed.

Looked like one of the mice had had enough. The rat was dead.

CHAPTER 7

WHEN THE POLICE ARRIVED they directed everybody to convene in the general purpose room. That meant thirty-five to forty people in all, counting Dr. Petroski and his staff. The director suggested they organize themselves into their usual group arrangements, by table. Those not already crowding the halls were wakened and told where to go.

Lots of people carried cell phones, but Dr. P told them to hand them over. He wanted no distractions, though from what was not made clear. Obliquely he reminded the group that one participant was on oxygen, another had a pacemaker, and sensitive electronic equipment was used with another physically challenged person who regularly checked his condition. The conference director wanted no health issues, nor risks of lawsuits if something went wrong. Sam Jones had said in the beginning that cell phones, iPods, Droids or any other gadget including electronic games and Kindles should be left in the dormitory in their private bedrooms. Now his order was extended indefinitely.

En route to the assembly room, Aggie glanced down at herself, appalled. How long would she be stuck wearing nothing but a nightgown and Isabelle's purple and lavender shawl? Could be half the night. She returned to her room to don a robe. Quickly, before they discovered her missing, Aggie called Joan. She knew her daughter would come instantly awake, no matter that it was late.

"What in the world? What's the matter, mom?"

"Oh, Joan, there's been a murder! If I were superstitious, I'd think we wished it on him. You and I, with all our complaints about that pitiful man."

"Who? This is awful. Mom, who was killed?"

"Sam Jones."

"Ahh. At last some little worm turned on him, eh?"

"If you mean some woman he molested, I might have agreed earlier, but I've also discovered he could have been blackmailing somebody." Aggie quickly shared her encounter with the red-headed Delano pair in the woods. "If Jones threatened them, it could have been a regular practice. There could be other victims, too."

Joan interrupted with a snicker. "Did you tell everybody how you foiled that escaped convict, right in your own home? Also the twin bank robbers? If you did it twice, you can do it a third time. Catch a killer, that is. How about volunteering your expertise?"

"I hardly think this is the time for jokes, dear."

"Yes, ma'am," said Joan, with not a speck of sincerity in her voice.

A pounding on her door alerted Aggie they'd discovered she was missing.

"Out, ma'am, out. You must join the others."

"Yes, of course, officer." Confronted with his scowl and polite but harsh voice, Aggie was embarrassed.

The first person Aggie ran into was Olaf Swenson. She knew Grandpa's name, now. A retired professor of art, he glommed onto her, clutching her arm and leering. "Soon as we get out of here, Aggie, I've got some paintings to show you."

She gasped, thinking right away of etchings. Olaf was a spider come to sit down beside her. "Later," she murmured, scooting away, like Miss Muffett sitting on a tuffett before she was frightened off her curds and whey.

The original assignment was eight people per group. With Joan gone, that left six in her cluster besides herself. Each of these small "families" now tended to huddle together as if their initial bonding made them immune to the plague of suspicion. Everybody else, by extension, was suspect. People looked around nervously. Somebody among them must be the killer.

Kristi rubbed her hands together as if to stimulate circulation. Aggie knew the feeling. She too felt numb all over. "What will they do with us?" Kristi said.

Aggie rightly concluded that they were being held captive for two reasons: for questioning, and to ensure that everybody was accounted for, that nobody escaped. She assumed that the crime scene had been secured and, even as they huddled in this room apart from the gory hallway, a team of technicians must be busily gathering evidence.

Turning aside Aggie scrutinized the officer in charge. Wearing a rumpled brown suit, white shirt and brown tie with red stripes, he glowered from his place in front of the room. Detective Whitehall, like Fletcher out home, was tall, wide, and well muscled. The officer who'd come to her door stood with two more around the room. These three wore brown uniforms complete with badges, batons, and holstered police-issue revolvers. Of the latter two, the man was African-American, the other a woman with the Italian name of Battisti.

The room had taken on an eerie late-night glow. It was no longer their familiar meeting center but felt more like an interrogation chamber. Each little group had its own table, both in the classroom and in the dining room. Some people, for some reason, had brought with them their notebooks, as if convening for more magic from Dr. P instead of to contemplate the malice done to Jones.

Glancing at the notebooks, Aggie again felt guilty, only this time over a minor issue. She hadn't brought her journal, but what if the officers wanted to check everybody's? The back section of hers contained all those revealing comments about Jones, how cruel and crude he was, how mean and nasty. Could that put her at the top of the suspect list?

Naw, not to worry. The cops would need search warrants, surely. Her journal was safely stored in her room.

Dr. P sat behind the head table facing his mentees. The empty chair beside the director stood out, in the manner of a lanced carbuncle that's been removed.

"I don't like it," Kurt Delano whispered beside Aggie. Next to him sat Don, who nudged his cousin into silence.

On Aggie's other side, Penelope, pale and shaken, kept dabbing her eyes with a wad of crumpled Kleenex. She didn't like being called Penny, she'd said that first day, but that's how Aggie thought of the plain, shy girl with the thin, wispy, washed-out, once reddish hair. At first a shiny penny glistening bright with hope and expectations, Penny and her copper hair had faded and diminished like a coin exposed for too long to too many dirty hands.

Conversely, Tom Carson, who invariably called his niece Penny, despite her repugnance, appeared excited, exhilarated. This pair from Arkansas was an anomaly among Aggie's group. Quiet, retiring, the young computer director in the Arkansas state department was no match for her loud-mouthed uncle from the state university. Aggie had wondered all along what *relationship* the Carsons needed or wanted *to improve*. Tom could simply have sought acceptance in the program to enhance his vitae, one more rung on the ladder leading to tenure and promotion to associate professor. If so, why had Penny cooperated by agreeing to sign up for the relationship seminar?

The remaining two members of Group Four, Kristi and Reginald, were staff members, who, they admitted, had begged Dr. P to include them in his program whenever they could make time. The program's computer director might have something in common with Penny. Perhaps Kristi could draw out the quiet, shy girl, help her get acquainted. Aggie didn't know why, but she felt her motherly, nurturing feelings surface whenever confronted with Penelope.

Both Kristi and Reggie were tall, dark, and handsome. If Kristi's beauty didn't intimidate the thin waif, Penny might find a friend in the staff member.

Detective Fred Whitehall droned on with instructions and admonitions. They must all remain together in this meeting room; anybody with clues should come forward; they should expect to be interviewed one by one and group by group throughout the night. Dr. Petroski had apparently described the cluster concept.

"I'm so frightened," Penelope mumbled to Aggie.

"Why, for land sakes?" Tom boomed, loud enough for everyone in the whole room to hear. "You didn't do anything, except find the scummy S.O.B. Frankly, my dear, me thinks the bastard deserved to die."

A collective gasp arose from their table like a puff of smoke to the ceiling.

"Quiet, over there," Whitehall called from his position standing near Dr. P.

Aggie knew she was biased in favor of Walt, but this detective was no Fletcher. She missed her old friend and the comfortable familiarity of her home state, where she was known, if only because both her grandmothers were famous settlers, and Nasty Three, in present-day time, was the Secretary of State.

Studying the policeman in charge here in Vermont, Aggie made comparisons. Both Whitehall and Fletcher were of similar physique; tall, with bulky shoulders threatening to burst out of their jackets. Even their sandy complexions and crew cuts were similar. Where they differed markedly was in countenance and competence. While Walt Fletcher was comfortable with his role and record, which showed in the warmth of his eyes and friendly facial expressions, like an old faithful dog, Fred Whitehall was a nervous puppy determined to prove himself, show that he was clearly in charge and knew what he was doing. His sidekick, Officer Malcolm Thompson, was the cop who'd come pounding on her door. Thompson exhibited the same blustering anxious demeanor as Whitehall. The other two officers, the woman and the black man, were both middle tall, middle girth, and blocky. They both wore watchful but otherwise bland, unreadable expressions.

"You must all remain in this room until you're called out one by one for interrogation," Whitehall said.

"Couldn't he at least have used the word *interviews*?" mumbled Kurt.

"Excuse me," Dr. P interrupted. "Can't they return to their rooms?"

"No, they can't!" barked the detective, oblivious to physical needs. Then, possibly remembering, he added lamely: "Uh, for visits to the, uh, facilities, the women will be escorted by Officer Battisti and the men by Officer Akunda."

Aggie smiled. The female cop must be Italian, or possibly Sicilian, like Aggie herself. That might prove to be a common bond.

A collective sigh escaped from Aggie's neighbors as Whitehall explained that the interviews would be conducted in consecutive numerical order by group. Which meant that Number Four, theirs, was dead last.

"Long wait," Kurt muttered from beneath his red mustache. He got another nudge from Don. "At least he said *interviews* this time," Kurt added.

Just then one of the police technicians, or perhaps a coroner, slipped in the side door to whisper to Whitehall. Although nobody could hear the message he conveyed, Aggie's lip-reading skill put her in the know.

"Jones was stabbed in the ear with a hatpin," she reported to her group before catching herself. Oops, too late to bite her tongue.

CHAPTER 8

DETECTIVE FRED WHITEHALL AND Officer Malcolm Thompson conducted and recorded the interviews in a small classroom, which left Akunda and Battisti in charge of the tired, irritable conferees and staff members. People complained for lack of cell phones, iPods, and Blackberries. All over the room laptop computers opened and the people commenced pecking away. Sending and receiving e-mails was one means of communications with the outside world.

Kristi Falstaff hovered close to Penny, possibly offering comfort or the distraction of computerese. Penelope mostly ignored the center's computer operator. Kurt and Don Delano spoke only to each other. Kurt ran long fingers through short red hair. Don wrinkled his brow and scratched his head. Officer Battisti left to escort one of the Bailey sisters, the one with the warty nose, to the restroom. Lucille looked lost without her big sister. Or perhaps relieved. The woman bit her lip as if to hold back some emotion.

That was when Aggie dropped her bombshell. With the word "hatpin" said aloud, she clapped both hands over her mouth as if to take it back.

Although he addressed Aggie, Tom's loud voice boomed across the room. "Makes no sense. How can you kill somebody with a hatpin?"

Shushing him came too late. In the hushed room, many people overheard and jumped out of their chairs. Grandpa Swenson knocked over a cracked-leg chair to bang and bust on the floor. People quickly crowded around Aggie's table. Officer Akunda stared, momentarily speechless.

Aggie blushed. She wasn't about to admit to lip-reading. "Uh, perhaps I overheard. Could be just a rumor, of course."

The issues of who did it, why, and how were open to the conjecture of all.

"Take your seats!" shouted Mishka Akunda, pulling out and waving his baton. Beneath Akunda's glare, Penny burst into tears. The uniformed officer swiftly assumed a herding role, not as a gentle shepherd with a flock of sleepy sheep but as an animal trainer with a cage full of snarling tigers.

Good grief. He surely didn't think they were all dangerous beasts, about to pounce and claw him to pieces. Aggie figured Akunda to be an inexperienced rookie, out to prove he could keep his "prisoners" under control. Perhaps she should chat with him.

"I have to go to the bathroom," Penelope wailed, seated as she was at the end of their table, just inches below Akunda's waving wand.

The officer calmed momentarily, visibly switching roles from a wild-eyed keeper of animals to an understanding fellow human. "Uh, okay. Officer Battisti will accompany you." Battisti and Maude-with-the-mole were back.

People returned to their seats to resume where they'd left off. Some with heads down on folded arms trying to catch a few winks, others to whisper quietly to one another. Obviously Aggie had given them something to talk about.

The quiet mood didn't last long. The people at table one reorganized themselves into two groups, each reassembling around a card table to play bridge. These were the "beautiful" people, Aggie supposed, identifying them from their well-styled haircuts and expensive clothes. And further guessing that they had paid their own way to attend.

Soon laughter broke out at one card table and a light-hearted squabble at the other. One would never guess a murder had taken place a few short hours earlier. One thing was obvious--nobody cared about Jones. Or, the violence prevalent in movies and the evening news had inured them to the real thing.

Olaf Swenson quietly approached her table, laying an arm over Aggie's shoulders. Nimble as Jack, she could have jumped a candle stick, quick, had one been at hand. Instead, Aggie scowled and pushed Olaf away. Couldn't the man take a hint? Apparently not, as he stayed put, leaning ever closer. She turned, she breathed, she thought she'd faint from his halitosis. Good grief. At Akunda's motion to return to his seat, Swenson left, but with a "See ya, doll."

Aggie decided to collect names and addresses. She went from table to table requesting business cards, giving each a glance before tucking them in a pocket. Good reminder of who was whom, where they came from, and what they did.

They not so patiently awaited their turns to be called into the interview room; or, as bearded Tom Carson put it, "the torture chamber." Dressed in various attire, from sleepwear to casual clothes--as among the late-night party people--they appeared a motley bunch; except, of course, for table one. Lines of fatigue and bags below the eyes and smeared makeup made many of their faces appear less familiar, more vulnerable and somehow rather appealing.

Soon the card games broke up. The members of table one grew sleepy.

Aggie squirmed along with the rest of them, she couldn't wait to get her hands on her cell phone. She shouldn't be calling Joan again so soon, not in the middle of the night. However, it would be nice to think she could if she chose.

Dr. P's objective for them of bonding between and among the partners and within their clusters could extend across the entire membership. Or, conversely, tear them asunder, as they began to suspect neighbors and kin of having committed this worst of all crimes. Perhaps nobody was safe, their guarded looks beneath hooded lids implied.

Aggie realized, suddenly and belatedly, that this terrible tragedy had done one thing, and that was to draw her out of herself. At last there was something a whole lot more important than her own private dilemma and the debilitating pity-party she'd let herself throw on her own behalf.

Besides, she was curious. Puzzle-solving was her forte and so was taking charge. Her record with chairing church and charity meetings out in Cheyenne proved that. Why, every year for the last twenty years she'd been responsible for organizing hundreds of volunteers to feed the homeless at the local homeless shelter. Then there was her ability to organize the clan for pleasure or serious business. Aggie Morissey could hold up her head in the hostess department, even against her social butterfly cousin, Lisa.

Aggie could actually feel the change in herself; from rejected, humiliated, betrayed wifey to the general in charge! It was a blooming, a flowering, a rush of adrenalin that seemed to have permeated her whole body from head to toe.

What sleuthing skills did she have, beyond lip-reading? Oh, fiddle-faddle, no time for self-assessment, not now. She wouldn't make concrete plans, just let things unfold as ideas came to her.

First, Aggie decided to snoop. Who would suspect a little bitty grandmother of playing detective? Better exercise caution, however, which sent her on a recall journey. That first day Dr. P had recommended *caution* when he said that in making voluntary changes we should "proceed one small and cautious step at a time." Now Aggie was taking her first cautious step as a spy or amateur sleuth.

First things first. Get to know the officers, draw them out, help them relax. Then she would attempt to slip through the cracks of their confidence, win them over; one, if not both. Battisti, especially, might inadvertently share what she knew or what Whitehall's plan of action entailed.

Aggie had learned a few things from the gossipy mother of double cousin Nasty. Namely, how to extract from others information you could use without revealing much about yourself or letting the talker know how much he or she was opening up to spill the beans. Wyoming's Secretary of State's mom was nothing if not an expert social detective.

Signaling her need to use the facilities, Aggie was accompanied by Battisti. Agatha managed to keep up the female's typical chatter en route to the ladies room, over the sound of tinkle, and returning to her chair. Officer Battisti gradually warmed up to the little lady. The moment Aggie reseated herself, Kristi scooted up close. The beautiful girl grinned and whispered, "So, what'd you learn from Officer Battisti?"

Hah, their computer director was quick on the uptake. Aggie smiled. "Not much about the case. Lots more about Battisti herself, however. Her first name's Sylvia and she's a single mother. This is her first experience with murder and she's nervous. Eager to do a good job." Aggie had said enough. She didn't share the rest, that Sylvia believed personally that the murderer was in this very room. "She did say this much: none of the cops suspects Dr. Petroski."

"Well, I should hope not!" boomed Tom Carson, having eavesdropped.

Kurt waited until his companions turned away before addressing Mrs. M, as he called Agatha Morissey. "Bet I'm at the top of their suspect list," he whispered, for her ears only. "Somebody's bound to have overheard my quarrels with Jones and reported me to the cops by now."

"You were pretty mad and loud with your threats," Don Delano concurred, apparently oblivious to the consternation his words produced in his cousin.

"Hey, Donald, you're no help," countered Kristi, listening in. "Can't you be more supportive?" That said, she turned back to pamper Penelope, whose Uncle Tom provided no comfort at all to his whimpering niece.

Reggie excused himself to go supervise their breakfast preparations.

Everybody from table one suddenly pushed back their chairs and stood. Oblivious to the others, they began marching around the perimeter of the room.

"What on earth?" said Donald.

"Exercise! We need exercise," barked the man at the head of the line.

"I wouldn't be surprised to see them doing the bunny hop," Kurt mumbled.

Half the group followed table one's example. The others ignored the action, among them Aggie. She captured a lost pen and some blank papers out of the center of the table. Her cluster mates probably couldn't read Gregg shorthand, so she could keep her scribbles private. For over thirty years Aggie had used the shorthand skill she'd learned in high school to take Randy's dictation while they were abroad, transcribing her squiggles into usable documents at the computer.

In enumerated format and recalling her notes about Sam Jones, Aggie listed the people known to have had direct, personal, and especially horrendous encounters with the assistant director. That could be just about everybody, herself included. She unwillingly listed Kurt Delano and Tom Carson first, because of their quarrels with Jones.

The murder weapon was unusual but not unheard of. Not if it was the very long, sharp tool of yesteryear, back when women wound their long hair atop their heads, on top of which they added the once popular gaudy hats. With all those feathers, flowers, fruit and other decorations, the big hats would have toppled or blown away without the long sturdy hatpins to attach hat to hair.

But where would Kristi, Penny, or any other among the younger women or men get a long, strong outmoded hatpin? In this crowd the Wisconsin Grandpa was the only one of an age to even know what they were talking about, much less be able to lay his hands on one. Unless the murder was premeditated. Unless somebody knew Sam already, and had specifically sought acceptance to the program, and packed the hatpin beforehand. Use the conference and its participants as cover. Commit murder and then hide in plain sight among his (or her?) fellows.

Aggie casually peered around. They had all been together for only three days and nights. Hardly time, with all the meetings and after-hour activities, for her to get acquainted with anybody outside her own group or from among the staff. Okay, so she'd start circulating. After breakfast and a shower, she would commence with the informal interrogating and sleuthing in earnest.

That settled, Aggie again consulted her list. Penelope had been sexually assaulted by Jones. So had Joan, but she was gone, thank God. Aggie would have hated adding Joan's name to the list of possibilities. Penny's Uncle Tom Carson, for all his vulgar posturing and bluster, might have been taking his revenge on Sam. Only where could Tom have come by an old-fashioned hatpin?

Kurt Delano, of course, had a secret he thought must be hidden, lest he lose his job in the Tennessee state department of education. His cousin Don could be defending Kurt's reputation, just as Tom might have defended Penelope's. Defending one's family members seemed like a pretty flimsy motive for murder; actually taking another human life and putting oneself at risk of discovery and incarceration.

Glancing over the edge of her papers, Aggie spotted Olaf again. Hitching up his pants, stuffing in his shirt, he stared at her from beneath bushy white eyebrows, licking his lips as he advanced. What was she, his piece of cake?

Hastily Aggie jumped up from the chair to ask permission to go potty.

"Again?" Akunda mumbled. Tired or distraught, the officer didn't bother to fetch Battisti. He simply nodded, thus effectuating her escape from Grandpa.

Safely seated on a bench in the ladies' room, Aggie returned to her notes.

She recollected the most obvious motivations: greed, sex, money, and jealousy; also power and fear. People wanting any of these things or who were afraid they'd lose them after they got them could, she supposed, be driven to kill. So fear for one's personal safety or fear of loss might be construed as motivation.

Suddenly her notations leaped from hypothetical to real and personal. She must return to Cheyenne and confront both Randy and Lisa. As tough as that would be, it beat divorce. Even infidelity now seemed minor compared to murder.

That settled, Aggie flushed the toilet she hadn't used and returned to her place. Idly, as people nodded off in the quiet room, she mused that she could have saved herself a lot of pain if she'd reached the decision to confront hubby and cousin a lot earlier.

Come to think of it, what if she'd been mistaken all along? Perhaps it hadn't been Lisa bouncing around on her bed or even Randy underneath the pretty blonde.

It might have been two strangers using her room. Two unfamiliar people who looked exactly like Randy and Lisa? Get real.

At last their table was called. One by one, their members disappeared to be interviewed. Aggie was last. Still in her nightclothes and her loose bedroom slippers about to fall off, she shuffled into the small room and peered about. The very small conference room held only a few pieces of furniture: a rectangular table about three-by-eight, two chairs on the one side for the cops, and a single chair for the interviewee. This arrangement must be designed to intimidate witnesses.

Aggie gulped nervously. She couldn't imagine what she could say that the others had not already said. No point in mentioning her secret journal or the shorthand-scribbled list, which was nothing more than conjecture.

Aggie had sworn not to tell anyone about Kurt's secret sex life. She did mention Jones' assault on Penny to the police, since neither the girl nor Tom had sought to extract her vow of silence.

Didn't matter, as the cops already knew. "She told us," said Thompson.

"Her uncle confirmed that Jones molested Penelope," Whitehall said.

Released at last, Aggie returned to the general meeting room, where the servers led by Reggie marched in with pots of steaming coffee. A collective sigh like the dispersion of fog emanated from the room's occupants. Sylvia Battisti left to get Whitehall's permission, she said, to allow them to vacate the premises.

In the dining room they were greeted with the delicious odors of bacon, scrambled eggs, biscuits and sausage gravy, and a variety of juices. And more coffee, both regular and decaffeinated. The tables as always were graced with clean white linen, polished silver, sparkling crystal glasses and bouquets of fresh flowers as centerpieces.

Dr. P announced that people should mix and mingle. "Get to know one another. We can't do much else until the authorities let us resume our program. Many of you probably don't feel like it, anyhow." He didn't say how he felt.

With that, the great man exited on Kristi's arm, presumably to take his breakfast alone in his suite; or, perhaps, to forego food in favor of a nap. The director had been the first to be interviewed and was now free to go where he wished within the center complex.

Their group decided to eat first, mingle later.

"Dr. P might wish to be alone to mourn," Kurt suggested, regarding the director's absence.

"Don't see why," Tom said, less loudly than usual. "Surely nobody will miss Jones or be sorry he's gone."

"'Dead'. He's not just <u>gone</u>. He's dead! Say it," Penelope squeaked, her tiny voice a full octave higher than usual.

"Mix and mingle," Don reminded his cousin. "We've got to separate."

Aggie thought Kurt looked devastated; panicky, perhaps afraid. Unless he was timid and didn't want Don to leave his side. Yet, Kurt was a knowledgeable professional, accustomed to interacting with secondary school administrators, teachers, teens and parents. He couldn't cope alone in this environment? Or, aware that Aggie knew his secret, he could be overanxious, afraid she would spread the gossip and he'd be ostracized, or named as a suspect, or fired; or, any and all of the above. All this supposing made her head spin.

They rose to mix. Aggie introduced herself around table two, catching the names of no more than half of her new compadres. Officer Battisti pulled up the next chair. "Mind?"

"Of course not, Sylvia; if I may call you that. You must be dead, uh, beat. On your feet guarding us all night."

"That, too. What's really bugging me, though," said the chunky cop as she prepared to eat--alone, since everyone else had finished, "is not getting in on the action. You know, with the techs and medical examiner at the crime scene. They finished with all that and removed the corpse ages ago. If they found any trace evidence, it would be on its way to the state crime lab by now. They'll check with NCIC, the National Crime Information Center, to match, if possible, any DNA data. But that won't do any good unless the perp's got a record; you know, has been DNA-tested previously. The NCIC also tracks guns by serial number and ballistics data."

Aggie didn't know about all that, but she presumed that the rookie officer was keen to show how knowledgeable she was with investigative procedures.

"Mishka and I are new at this," Sylvia said further, refocusing Aggie's attention on her state of mind. "Does it show?"

"You act confident. As for Officer Akunda, he seems to have relaxed a bit. He no longer treats us as collective murderers. Here we are, you know, all together in this rat's cage, as if ready to pounce on him."

"Exactly." Sylvia smiled, her black hair and eyebrows framing dark flashing eyes. She was eager to talk. "The interviews are finished. Detective Whitehall says we know who everybody is and where they're from. If the culprit escapes, we'd be on him in a New York minute. What with computerized data and the interlocking networks of state crime labs and police departments."

"Or her."

"What?"

"You said 'him'. Could be a woman."

"Right. Especially with that hatpin weapon." Battisti dropped her fork and her two hands flew to cover her mouth as if to eat not the scrambled eggs but her words.

"Never mind, Sylvia. I heard about the hatpin already."

"What! How could you?"

"Uh, somebody I overheard, I guess." Aggie wasn't ready to admit she could semi-read lips. That talent was her secret; could prove useful yet. As the police suspected, someone among them was likely the killer.

Battisti excused herself to go look for Mishka Akunda. Aggie returned to eavesdropping, studying her breakfast companions, and reading lips. Everybody was restless.

Detective Whitehall entered the room to be bombarded by the babble of questions and protests. "Yes, yes, you can go. But stay inside the complex."

He hesitated, but agreed the golf course was open, this side of the lake available for fishing and swimming. "But don't go far, we might want to call you all back."

And yes, they could collect their gadgetry, use their cell phones to call outside.

People pushed back chairs and rushed out of the room as if they could hear their phones' twitters and sing-songs beckoning. Aggie too was in a hurry, yet she couldn't help laughing. How quickly we have accustomed ourselves to the technology, she thought. Obviously we couldn't un-invent our conveniences, yet what would we do without our lifelines, all the stuff we collect to make life easier?

In the hall she ran into Officer Akunda, looking lonely. On impulse she invited him to play golf with her. "I brought my clubs with me."

Since he was off-duty for the time being, he agreed after a slight hesitation.

Towering over her, Mishka grinned down at the little lady. He confessed to keeping his clubs in the trunk of his vehicle. "I drove my own car out here this morning. Sylvia had already checked out the police car."

Looking around the room Aggie caught Kurt's eye. She motioned for him to come over. "Up for a game of golf? Mishka and I are putting together a foursome."

With one bent finger Kurt beckoned his cousin, and Don joined the trio. The Tennessee pair had also packed their golf clubs. "The brochure advertising the center described the recreation facilities," Don said, "So we came prepared."

The foursome dispersed to change clothes, collect their gear, and reconvene at the clubhouse. Aggie was eager for the exercise, but especially for a chance to watch the interaction of the three men. If Kurt really was intent on hiding his sexual orientation, wasn't it a bit odd that he'd agreed to accompany the officer? Don might not watch his tongue every minute, meaning that Mishka could read something into their exchange.

Oh, she was being silly. Gay people, no more than straights, didn't go around with their sexual exploits written across their foreheads. How about herself, for example, Aggie mused as she stripped nude in preparation for donning lavender sweats. From just looking at this little grandmother, would the casual passerby ever imagine that she was a multiple orgasm kind of person? How about ten to twenty, one right after the other? Aggie giggled.

Randy was one super lover, great in the sack. She couldn't imagine life without her sexy husband. Nosirree Bob, Aggie wasn't about to give him up to Lisa. Dammit all, if Lisa's husband Peter could no longer perform, let him take Viagra, or get counseling. Leave Randy alone, she wanted to shout at Lisa. Or any other woman who ventured too close. Contankerous thought he might be of late, Randy was hers!

On the golf course Aggie nearly forgot her goal of divining attitudes from watching behaviors. But she soon caught herself and began squinting from beneath hooded eyes—not just at the ball, her club, and the green, but at her companions. Mishka Akunda, the most proficient of the four, soon lost his expression of left-out hangdog in lining up his ball, setting his stance, and getting into the game. If Sylvia was right in suggesting both she and Mishka were being cut out of the investigation, you'd never know the black officer felt discriminated against. Confident and competent on the golf course, with his tall muscular frame and his well-muscled arms he smacked his balls straight down the fairway. In contrast to Don's, whose first three balls went into the rough.

Aggie's ball fell short of the green she was aiming for, it plopped straight into a sand trap. With Don and Aggie occupied lining up their shots to get back in play, Kurt and Mishka walked together, golf bags slung over their shoulders. From glaring at her ball, as if it had failed her on purpose, Aggie twisted to stare behind her. She saw the two men arguing. But of course she couldn't lip-read from this distance. Don got out of the rough and she smacked her ball out of the sand. Both advanced on Kurt and Mishka, who interrupted their tirade to move apart.

The officer called a halt when they'd finished the ninth hole. "Better get back," he said, hoisting his clubs and striding off. He might be on break, but he was clearly ready for action of some kind.

"Care for a beer?" Don suggested. Kurt nodded, Aggie turned away.

"Uh, wait a minute," she said. "What were you and Officer Akunda debating back there?" she asked Kurt.

"Debating?" Kurt said, clearly puzzled.

"Arguing about, then."

His grin lopsided, Kurt pulled rank, as if his position in Tennessee'd state government gave him a step up on her. "Not for you to know, young lady."

"'Young lady'," Aggie huffed. "I'll have you know I'm a great-great-grandmother." Then she realized the redhead was distracting her on purpose. Aggie reached up and tugged on one end of his handlebar mustache in playful rebuttal. "You're not going to tell me, are you?"

"Tell you what?"

"There you go again, changing the subject on me. I think I'll join you guys for a beer after all." Maybe that old saying, *liquor is quicker* worked on men, too. When Kurt had tipped a couple of cans of Coors, he might open up more readily.

The trio entered the club house just after opening time. It was a small daytime club, the bartender said, open for coffee and beer in the morning, sandwiches and turkey wraps at noon, and beer plus mixed drinks in the afternoon. "We close at five. They'll be expecting you people soon for lunch," he said. "Although I could serve you here."

Aggie recalled that this wasn't a public course or bar and grill. It was part of the center's complex, serving conference participants only. "They must have a continuous list of seminars and such scheduled here," she said politely.

"Yes, ma'am," said the barkeep, nodding and wiping glasses.

When Kurt excused himself to use the facilities, Don turned to Aggie. "What was that all about, between you and Kurt?"

"I saw him and Officer Akunda arguing. I asked Kurt what about."

Donald Delano frowned. "Kurt's a private sort."

"I suppose so."

"What's that supposed to mean?"

"Nothing in particular. But if he's not come out of the closet yet, I imagine he's accustomed to being secretive. About anything and everything."

"You got that right." Delano lapsed into silence.

He lifted his can and took a long drag, while Aggie daintily sipped from her frosted mug. Nothing like a cold beer after tennis or golf, though she seldom imbibed much. "I suppose we'd better be getting back. They'll be looking for us."

"Officer Akunda can tell them where we were."

"I suppose. But you don't know what the altercation between Kurt and Mishka was about, either, right?"

"Probably nothing. I wouldn't worry about it, if I were you."

The story of her life. Either because she was female or small, people, men, especially, often dismissed her concerns as of little or no importance. Yet Aggie would recall this encounter, and the fact that both men had sloughed her off.

Back indoors the Delanos joined the Houstons at table four. Aggie reseated herself beside Sylvia, who quickly excused herself, like Aggie had halitosis or body odor, and departed.

Suddenly, from out in the hall came a shrill scream. Closest to the door, Aggie pushed back her chair and ran out of the dining room through the same door through which Sylvia had just vanished.

Halfway down the hall and pointing to the floor, Officer Battisti moaned, then stammered: "It's Mishka. I th-think he's d-dead. What do we do?"

Blood pumped from a hit to the officer's chest.

"You're the cop, dear. You take charge."

CHAPTER 9

AGGIE HOPED THAT SYLVIA wouldn't recall her own blunders. A cop screaming and then asking a civilian what to do? Battisti would be so embarrassed.

If the cop was aware of her naivete, she didn't show it. A look of grim determination flashed across Sylvia's face as she barked fast commands. "I'll stand guard over Akunda's body, Aggie, while you go get Detective Whitehall." To the crowd that burst through the double swinging doors, Sylvia yelled, "Stand away. The crime scene must be secured. You there," she pointed to big bearded Tom Carson. "Get everybody back in the dining room and tell them to stay put. Order more coffee. Officer Akunda's down and I'm in charge. Everything's under control here."

Aggie might have grinned but this was neither the place nor the situation for frivolity. She pressed on; searching for the detective was not what she wanted to do. Discovering who might have been missing from the dining room was more to the point. She didn't know everyone yet, not even all their names.

Rounding another of those odd angles in the hall, Aggie's face smacked into Whitehall's chest. He reminded her of a sequoia, strong and fixed in place. "Oops. S'cuse me," she said, feeling like a child.

"Whoa, little lady, what's up?" the detective grabbed Aggie's narrow shoulders with his two big hands. "Where are you rushing off to so fast?"

She paused for a quick breath. The detective sergeant was indeed a huge man. Not that Aggie wasn't accustomed to coming armpit-high against big people; like Colonel Schwartzkopf, Lisa's husband, who towered well over six feet to Aggie's and Lisa's five feet-zero.

Pointing back the way she'd come, Aggie stammered, "Of-officer Akunda.

He's dead."

Whitehall didn't wait for clarification. Pushing past her, he raced back down the corridor. Aggie stood alone for a moment before whirling around to follow him. Except that she kept right on going, returning to the dining room.

Tom Carson's bass voice bellowing at full register sent the crowd cowering to obey. Everybody sat at the newly assigned tables. Slipping into her new seat at Table Two, Aggie retrieved her scattered papers and, with covert glances, began tallying attendance as if she were a school monitor assigned to take roll.

Somebody must be missing; namely, the murderer. But how to tell?

Ahh, among her regathered papers was a page listing conferees, including addresses, phone numbers, professions, and familial connection to their partners. By noting pairs she could reduce the number of people to identify, from thirty to fifteen, plus staff and Dr. Petroski. Eliminate her own group, numbering eight, four partners, and that left eleven pairs. Drat. People would be scattered all about from their mix-and-mingle assignment. Deal with matching mates later.

Now she noticed that Kurt and Don Delano were still missing. Perhaps they had taken time for a shower before rejoining everybody. Where else could they be?

Across the room Kristi stuck beside Penny. Reggie poured coffee. Tom Carson buzzed around the room fielding frantic questions, pompously and pedantically, as if Officer Battisti's order to him to corral everybody made the Arkansas assistant professor an authority on murder.

However, Aggie chided herself, she mustn't jump to the obvious conclusion. If not murder, what about an accident? Akunda the rookie could have been as inept with his shooter as she was, and shot himself.

In the chest? Not bloody likely. Aggie arose to go search for the Delanos. This time Kurt was going to 'fess up to his argument with Mishka.

But the woman seated next to Aggie squelched that notion. "I don't believe we've met," Aggie's neighbor said. "I'm Lucille, and my sister, across the room, is my partner. Her name's Maude. We're the Bailey sisters. I direct the women's center at West Virginia U and Maude's field is Chinese philosophy; same university."

Aggie nearly snorted at this very odd woman going on about herself in the face of the double murders. Besides, they'd already met, and how many times had Aggie given Lucille a chance to talk, only to be ignored.

Often aware of height and age, Aggie was reminded that Lucille was the tall one and Maude the shorter one; Lucille was the younger, Maude the older. Little sister was pretty; big sister suffered the albatross of that ghastly wart on her nose. Why on earth had she never had the thing surgically removed? Wart or mole, Aggie didn't know the difference, but she supposed that since hairs grew out of the middle that it was more likely a mole.

Across the room Maude waved at Lucille and jerked her thumb toward the door, signaling, it appeared, that they should both escape this scene. Might be a trip to the john to confer and commiserate.

"See you later," Lucille Bailey from West Virginia said.

Aggie wondered who would now escort people to the restrooms, with Akunda shot and Sylvia reassigned to a more active role in the case. Malcolm Thompson, Whitehall's partner, had disappeared, too. On assignment from Fred, perhaps.

Jerking, as if she'd lost control of her muscles, Aggie began to berate herself. She felt remorseful. Here she was treating these murders like a simple puzzle of logic; a game, a jigsaw or crossword puzzle. With no more feeling than this toward the loss of human lives, she deserved a spanking with a wet noodle. Perhaps it was shock that had set in to provide a bulwark between reality and mystery solving.

With that realization Aggie began to feel some empathy with those among her companions who were acting oddly, giggling inappropriately, speaking of mundane things, ignoring the double tragedy. We can't go around shrieking every minute. Nobody even liked Jones, and they didn't know Mishka.

"We're a father-son pair," said the man across the table, repeating himself as Lucille had done earlier. "Mick and Max Houston from Boise." Max laughed loudly, as if he'd said something funny. "Now don't confuse us and call us the Boises from Texas. He hee."

Aggie still didn't know which was the father and which one the son. "You are the father, and your name is Mick?"

"No, Max. It's alphabetical, see." Another titter followed the description. "Father came first, then son. Max before Mick, get it?"

"Yes, I got it. Your son is the one with the leg." Oops, how rude.

"The leg? You bet, little lady. Mick has both his legs."

"Never mind."

Good grief, another example of strange behavior, both hers and Max's. Aggie had already met the Houstons, same as she had the Baileys, and the men, too, had ignored her at first. Talk about preoccupation with oneself. Both men were small, compact, slender, sandy complected, and fit. They could have passed for fortyish brothers.

"And?" Aggie said, awaiting more input.

"I'm an info-tech-support consultant at the University of Idaho and my son Mick's a physicist. Just left his job with NASA in Houston--Texas, that is. Yup, you'd be right this time in your 'Houston from Houston', he hee."

"And?"

"And? Uh, Mick's between jobs. Got interested in Dr. Petroski's theories and goals. Don't ask me why." Max Houston from Boise scratched his head vigorously, as if he had a bad case of dandruff. "Mick hopes to sign on here."

"Interesting. I wouldn't have thought Dr. Petroski would have need for a physicist. Mick's already been hired? As a consultant doing what?"

"Beats me. Mick's burned out, he claims. Wants a mid-life career change and he's barely in his thirties. As for joining the Corner for Cautious Change? Uh, that's up in the air right now."

"How's that?" Aggie didn't see what his reply had to do with anything, but common courtesy if not suspicion suggested that she ask him.

"Well, Mick applied and Dr. Petroski invited my son on board. With great enthusiasm, I might add. Mick quit his NASA job, sublet his apartment, packed up and was ready to leave…"

"And?" Why did Max make this so hard? Carrying on a conversation with the scalp-scratching, he-heeing computer techy was as tough as pulling mullein weeds--the herb that sold for twenty-four dollars a pound in Bulgaria but made Randy crazy at home, because it kept ruining his lawn.

"Uh, well, we're not sure what's going to happen now. See, after Mick got Dr. P's phone call so full of warmth with the oral offer, along comes a letter from Jones, saying 'no way'. In effect, 'forget your dream to join our exclusive team'. By then Mick had resigned, of course, so he came home to Boise; got an interim job at the U in the physics lab. Messed around there awhile, stewing over his lost chance. In desperation--the poor lad was suffering some deep emotional trauma over his rejection, it seemed--I applied for this conference and we got accepted. End of my sad tale."

"So, with Jones out of the way, the obstacle to Mick's employment has vanished."

Max's expression changed to one of confusion. The camaraderie exhibited, perhaps simulated, switched like a train to a new track. "Uh, could be." Max Houston from Boise pushed back his chair. "Pardon me. Got to go mix and mingle."

Not exactly mixing and mingling, people at least were moving and milling. Getting up, sitting down, circulating, and demanding restroom visits (too much coffee). Tom Carson either gave up on controlling the crowd or no longer cared. Aggie caught him looking around, presumably searching for Penny; to berate her again about something? Perhaps she'd made another restroom visit. With her jangly nerves, she'd need it.

When Penelope returned, Aggie noted Tom's body language and tried reading his lips. Good grief, he expected Penny to control her emotions? The poor lassie hadn't even had time to adjust to seeing her molester knocked off his horse before the caravan galloped over him and down the incline to run pall mall over Akunda, the single black face present. She'd asked about that. Kristi had explained that the only African-American pair who'd applied and been accepted had failed to show.

Aggie was tired. Too little sleep, too many traumatic happenings, too much input too fast. She needed a respite to recuperate and reconnoiter.

Peripheral vision perked her senses. The Delanos were back. As Kurt and Don passed her table, Aggie smelled tobacco. Ahh, so they were smokers. After getting interviewed, they'd got permission, no doubt, to go outside in response to the demands of their habit. That explained why they were late returning to the fold following their golf game with her.

Slipping quickly into adjacent seats at table two, the Delanos clasped hands under cover of the white linen tablecloth. They were both gay, then? Mates in more than their cousinly connection? So what? Unless, of course, their romantic liaison pushed one or the other higher on the suspect list. Suppose Don had got rid of Jones to protect Kurt, or vice versa. To save both their jobs and their reputations down in Bible belt country?

But why kill Akunda, too? Unless the rookie cop caught them talking about the murder, trying to cover up. If so, little wonder neither Don nor Kurt had confessed to the topic of Kurt's altercation with Mishka. Aggie tried valiantly to read their lips but the Delanos were cautious. Heads dipped low and close, their mumbles beneath matching mustaches were indecipherable.

Either Don or Kurt Delano could have a motive, no matter how slight it seemed to her. The same could be said of Tom and Penny; a small motive, very slight. As for opportunity, everybody was pretty much in the same boat. They were closeted here together.

Two other sets of partners came to mind, but only because they had just introduced themselves to her--the Bailey sisters, Maude and Lucille, and the Houstons from Idaho. She must collect and record more data on the latter four people, while continuing to poke around over Don, Kurt, Penny, and Tom. Too many people, eight in all. Slowly but surely, she must eliminate potential suspects.

Until then, she must protect her own back. Should the killer come to suspect Aggie of snooping, she could be the next victim.

CHAPTER 10

DETECTIVE WHITEHALL WITH OFFICER Battisti at his side arrived to give the conferees permission to go to their rooms for a long-awaited rest. "Be sure you don't leave campus. And be back here for lunch. One o'clock, sharp." Whitehall paused to glance at Reggie for confirmation. The food manager nodded.

They were reminded they shouldn't stray far from the assembly room. However, said Whitehall, although faced with another murder, the police were loaded with plenty of personal scoop. As for alibis, everybody had the same one. They were supposed to have stayed together, but apparently not. Just as Aggie had left with the Delanos to play golf, somebody had gotten free to kill again. When and if confronted, Aggie expected to explain that Akunda was with them. They hardly needed permission from anybody else to leave.

"If we need you, we know where to get you," said Fred Whitehall.

Malcolm Thompson, the detective's sidekick, made a show of flipping open his notebook, his tone echoing the flamboyance in his gesture. "We got plenty a data 'bout you guys right heah."

The Delanos invariably ridiculed the Vermont accent, from *Shu-ah* for "sure," to *idear,* to *heah*. "They must be fond of H's," Kurt mumbled to Aggie.

Dr. P. said the program would resume the following day. With that announcement, most of the attendees looked pleased, or at any rate they were using the conference as an excuse to get off work. A grant had funded the tuition for everybody except for those at table one. Those people were the paying participants and, of them, a half-dozen demanded refunds. They were leaving. Without Jones to run interference, Dr. P sighed and agreed. He directed Kristi to issue checks.

After Officer Battisti passed the pair of officers at the door, she whispered to Aggie, "Talk to you this afternoon, okay?"

Aggie nodded and went to her room where she meant to collapse on the rumpled bed. However, she really ought to call Randy. Beat him to it, before he called her and rattled her timbers. She preferred being the one in control.

No reply on his end. Wherever he was, her husband might not be able to get a signal on his cell phone. And he had left her no list of alternate land line numbers. Her geologist husband could be anywhere—in any of those little *stan* countries, that is.

Next, Aggie checked the drawer for her notebook. Missing!

She pawed through drawers and closet; couldn't find the journal anywhere. Now, what? If merely absentminded, Aggie supposed she could have left the notebook over in the main building. Aggie yawned. She'd look for it later. Right now the sandman was calling.

Shower forgotten, Aggie fell onto her bed to sink into a deep and dreamless sleep.

Then her cell phone buzzed, awakening her at five minutes before one o'clock. It was Joan with news of Randy. "Dad called me. He wanted to know why he couldn't reach you. Or, as he put it, 'Where th'hell's your mama got herself off to?'"

Aggie gulped and jumped off the bed to stand in the center of the room, phone at her ear. One call, one word from or about Randy, and she felt herself sliding down that long tunnel into a hole where she didn't know who she was. Up here in the light, she was her own self, competent Aggie Morissey. Down there in the mud, she felt like a doormat for Randy to wipe his feet on.

"Why didn't he call my cell phone?"

"He said he did, but you must have turned it off, or forgotten to recharge it. He paged you, too, but you didn't call him back."

"I most certainly did," Aggie said. Stammering, she turned her ire on her daughter. "Uh, what'd you tell your dad about me, Joan?"

"I told him the truth--you went with me to the Vermont seminar but I had to return home. He said I should have brought you back with me."

"And?"

Joan laughed. "I told him you're a big girl. Of course that did no good. You know what Daddy's like. So I promised him I'd get hold of Lisa and send her back there to be with you."

Thank goodness Joan couldn't see her face. Aggie's mouth stretched open a mile. Aiming to sit back down on the bed, she missed the edge to plummet onto the floor. "Oh, no." Then she caught herself. Joan would expect her mother to be delighted. "Uh, that's nice, dear."

Apparently her daughter missed the reaction. Joan had already changed the subject to talk about her own affairs. She was still working on Cherri Chavez's admittance to her fall program, she said. No dice, yet.

While Aggie, only half-listening, tut-tutted in the phone, Joan suddenly interrupted herself. "Mom! Nicole's here! Gotta run."

"Wait! Let me talk to her." Aggie couldn't call Nickee, nobody could. Her hateful husband had smashed Nicole's cell phone with a brick, the nice camera-phone Aggie had given her so the family could follow Stevie's growth, his cute little sayings and shenanigans. Now Aggie waited until John handed over her phone to her daughter.

"Nickee, darling, how are you?"

Nicole babbled her news so fast Aggie barely caught it. "You're leaving him for good this time?" Probably not. After listening to her granddad rant at her mom all those years about being true to one's marriage vows, Nicole was determined to stick by her man. Nobody liked him. Joan couldn't stand her son-in-law, and neither could Joan's ex, Nickee's father. The rodeo cowboy had dragged Nickee off on an impulsive elopement when the child turned sixteen. Now the couple, with baby Stevie, roamed the western rodeo circuit living out of a trashy trailer on dusty back lots with neither water nor bathroom facilities. Stevie's daddy was abusive, and Nickee put up with it.

In Aggie's ear, Nickee sighed. "You know I can't stay here with mom, Gam. She'll try to get me enrolled at the U. My husband will know right where to look for us."

"You still haven't tried a safe house somewhere?"

"Naw. I can handle him. He's never laid a hand on Stevie."

Following another five minutes on the phone, mostly about adorable Stevie and how much Aggie missed him and Nicole, Joan grabbed back the phone. "Gotta run, mom. Talk later. Meanwhile, Lisa will be with you soon."

Aggie did not protest Lisa's potential arrival. When and if she heard from Lisa herself, she'd worry then about how to put her off.

Aggie looked around the room. Something she'd meant to do before napping, something other than a shower. Ahh, of course. Now she remembered. She'd planned to search once more for the misplaced notebook.

First, though, she must get that bath and return to the center. It was already past time for the group to reassemble. She signed off with Joan.

When she re joined her table, Aggie was delighted to discover Reggie's menu. He had directed the kitchen staff to concoct a light lunch of fresh spinach salad with lots of other veggies, cold shrimp with sauce, and hunks of French bread fresh baked from the oven. Kristi asked her if she was frightened.

"Of what?"

"Two people have been killed already." The girl shivered. "Who's next?"

"Wouldn't we have to be guilty of something to get on the hit list?"

A look of amazement passed across Kristi's face, like the thought of bringing on one's own death had not occurred to her. "Like what?"

"Inappropriate behavior, I should think." Drat, she hadn't meant to come off sounding like a pundit, or as that blase, either. "Criticism."

"I don't get it."

"Suppose the victims criticized the killer and he took revenge. Or perhaps the motivation for murder was infidelity. Or blackmail,"Aggie suggested next. She knew she was reaching. This whole conversation sounded lame. What was she thinking?

Kristi continued to stare at her, like she'd gone daft in the head. "Could be random, Aggie. Maybe a psychopathic serial killer is loose among us."

That was a new idea. If Kristi were right, they could all be in danger.

Aggie's nerves twitched, her hand jerked. She spilled sauce on her clean lavender silk blouse and the purple linen skirt.

"Oh, dear. Excuse me, Kristi. I must go to the dorm to change again." Visions of Lisa burst onto Aggie's horizon. Tidy Lisa would fret and stew anew and have a fit. Just like Randy. Perhaps the pair deserved each other.

Back in her room once more, Aggie slipped out of the soiled garments. Now she must take time to search more thoroughly for her misplaced journal. She looked high and low, in desk and closet, and bureau drawers, but couldn't find it. That was odd. Hmm, must be here somewhere. She'd fine-tune the job of hunting better later.

Back again in the dining room, this time Aggie joined the Baileys. Her people had already left their table. Smiling, Reggie set out a new salad for her.

"Mmm, it's delicious," murmured Lucille. "You'll love it."

"Nutritious, too," said Maude. She looked at Aggie around her mole, out of which two hairs waved. The woman ought to be cross-eyed by now.

Trying hard not to stare at the tip of Dr. Bailey's nose, Aggie said, "Your field is Chinese philosophy, am I right?"

"Yes. In fact, I'm one of your two guest speakers tomorrow. The other is Chinese. Dr. Yu should be here sometime today." Maude glanced past her mole to glare at a big timepiece with an oversize Disney figure on her left wrist, as if Mickey Mouse would reveal the exact minute when the Asian professor would arrive. "Never mind," Maude added, a look of disgust on her face. "I'm not supposed to be giving away secrets."

Startled, Aggie cried out, "Secrets!" Her mind occupied with the double murders, she half-expected Maude to reveal some clue that would unlock the box of solutions. Sylvia then need only to reach in and collect the precious jewel; identify the murderer, solve the crimes. Send us back to the conference.

The conversations buzzing throughout the room sounded disharmonious, out of sync with the canned background music; designed to soothe the savage beast among them? Or was it *Calm the savage breast?* She'd forgotten the exact quotation. Naturally Lisa, the English Lit major, would know.

"Never mind, Aggie," Maude hedged. "Our presentation topic is a surprise, a treat I'm not supposed to mention ahead of time."

So that's what mole-nose had meant. Her secret had nothing to do with the murders. So what? Aggie couldn't imagine that she could possibly care less.

Max and Mick Houston from Boise brought their after-lunch coffees to the table with a quick "May we join you?" offered innocuously. Another set of doubles, Aggie differentiated between the two Houstons from the father's perpetual scratching. Max regularly gave his scalp a rub, Mick didn't. However, she remembered with disgust, Mick was the one with the annoying pump-and-thump habit, and, once seated, he began again: pump-pump went his leg, thump-thump went his foot.

Oblivious to the Houstons' intrusion and also to her vow of silence, Maude continued to deliver in monotone format some of her pet theories from Chinese philosophy. Aggie supposed that's what Dr. Bailey was doing. She couldn't really hear all that much. She would never be able to decipher Maude's lecture the next day no matter how hard she strained to hear. Reading lips wasn't possible, either, if the speaker didn't clearly enunciate. Muffled Maude's lips barely moved.

When Maude took a breath, Aggie asked Lucille if she'd met the others among her first group. As the Delanos along with Penny and Kristi descended on them, Aggie stood to issue an invitation for them to seat themselves.

Aggie was immediately bombarded with service, followed by questions. Kristi shoved Aggie back down. Don refilled her coffee cup. Everybody pulled out chairs to gather around. Now the Baileys and Houstons, with Mick's pump-thump, were hemmed in. Surrounded by all these people eagerly hitting her with their conjectures and, apparently, seeking confirmation of their guesstimates, Aggie wondered if she looked like Sherlock Holmes. They sounded like a choir of magpies all speaking at once.

"Do you think Dr. P is okay?"

"Dr. P must be taking Jones' death pretty hard."

"Why?"

"Why not, they were pretty close."

"Don't kid yourself."

"What does that mean?"

"What do you mean, what do I mean? What do you think, Aggie?"

"Why ask me? I don't know what you're talking about."

"I'm talking about the twinnies, Dr. P and Jones, how close they were. Why, they could have been Siamese twins," said Don.

"I disagree," said Kurt, who understood and could recognize the closeness, or lack of it, between two men. "It seemed to me that Sam pushed himself on Dr. Petroski, and our leader simply tolerated him like a pesky gnat."

That set off another batch of ideas, each person determined to get his or her theory on the table. Aggie thought it was annoyance she caught shooting between and among all four of the Baileys and Houstons. The two pairs stuck together like next-door neighbor kids at their first summer camp, yet they didn't seem to find it easy tolerating one another. Pump-pump, thump-thump. She wanted to plug her ears.

The afternoon waned with no sign of Dr. P. Aggie joined Kristi and Reggie for a walk around campus between and among the buildings. She had pushed herself between them, impolitely to be sure. Picking their brains for their impressions took precedence over sensitivity right now.

"What do you think?" Aggie asked Reggie.

"About what?"

"The murders, of course."

"I think it's none of our business."

Kristi was more forthcoming. "Now, now, Reggie. Aggie is only trying to be helpful. She and I talked already. Reggie, it's like identifying the killer for the purpose of saving our own necks."

"I don't get it. How so?"

"If Officer Akunda was murdered because he saw or learned something and the killer was forced to shut him up, it could happen to any of us."

"Then why prowl around getting into trouble?" said Reggie. "I'm steering clear of the whole mess."

Aggie pressed on. "In other words, you don't know anything, you suspect nothing, and if anybody asks, you're minding your own business."

"Yup."

Reggie's sentiments, Aggie realized, was probably echoed by the majority.

She left the young people to return to the center. Glancing over her shoulder, she saw them holding hands. My my, a budding romance. How sweet.

In the foyer of the main building Olaf Swenson caught hold of Aggie's arm, giving it a squeeze and bringing a wince. She pulled away.

"The paintings, Aggie, I want you to see the paintings." The elderly professor emeritus clutched her arm to drag her off with him. Not by a hank of hair to his cave, she trusted. She wasn't up to studying his *etchings*.

Picking his nose with the little finger of his right hand, he clung to her with his left. "Right this way, doll. I want you to see the really excellent abstracts by that young artist, T.J. Jordan, from Independence, Missouri." He might be retired, but the art professor apparently still cared about his product.

He thought she was blind as well as half-deaf, perhaps. Of course she had noticed them. The paintings were extraordinarily beautiful. Aggie thought the abstracts were appropriately named and had, in fact, already bought several to have shipped home as gifts: *Acid Rain* for Joan; *Simple Truth* for her granddaughter, Nicole, and *Malicious Intent* for herself. She'd spent a blinkin' fortune, but it was her money to spend; at least she hoped she had some money left. If Randy hadn't blown it all on his mistress. She had pondered over *Night's Passion* as a gift for her husband, but figured he would just throw a fit at her frenzy of buying. "I don't think you were listening, doll," said the old coot beside her.

Aggie didn't even apologize. Instead, she scooted off to the ladies.

Back in the central meeting room, Aggie noticed that Tom, with booming bass, but still with sunken chest, had taken charge again. He made brief, sometimes lengthy, announcements and, like docile sheep en route to the shearing barn, many people mindlessly obeyed. Carson had gotten the straight scoop from Whitehall, he said, making it sound like an important and next-to-impossible feat. No afternoon sessions were scheduled, Tom said further, making his announcement sound super official, and no small-group interaction or role-play activities, either. As for their personal rules, there was no leaving campus, but they could wander throughout the center and the dormitory.

Seemed strange; first they were given permission to leave, then they were told what they could and could not do. Carson had probably garbled the instructions passed down from the detective. Oh, well, might as well watch and see what would happen as a result of his pronouncements.

Aggie was curious to see how these professionals would react as time went on, especially having their freedoms and rights removed all over again. The night before didn't count; people were too tired to resist and perhaps too frightened as well, as they waited to be interrogated. But now that most of the afternoon had passed, even with the second murder, they resisted being treated like prisoners or horses herded into the corral.

Aggie watched for character flaws, for unusual behavior. Might learn something of note. Circulating, she checked name tags, made small talk. Who among them could possibly be the killer? Conversely, who could be trusted? Or not. Especially the latter.

By late afternoon it happened, the first eruption; evidence that somebody had had enough. "Hey," said Houston from Boise. "Why are we here?" Since he scratched but failed to thump, he was obviously Max, the father.

That's all it took--the first leak in the dike before the flood flowed fast. People stopped sipping coffee, talking, walking, or moseying around the big room to admire and comment on T. J. Jordan's spectacular canvasses.

"We've got rights. I want to call my lawyer."

This time, Battisti whispered to Aggie, Detective Whitehall had instructed his sidekick to confiscate the cell phones. Every last one of them rested in a big pile on the sideboard. First one and then another among the crowd looked longingly at their missing links to the outside world. Aggie wondered at the absence of laptops. Sylvia explained that during Aggie's absence to play golf, Malcolm had gathered up those, too.

"Why don't they arrest somebody and let the rest of us go?"

"Why doesn't somebody sue? They can't take our phones and computers."

"Oh, yeah?" snarled Thompson. "We can do anything we want. We're the law."

"Shut your mouth, Malcolm," mumbled Whitehall.

This was absurd, somebody yelled.

They'd already been released once, and half-a-dozen had been allowed to leave, shouted another.

"Well, of course they got permission. That was the rich bunch. Rich people are allowed to do anything they please. But not us lowly peons."

Odd term to call a group of professionals. Then Aggie recalled something Randy had said more than once, that government personnel and other agency bureaucrats are often whiners; thinking, Randy supposed, that if they didn't complain about their low wages and their lowly lot in life, the taxpayers would resent their salaries. Gripe long and loud enough, Aggie figured, people eventually start believing themselves, no matter how absurd their complaints.

Aggie wondered further whether these people typically modeled themselves after each other, following the most outspoken as if they were zombies. Perhaps she ought to say something to jog them loose from their pity party. No, better to wait and listen awhile longer, before deciding whether to insert her two bits. They could mob her next.

"Yeah, who do they think we are? I'm outta here, man."

"We're innocent bystanders."

"You, too? I know I am!"

"Somebody isn't," Aggie said quietly, unable at last to resist. "Murder has been done, not once but twice. Obviously we're not all innocent."

People turned to see who'd spoken, ready to descend with claws at the ready, like buzzards over a fallen bison. Just as quickly, the members of Aggie's groups--the originals plus her new acquaintances--grabbed chairs to circle around her like covered Conestogas in a western wagon train positioning themselves to protect their own from marauders.

"You better not be accusing me," barked a burly boy from Kentucky.

"You know something you're not telling?" burbled a brawny broad from Utah with sun-wrinkled face pulling in so close to Aggie she could see up her nose.

"Tell us what you know, Mrs. M," squealed a tiny blonde from South Dakota. Was she overwrought for a reason beyond strung-out nerves?

"She doesn't know anything," protested mole-nose Maude, a protective arm around Aggie's shoulders. Aggie pulled away slightly, wondering what made Professor Bailey assume that kind of knowledge, and why was she hovering so closely?

"We had our chance to leave, remember," said Aggie.

Now they sat back, startled, staring at each other. Of course. They had stayed because they didn't want to miss the rest of the program. Glances dropped, hands twitched. She smiled. Every single person acted guilty, but she suspected it was merely that they'd been caught out, by her. Joan's idea that some of the people had enrolled and others had lingered following the murders, was not because of interest but to get away from their own workaday jobs.

Gently shrugging herself free of the overzealous Maude, Aggie stood to raise one small hand. Not beseechingly; rather, calmly and authoritatively. She could have been chairing a charity function or political fundraiser out home.

"Quiet, everyone. Pull your chairs back up and gather around. Since the rest of us here agreed to stay, let's make the best of it. No doubt the program will resume tomorrow. Meanwhile, let's speak rationally, one at a time. Pool what we know."

Just like that, they obeyed as one body. Sheep, to be led by the good shepherd. Randy and Lisa should see her now.

Aggie didn't always play the dumb dodo, a doormat to her smart aleck of a husband, or the sloppy second to her organized and efficient cousin. Free of her picky *loved ones,* she could climb mountains! Swim oceans!

"I hope you're happy now," Howie said.

The Holloway brothers sat pushing back and forth on the porch swing, their feet propped on the porch railing, along which sat a row of pink geraniums in clay pots. Harris sipped a martini, up, and Howard periodically gulped his Scotch-rocks. They passed the binoculars back and forth, pausing from their rocking to stare through the lens.

Harris gloated. "I hadn't planned the murder of that policeman. But, yeah, any time a cop gets killed, that's fine with me."

"Who's the next civilian on your agenda?"

"Why does it have to be a civilian? Might as well wait it out. Go for the gold."

At ease--with his brother, himself, and the situation--Howie made no objection. "Okay by me, little bro. This is your drama, you're the director. Play it out."

CHAPTER 11

LATER THAT EVENING AGGIE and Sylvia left the premises by the back door for a walk in the woods. The night was cool, the air damp. Beyond the trees they could see the glimmer of moonlight dancing across the lake. The women sniffed the fresh air, scented with the sweet fragrance of pine and fir trees.

They hadn't seen Dr. Petroski since lunch. By then his haggard appearance belied his suggestion that the conference would resume on the morrow. Nevertheless, the reminder that they were free to leave, but had voluntarily agreed to stick by Dr. P, apparently pierced the fog of numbed brains. Aggie was tired, too, but her peers' reactions were almost funny. She had dismissed the more disheveled members whose nerves were as unraveled as Aunt Hepzibah's knitting yarn. Aggie's soothing words, Don Delano said, freed everybody to resume acting human.

"What do you think, Aggie?" Sylvia said after their opening exchange about how great it was to get outdoors, breathe the fresh Vermont air coming off Lake Bomoseen, and get away from the crowd. "I know you spent the day acquainting yourself with your companions, because I peeked in several times. I spotted you milling about, getting people to talk. You'd make a good investigative interrogator."

By then they had reached the lake. Side by side they strolled casually, pausing beneath the moonlight to pluck a few wildflowers, smell them, pass them back and forth. They kicked rocks, they looked heavenward and identified constellations. They paused to lean against a tree.

Meanwhile, Aggie ignored the compliment, if that's what Sylvia intended to convey in saying she had investigative skills. She recognized the technique. Put a person at ease, off guard. Aggie wasn't buying. Yet she was as eager to

73

extract information from the chunky officer as the other way around. So she took the first hesitant step. "I don't know, Sylvia. Jones was not well-liked…"

"To put it mildly. That was clear from the interviews. Detective Whitehall let me listen to the tapes." Sylvia paused to push back some long, low limbs leaning over the path like a crippled old man holding up a supermarket's checkout line. "Detective Whitehall came over from Rutland. His ulcer makes him cranky, or appear anxious. But he's good at what he does. He's experienced in dealing with the press and with murder investigations. Malcolm Thompson and I are from Castleton; Mishka, too. Uh, he was, rather. We're just small-town cops, with Malcolm the senior officer."

Aggie turned to face Officer Battisti, her profile outlined in the moonlight. "The press, right. We've been so cooped up, isolated, I'd forgotten about the media. We haven't had access to radio or television. The papers must have the story, too, by now."

Having reached the lake, they no longer needed to walk single file. Sylvia stepped forward to stroll beside Aggie, who stopped to lean against another tree. She was so tired and Sylvia must be half-dead, too. The blocky well-muscled Italian must work at keeping fit. Sylvia droned on about Dr. P's reputation, most of which Aggie knew.

Sylvia was right about the press. They'd been denied access to the complex. There went their chance to interview conference participants, who stayed cozy and safe indoors. Aggie could imagine what they'd do when allowed to enter. The reporters would no doubt swarm like maggots over a long-dead corpse. Oh dear, what an ugly comparison. Armed with a list of staff and participants, the media's researchers could be studying individual backgrounds.

The police, too, of course. Aggie asked Sylvia about how extensive their resources were in this rural state. Vermont was a mere one-tenth the size of Wyoming. Yet Vermont must beat Wyoming in population of under half a million, perhaps by three times over.

They reached a bench and paused to appreciate the moon's glow across the shimmering water. Resuming their slow walk along the lake shore, Sylvia replied that of course Vermont's forensic, pathology and investigative departments were all involved.

"Sylvia, you already know that I've heard about the hatpin that killed Jones…"

"Gun, too. Jones was also shot in the head. I expect it was the same revolver as used on Mishka. The ballistics analysis report will prove that."

Aggie gasped. She remembered now. Early to arrive on the murder scene, she had seen Jones lying face down with a lot of blood seeping around his head and shoulders. "Two weapons, then? Which means you're looking for two murderers?"

"Let's walk over to the golf shop," Sylvia said, as if reluctant to speak further.

Aggie shivered, though not from the temperature. She couldn't believe it. Two murderers. Possibly they were both among those who had left. She fervently hoped so. However, if that's what happened they might never discover the motivation.

Though late spring, the night air was cool and damp. Dew covered the grass. They reached the back porch of the golf club near their complex. Extending behind them were the greens, sand traps and water hazards of the course that was surrounded by and dotted with many trees. Altogether the area was a beautiful and ordinarily peaceful setting. Ideal for recreation with swimming, fishing, canoeing and boating, along with golf and tennis. The initial schedule had provided time for exercise and outdoor exploration during the late afternoons and early evenings.

No longer. Though fewer than twenty-four hours had elapsed since Jones' murder, it seemed like they'd been cooped up for weeks.

"Let's sit for awhile," Aggie said, dropping onto one of the lounges.

She sat upright in her chair. The clubhouse was locked and dark, having been vacated shortly after sunset. She'd noticed earlier in the week that it was not a country club, per se, but just a small building containing pro shop with golf equipment and sports clothes offered for sale to guests and participants of various scheduled conferences. The tiny snack bar was limited to soft drinks and sandwiches, chips and other junk foods.

"Jones' eardrum and brain were pierced?" Aggie asked. "Which was followed quickly or soon thereafter by a shot to the head. Or was it vice versa? Whichever; I suppose you won't know until the lab reports come back. The second killer didn't know about the first, maybe."

"Right, we won't know until we've got the reports. As for Akunda, that's a pretty straightforward killing, surely. He was shot once in the chest. A lucky hit--for the killer, I mean--straight into the heart. Unless the killer knew exactly what he was doing."

"He or she."

"Or both. Has to be some pretty strong motivation," Sylvia continued. She stood, a clear indication their talk had reached its conclusion, if not any mind-bending resolutions. "I need sleep. You, too, Aggie."

Returning, they no longer strolled leisurely while talking and sharing possibilities. Sylvia set a brisk pace. She stopped by her police car, parked near the golf course, to pat the holstered gun on her hip. "I'll escort you to the dorm, Aggie."

"Not necessary, Sylvia. I'm okay."

The uniformed officer got in the police car and started the engine. "Get some rest, Aggie," Sylvia said through the open window. "See you early tomorrow."

Aggie stood there a few moments watching the taillights disappear down the narrow tree-lined gravel road. Then she turned toward the center complex.

Unaware that she was being followed, Aggie didn't see the man dressed in dark clothing creeping up behind her on stealthy feet. Not that she could have identified the man had she spotted him. The Holloway brothers had neither enrolled in the seminar nor been invited to join the conference that their newly funded foundation had sponsored.

A lot of vehicles and tents were parked between her and the campus. Probably the press, Aggie mused. Mind awhirl with Sylvia's new input, Aggie walked slowly, circumventing the media circus with the goal of going indoors through the back door. The idea of two murderers was mind boggling, unless it was one killer all along, who used two weapons to make sure Jones was dead.

Lost in thought and oblivious to her surroundings, Aggie neither saw nor heard her attacker. Smack on the back of her head! Out like a snuffed candle, she crumpled to the ground within sight of the complex.

CHAPTER 12

OUT IN THE WOODS where she'd been dragged from the parking lot, Aggie opened her eyes. Carefully, cautiously, because a brass band with percussion predominating marched and blared inside her skull. She tried to sit up, but found herself pushed back gently with a soft admonition of "There, there, my dear."

Aggie rubbed her eyes, believing her double-vision affliction had returned.

Standing just past her feet, bending forward, tut-tutting, and wringing their hands uselessly were the look-alike, father-son pair--the Houstons from Idaho.

She blinked, looked again. A big wart, so close she thought she'd go cross-eyed, nearly touched Aggie's nose. Maude pressed an opened bottle of water to Aggie's lips. "Call emergency service," she barked at the Houstons.

"In jerkwater Castleton? Think again."

"A doctor, then."

"Call Rutland."

"Get the police."

With everybody putting in their two bucks worth and getting no consensus, Aggie sat up. "Forget it." She scrambled to her feet. "I'm hungry." What she really needed was a fistful of aspirin and a helping hand, but at this rate they'd fight over who'd get which duty and knock her flat again.

"What happened to you?" "What were you doing out here all alone?" "Were you here all night?" "Are you hurt?" "Did somebody bonk you unconscious?"

Why couldn't they speak one at a time? Aggie felt like a dartboard and wished they'd stop hitting the bull's eye. She didn't respond to any of their questions because for the moment she had no answers. Her first coherent thoughts materialized as questions: Where was Sylvia? Was she attacked too? If so, was she dead or alive?

Then her memory returned as surely as the sun over the eastern horizon. She'd gone walking with Sylvia and, afterwards, had stood watching the cop car disappear. She'd begun walking down the dark path beneath an umbrella of low-hanging leafy branches, thick foliage on both sides. That was the last she remembered.

Slowly, as if her arms were being operated by an inattentive puppeteer, Aggie lifted both hands to her pounding head. She managed on her own to rise.

"Beats me," she said. "I must have tripped and fallen while out taking a walk."

The group of five--Aggie, plus the Houstons and Baileys--arrived at the Center in time for Whitehall's press conference on the front steps. Behind the throng of media representatives, the fivesome clung closely together, like a basketball team in a huddle, as if to get further instructions and draw strength from one another.

The media, as predicted, fed on the double murders with a frenzy, like a pack of starving Somalian exiles over packets of food air-dropped from American planes. Not yet admitted to the central building and dormitory, the press waylaid their prey coming and going between dormitory and center, poking microphones in faces, shouting questions and demanding answers. Reporters and photographers pushed forward, flashes flashing, videocams humming.

With the parking lot full of conferee and staff cars, the press had opted to mash down all the grass on the incoming side of the center with their food and materials tents, and their high-tech vehicles sprouting antennae like giant prehistoric bugs on the lookout for food and danger. Satellite dishes on the roofs rotated slowly. Thick cables connecting equipment snaked everywhere.

All this commotion had commenced moving in the previous day, although the people incarcerated inside were mostly unaware, closeted as they were behind heavily insulated walls with dark drapes drawn over the windows. Whitehall, with Rutland's police chief and the governor's enthusiastic approval, had asked for a news blackout. Of course they didn't get it.

This was a big story, though not as yet fast breaking. A cop killing wasn't taken lightly among their own, an African-American, no less. Although Jones was neither well known nor particularly newsworthy, the same couldn't be said for his boss. A blind psychologist, author of several best-selling books in the trade and business sectors. Great players, in the media's opinion; a double-murder drama unfolding in the quiet backwaters of Vermont, a place where, supposedly, "nothing much ever happens."

When Whitehall showed his face he was buffeted on one side by Officers Battisti and Thompson, and on the other by the Rutland chief of police, the Castleton mayor, and the Vermont governor. The detective acknowledged the two murders but resisted the notion that a serial killer was responsible. Then came the usual disclaimers: the police were doing everything possible--gathering and analyzing evidence; overlooking no clues; interviewing conference participants, and so on and so on. Whitehall begged the press to include in their broadcasts and articles a plea for anyone with any knowledge or clues to please come forward. Beside the detective, Malcolm held aloft a placard with telephone numbers and email addresses for both the Rutland and Castleton police departments. Upon conferring with the mayor, the governor, and his own police chief, Whitehall added that it was too early to release any further information.

"Not even the murder weapon or weapons?" a CNN reporter, identifying herself as Marci Carmichael, shouted from the rear. "Was it a gun?"

"Yes, a gun was involved," Whitehall admitted reluctantly. "We're also in the process of locating kin, if any, of the deceased. Bear with us, please. We'll keep you updated as we know more ourselves." With that, Whitehall turned sharply to reenter the center, followed quickly by his band of supporters.

"Well! What do you think of that?" Lucille said to nobody in particular.

"Not surprised," said Max, scratching his scalp. "The media invariably show up en-masse at the first sniff of an unusual story."

"What's so unusual about murder?" Wart-Nose demanded. "Happens every few minutes in this country."

Aggie noticed that Lucille and Max were never standing near one another. They always seemed to keep Maude and Mick, preferably both, between them. Could be something significant about that, but Aggie couldn't think what.

"In rural Vermont? Murdering a cop and a well-known professional?" Mick countered. "Usual? Typical? I don't think so."

The quartet had apparently forgotten all about Aggie. She gingerly parted her hair with trembling fingers to explore her tender head. The egg-shaped lump on the back of her head seemed to be enlarging on the outside and raising a cacophony inside her skull.

With none of the authorities any longer available to catch on film, CNN's Marci directed her photographer to focus on a woman in the back. Reading the reporter's lips, Aggie realized they meant her.

"Ma'am? Oh, ma'am," said Marci, shoving a microphone at Aggie's mouth before she could get away. "How do you feel about these murders?"

Distracted by her pain, shooting like fireworks through her head, Aggie caught only the first few words. "How do I feel? I feel awful! But, how did you find out so quickly?"

"Uh, find what?"

"About the attack, the sock to my head," Aggie blurted without thinking. "Never mind," she said, reassembling her wits; gingerly, like gathering fresh eggs from beneath cranky hens. Tripping and stumbling, she ran away as if she were the Preble's Meadow Jumping Mouse, a protected specie in fear of going extinct.

"What was that all about?" Marci's hand-held microphone leaped like a skittish bullfrog from the Baileys to the Houstons. Philip homed in with his camera to record their comments for posterity--or until this particular film segment met its death in the cutting studio and the rubbish bin.

Which was how word of the attack on Aggie Morissey out in the back woods of rural Vermont reached the international airwaves. The media made it sound like she was the intended third victim. Marci's news flew around the globe by satellite, hopped like the Preble Mouse from network to cable, from the Internet and email and into newsprint.

Out in Wyoming they even heard about the attack on one of their own; namely, Agatha Morissey. She was, after all, descended from two of their own pioneer women.

Chapter 13

THE BAILEYS AND HOUSTONS wanted to call an ambulance. Aggie shook her head. She wasn't about to go traipsing off to the emergency room. She was just fine, thank you. Nothing wrong that an aspirin and a nap wouldn't fix. Aggie left the crowd quickly before anybody else could start fussing over her.

The buzzing of her cell phone hauled her back to reality. Agatha had dozed off after downing three or maybe four fast-acting Tylenol.

"Mom! What on earth?" Joan wailed in Aggie's ear.

"What are you talking about, dear?"

"Murder! Not one but two, and you were the third intended victim?"

"Really, dear, aren't you exaggerating? Anyway, how did you know?"

"How did I know? Mom, the whole world knows. Dad saw it on the news at the airport bar at Heathrow. He had a layover on his way home from Turkmenistan and called me from London. He's fit to be tied."

"Yes, well. A cop and that assistant director you hated so much were killed. But what does that have to do with me? Except that I happened to be here. You were here, Joan, you know the scene."

"Daddy said that wherever trouble reigns as king, there you are, queen of chaos. What happened to you, mom? That's why I called. And why wouldn't you talk to Dad when he called you?"

"Guess I didn't hear the phone buzzing. I was knocked out, er, from taking Tylenol and falling asleep."

"So, you were attacked! Naturally you refused to go to the emergency room or even see a doctor, right?"

"Please, dear. Don't shout. It makes my head hurt. And don't carry on, so. It was just a bump on the head, no matter what you heard." Aggie rubbed her head. "How could you have heard, anyhow? The only people who knew were a few of the new friends I've made here. You recall, Joan, you went dancing with the Delanos--Kurt and Don. Then there's Tom and Penny Carson. Joan, we got reshuffled and remingled and reseated at completely new tables, so now I'm also friends with the Boises from Houston, oops, the Houstons from Boise, and wart-nose and her sister Lucille from West Virginia. Oh dear, I shouldn't call Maude that. Maude's a professor of Chinese philosophy and she's one of our speakers, or supposed to be, except that she mumbles, speaks in a monotone, so of course I won't be able to hear her presentation."

"Mother, pul-ese! You're rambling."

"If you'd let me finish, dear. The Houstons and the Bailey sisters found me in the woods. Then we hurried back to the complex. Yes, I remember now. Reporters were all over the place, so those two pairs, the Houstons and the Bailey's, must have given an interview to the press. The doubles would have done that after I left for the dorm."

"The what? *Doubles,* you say? Don't tell me your double vision is back. I knew it, that whack on the head did it. Hie thee to the doctor, quick, mom. Listen to me, Mother. Pay attention, now. You must have suffered a concussion. Don't you dare fall back to sleep. Stay upright, walk. Keep walking. Get a medical examination…"

Agatha stopped listening. Joan had misunderstood. Surprisingly, given the thump she'd taken, Aggie's vision was affected not at all. Other than a headache, she was just fine. She felt rested, too.

"No, dear, I didn't say I was seeing double. What I meant was, I've nicknamed two of the fifteen partners here *the doubles,* because they look so much alike. Well, not all four of them. Lucille and Maude, sisters, are tall and short and Maude has that hairy mole. No, they don't <u>all</u> look alike. The Houstons from Boise--there, I got it right that time--are the look-alikes, the doubles; they're both apple-cheeked blondes… Now where was I? Oh, yes, Max and Mick. Maybe Max cloned himself in Mick, wouldn't that be funny? Maude's the one with the mole, so big you wouldn't believe. The Delanos are doubles, too. Redheaded, red mustaches; you remember."

Aggie switched the phone from her right ear to her left and looked down at herself. She felt grubby, unkempt. Her once smart outfit of purple-trimmed lavender slacks with matching vest, plus a purple silk blouse, were all torn and dirty.

Hey, that's right, she realized with sudden clarity. When struck on the head, she'd been walking the path. The doubles had found her deep in the woods. She couldn't think how that had happened. Perhaps the murderer meant to kill her and had left her for dead, or to die--lingeringly and pitifully, alone--like poor gay Max Shepard out in Wyoming. Or maybe the hit was merely meant as a warning. To cease what she'd assumed was a secret investigation, but apparently wasn't.

"Mom, you didn't hear a word I said, did you?"

"Frankly, no. I wasn't listening, my darling daughter." The endearment was designed to temper her honest but possibly hurtful reply.

"You're not making any sense, mom. Doubles, clones, the Boises from Houston."

"No, dear. I may have said that, but if so I was mistaken. Max and Mick Houston are from Boise, not the other way around."

"Good grief. What does it matter?"

"Joan, somebody else lived in Houston; let me think. Mick, that's right. Max's son Mick, a physicist, worked out of Houston with NASA but quit because he thought he had a job here with Dr. P; only Jones cancelled the center's so-called commitment, so you see, dear, that makes Mick a suspect, too, doesn't it? If he were so upset over not getting hired after all, is what I meant to say. Now that's perfectly clear, isn't it?"

"No, it isn't! Nothing's clear. Go see a doctor before you collapse. And then, dear mother, please come home."

"What? What are you talking about now, Joan?" Then Aggie remembered the best news of all. "Nickee! Is Nicole still home with you, Joan? How's Stevie?"

"They took off again. Right after she got here, Nicole packed up Steven and left for the ranch. I told her she can't hide out there, either, Billy will find her."

"Her dad and granddad will want to see her and Stevie. Leave them be, dear. The men will look after Nickee and Stevie. Your daughter needn't be afraid of an abusive husband when she's there under their protection. Nicole can ride her horse, feel safe for awhile. And of course little Stevie will be happy on his pony."

Aggie nearly blurted out a new decision. She had suddenly decided that when all this blew over and she had made peace with Randy—or kicked him out—she was heading for Nicole. Find her granddaughter from wherever she had decided to hide out, and bring her home. Nickee didn't have to live with an abusive mate, no matter what Randy said about married women sticking with their marriage vows.

"Meanwhile, mom," Joan continued. "You must leave right away before you're killed too. Oh, mom, don't you understand? Somebody tried to kill you! Everybody agrees with me."

Now Aggie knew why her mind had completely leaped the track, like a derailed train. With daughter Joan raising the fear of her mom's potential attacker, Agatha had abruptly switched to worrying about granddaughter

Nicole and her son, Stevie. Of course they would be all right. Every last one of them. People didn't pop out of the woodwork every five minutes to stab and shoot other people. There were plenty of other ways to settle one's differences. Like learning to accept a philandering husband? Maybe

At last Agatha returned to the conversation at hand to reply to Joan. "By *everybody,* do you mean every last person in this big extended family? My darling daughter, you can't really mean that *everybody* agrees with you. I thought you said you were calling from Laramie."

"I am. But don't you know, can't you imagine, that my phone and fax have been ringing for the past half hour? Lisa and Peter, Beth and Brad, Daddy from London, all three Nasties--Nasty Three from the capitol--Ned Fleetfoot from the laundromat, even old Hepzibah and Isabelle. Yes, mom, *everybody* is worrying their head off over you."

"You didn't mention Teddi." Aggie referred to an absent niece, the daughter of Teddy Roosevelt and Isabelle Vicente, a grown-up girl working as a flight attendant out of O'Hare. Agatha was starting to get a kick out of this conversation. She could have mentioned her two brothers, but didn't. Dale made pizzas in his string of Texas shops, and Russell was in Tucson telecommunications, something like that, maybe satellites.

"But not President Davidson?" Aggie giggled, thinking of her old friend, Dom. Joan was too distraught or stubborn to acknowledge her mother's typical reaction to a crisis. Sweep it under the car, drive over it, turn somersaults, giggle her head off.

"Honestly, mom, there's no getting through to you. If you won't come home, then Lisa said to tell you she's coming back there to join you."

Aggie gulped. Next to Randy, Lisa was the last person she wanted to see. Now she'd have to tell more lies and continue to play the pretend game with her favorite cousin. That, or confront Lisa, demand to know when she had started boffing Randy. Aggie tried to think, just when was it her husband had stopped making love to her? Instead of two or three times a week, their lovemaking had dropped off to twice a month, then once, now it was every other month. A big change that had emerged so gradually she hadn't given it much thought at the time. Withholding sex from her, that could be punishment for some petty infraction, some little thing she'd done or failed to do that had upset him. Or, how about this? Randy and Lisa had fallen into each other's arms because Peter had failed Lisa. Everybody knew that when a man took a mistress, he backed off with his wife. Wasn't that the way it went?

Joan was still carrying on. Aggie hoped she'd muttered Mmm and hmmm at the appropriate places. Better to pick up the pace now or Joan would catch on her mama wasn't listening at all. Better yet, turn the conversational ball back on her daughter.

"That's nice, dear," said Aggie. "Meanwhile, you didn't answer my question. How did you hear so fast? About the murders, I can understand. What about my head?"

"Really, mom. Doesn't everybody listen to the radio, watch the TV news, read the papers? Daddy heard in London and Nasty Two in Cheyenne. Nasturtium the Second called her mom down in San Miguel de Allende, so Nasty One is flying in here tomorrow

"That explains it. The minute Nasty Two knows something, the Family Gossip gets in touch with every last clan member she can reach--by cell phone, e-mail, fax; or, presumably, by carrier pigeon."

Joan laughed despite her serious intent. "Lisa will be with you soon."

Aggie bit the bullet and told the truth. "Tell her not to bother."

Joan didn't hear. She had already disconnected.

Aggie flashed back to the day when Joan had taken her first baby steps. She would willingly walk to Aggie but not to her father. Agatha recalled the absolute pride on Randy's face the day Joan had walked into his arms. Yes, Randy had been a good father, despite everything. And now Joan was a grown woman who had made all the right choices in life. Well, except for her divorce. Agatha loved Big Jack like a son, to this very day. Aggie suddenly missed her daughter, her ex-husband, and his dad, too.

Trouble was, hard as both of them had tried with Nickee—and, yes, Randy as grandfather and Jack as father to Nicole—they'd all slipped up, somehow. Aggie worried now that young Nickee, traipsing around the country with her rodeo cowboy husband, never would get her own life back on track.

Following a quick shower, Aggie left her room for the center. Too late for the breakfast of pancakes and sausage, the mouth-watering odors lingering in the dining room. Reggie brought her a bowl of raisin bran with a small pitcher of two-percent milk, a glass of chilled orange juice, freshly thawed from a frozen can, and a pot of hot coffee.

Still headachy, Aggie ate slowly and deliberately. Any abrupt movement made her head hurt. The delicious aroma of leftover breakfast commingled with pork roasting and fresh bread baking for lunch would normally have made her mouth water. This time she felt nauseous. She might have been pregnant with morning sickness.

Late for Professor Bailey's session, Aggie slipped into a chair at table two.

She couldn't hear Maude's monotone and had no interest in reading her lips. Pretending to pay attention, Aggie wondered again about her missing notebook. A shrug, a sip of water, and she occupied herself with studying her peers and contemplating possible motives.

Penelope's Uncle Tom might have done it. Carson had both the strength and the anger. In fact, he appeared perpetually angry, at everyone, Penelope especially. Another unanswered question was whether he'd killed Jones in defense of Penny, or for other personal reasons, and then had taken out Akunda because the cop was on to him.

Then there were the Delanos. Aggie couldn't get past the notion that either one might have killed to protect the other, and also in defense of their jobs. She had uncovered no motivation for Kristi or Reggie to do murder. Of course Sam was their boss, and neither had expressed any particular sorrow at his demise.

The nature of Dr. P and Jones' relationship was still a mystery. What had those two meant to each other, if anything beyond the obvious--Dr. P leaning on Jones because the assistant director could see. If so, how had Paul Petroski managed before Sam Jones came into his life? Or had Jones been there all along--through all those degrees that Dr. P took, seemingly on his own; and, thereafter, on the corporate stage?

Aggie spotted Olaf creeping up on her, one chair at a time. When he caught her eye, he grinned. Aggie got up and moved to another table, closer to the front, farther from the Wisconsin Grandpa.

Aggie tilted her head, ear toward the speaker. Just as well she had lingered on the phone with Joan. Aggie didn't mind missing what she couldn't hear. Professor Bailey was a mumbler.

Penny scooted her chair closer to Aggie's and turned back a few pages in her notebook, presumably so Aggie could copy what she'd missed. Aggie smiled and nodded a Thank-You at the shy girl. Then she noticed: shorthand mixed with longhand. Shorthand? Just as well she'd lingered on the phone with Joan.

Dr. Yu, the Chinese medical doctor-philosopher from Bejing, was scheduled next as their "special treat." She hoped he would speak louder than Maude did. Aggie glanced over her shoulder. Whew, Olaf had advanced no closer. Perhaps he was finally getting the hint that she wasn't interested in him.

At the conclusion of whatever it was mole-nose had mumbled, the applause was polite but half-hearted. Mick Houston, however, exhibited great but puzzling enthusiasm. He stood to shout "Bravo! Bravo!" When Maude returned to their table, he pulled his chair close to hers. The two quickly put their heads together, Mick mumbling in Maude's ear, Maude nodding and muttering back.

Hmmm, what did we have here? A private conference or a budding romance?

She must try to separate this foursome, talk to them one at a time—Max, Mick, Maude and Lucille.

With Maude lingering to wait for Lucille and accept a few plaudits (darn few) for her speech, Aggie followed the men out of the room. She hoped Max and his son would separate so she could trail one or the other. She was determined to corner the Houstons, get them talking, find out more about each of them.

Max and Mick strolled on past the dorm through the trees. Soon the pair set out running. No problem. Aggie and Lisa had run the Boston and San Diego marathons. Aggie had no trouble at all keeping up with the Houstons. When they paused so Max could catch his breath, Aggie did, too. Max sank down on a fallen log and Aggie slipped behind a tree. She hoped that one of the two men faced her way so she could read lips.

"Okay, dad," Mick said, standing behind Max and facing in Aggie's direction. "What did you want to talk about?"

"Who, me?"

"Yes, you. You're no jogger, so when you invited me to join you in a run, I suspected you of having a hidden agenda."

"Uh, well, I thought we could talk about the liberals and conservatives. You know, politics." Max, too, faced Aggie. Apparently neither man wanted to look each other in the eyes.

Mick chuckled on a false sounding note. "The liberals keep talking sweet stuff. You know, about horrifying experiences to babies and the heroes who save them, about oldtimers bereft of medical insurance and the organizations out to protect them."

"Yeah, well, if the liberals are sweet talking, the conservatives are talking even sweeter, except about saving the country from terrorists, from the Muslims' Jihad, from the oil-hoarding Arabs."

Aggie's mind tripped half-way round the globe as if to drop in on her sweetie. What was Randy's mission in Eurasia this time around? Perhaps she should have accompanied him instead of following her daughter's wishes in heading for Vermont. But, then, Randy hadn't invited her. What could she do for him anyhow, except take his dictation, and she could do that by phone; transcribe it, too, forward it on to recipients by e-mail or fax. After so many years she was expert at forging his signature, so no problem signing his letters, even legal documents. She couldn't make love to him long-distance, and even if she showed up on his doorstep, Randy was no longer interested in their physical relationship.

Busy with daydreams, Aggie nearly missed the change of topics. Suddenly

Max was accusing Mick of something; the son was defending himself, rather ably, it appeared.

"You didn't have to come after me, dad. I knew what I was doing."

"You'd been recruited into a cult, son! That's what was happening. I had to get you out, and get you some sound counseling."

"Kidnapped me, you mean. You still don't realize how embarrassing that was."

"Who cared? I was fighting for your sanity. I never did trust those survivalists who bought into that camp over inWyoming."

"For cryin' out loud, dad. You're an atheist, what do you know about the fundamentalists?"

"Agnostic, perhaps, not an out-and-out atheist, son."

"The fact remains, you hate fundamentalists."

"I thought they were evangelicals."

"Evangelicals, fundamentalists, survivalists—you've got a whole repertoire of labels to stick on people, haven't you? If you'd just waited around long enough, got to know them, you might have accepted our hosts' beliefs, seen the light, been converted."

"The hell you say."

"As a matter of fact, you did listen to their spiel awhile. Admit it. They cornered you. In fact, Harris Holloway did hypnotize you. You could hardly turn off your brain under the influence of his power."

"Oh, yeah?"

CHAPTER 14

AGGIE DIDN'T KNOW WHAT that was all about, and didn't much care. Politics, religion, neither one an issue right now. She couldn't see how the Houstons' differences could possibly play with Jones' murder, much less Mishka's.

Aggie returned to the center and sat back down in the assembly room among the remaining conferees. She hoped she was in time for the next speaker scheduled following the long mid-afternoon break. Maude hadn't offered much, not when Aggie couldn't hear her, but now Agatha had high hopes for the rest of the day's program.

Just then Officer Malcolm Thompson lumbered in, crossed the floor, and tapped Aggie on the shoulder. Startled, she jumped and looked up into the stern expression of the big man looming over her.

"Detective Whitehall wants to see you."

Aggie sat immobile.

"Right now."

"You're going to make me miss our special treat," Aggie said to Whitehall.

"Never mind that." The detective scowled down at her. "I want some answers. What were you doing outside so late last night? Tell me what happened before the attack." He pulled up a chair facing her across the table. When Reggie poked in his head, Fred called for coffee.

"You've listened to the television news, I suppose." If Randy across the Atlantic and her family out in Wyoming had heard, everybody must know.

"Not me. I've been here most of the night. Officer Battisti told me. She was listening to the radio in her car." Whitehall stopped talking to nod his

89

gratitude at Reggie, who poured the fragrant, steaming coffee into two mugs; one for Whitehall, the other for Aggie.

Aggie didn't have much to report. She saw no point in describing her chat with Sylvia, which could get the rookie cop in trouble. Surely Battisti had revealed to Aggie more than she should have. "I was out walking, alone, getting some exercise, enjoying the night air off the lake," Aggie said, only half-fibbing. She was returning to the dormitory, she said, when she got hit. That's all she could recall. She wondered again who'd socked her, and equally important, why?

Dissatisfied but unable to squeeze truth from a turnip, or in this case extract any more information from Aggie, Fred dismissed her.

Agatha missed the introduction, but was in time to hear most of Dr. Yu's lecture on Chinese medical philosophy of holistic, preventative healing. As Joan had requested, she took copious notes.

"The body, mind, and emotions are interactive," Dr. Yu said. "When in complete balance, both our physical and our mental conditions are more likely to be healthy, given the absence of internal and external conflict or trauma. The primary, most primitive affectors come from our relations to and our interaction with self and with our significant others: mate, children, parents, extended family members, friends, coworkers and colleagues, neighbors; and, finally, with the members of our various groups and the country at large. By *groups*, think of all the people you interact with during a given day or week—work group, religious or political group, civic organizations, strangers and other passers-by, clerks and service personnel, tradesmen, repair persons, and what-not."

Her mind drifted. If Randy wanted a mistress, did he have to hurt her even worse by choosing her own dear cousin, Lisa? Or, turn it around. Aggie had always supposed Lisa and Peter Schwartzkopf had the perfect marriage. Now Aggie imagined that Lisa's libido was every bit as strong and demanding as Aggie's own. Yet, in the entire span of their life together, they had never once discussed their sexual needs. Humph. What occurred to Aggie now was that if Lisa needed a lover, why did she have to take Randy?

"To help prevent illness, look at the health or absence thereof of your personal and most meaningful relationships. To seek healing--the alleviation of physical pain or mental anguish--address the health of your relationships. When these are in turmoil, in conflict or danger, the whole body-mind-soul suffers. What do we get? Ulcers, high blood pressure; or, at the extreme, cancer, stroke, heart failure, and sooner rather than later in many cases, death itself."

Good grief. With the betrayal and humiliation she'd been suffering over the past couple of weeks, she too could be subject to any of those awful ailments. Hate and hurt again suffused Aggie's whole being. It wasn't fair! Go along her whole life doing what's right, but instead of the rewards of praise and appreciation, she'd got socked in the gut.

"Treat the body badly," Dr. Yu said, "batter it with frequent overdoses of drugs, alcohol, junk food, sweets and fats, too many calories, too little exercise or sleep--and not only the body but also the mind and emotions rebel. Leading to, among other things, conflicts with and the breakdown of once healthy personal and familial relationships."

A new idea dawned, like the sun rising in Aggie's brain. Adultery was more than a sin against her and Peter. It could be harmful to the adulterers, too. She wondered if both Randy and Lisa had suddenly come down with mental illness.

Dr. Yu quoted from Kaptchuk's *The Web that has no Weaver* to help them appreciate the benefits of a common Chinese medical practice; namely, acupuncture. Aggie, along with a number of others, she noticed, tuned out.

The next topic--*Sex!* Aggie shuddered. Yu was getting too close to her current troubles with Randy for comfort.

All over the room people perked up and sat up and leaned forward, their arms on the tables or holding up sleepy heads. This time Yu quoted from Dunas and Goldberg's *Passion Play: Ancient Secrets for a Lifetime of Health and Happiness through Sensational Sex.*

"Sex is good medicine," he said. "Fantastic sex can bolster one's immune system, strengthen internal organs, and secure emotional well-being. Using traditional Chinese medicine, Dunas offers sexual prescriptions for common Western ailments, such as how to strengthen overtaxed kidneys, and how to fire up an emotionally distant relationship."

Phooey on that stuff, it didn't even sound romantic. If Randy sensed an "emotional distance" between them, he had good reason. A perpetual bully could not expect unrelenting and uninhibited passion from the woman he tries to dominate. Ahah, and how about her granddaughter? Aggie didn't even want to contemplate Nickee's relationship with Billy, the skinny creep who strutted around like a little bandy rooster.

When Aggie tuned back in, she caught the words yin and yang. Joan had once defined those for her: Yin--the passive, female cosmic element, force, or principle that is opposite but complementary to yang in Chinese dualistic philosophy. Yang--the active, male cosmic element, complementary to yin. The Chinese didn't put men before or above women, Joan had said, but saw them as complementary. Randy ought to hear this.

Aggie no longer needed to ponder, as first she had, why this particular conference of Dr. Petroski's focused on family relationships; good, bad, or indifferent, their impact affected too many other aspects of one's life. The big

91

question was why had Joan insisted on her attendance. Her daughter was nuts if she thought these insights could make a difference in her parents' marriage. How could she hope to change Randy now? A decade older than she was, his personality seemed frozen in the Russian tundra.

Dr. Yu quit the stage, to be replaced by the director. The cause of Dr. P's warmth and charisma, his mesmerizing effect on his conferees and clients, was becoming clear. He cared--passionately and compassionately. About individuals, at work and at home. About corporations--their workers and their stockholders. And, by extension, about the world and society at large.

Turn it backwards--he hoped to help people develop healthy relationships in their marriages. If only she could. Paul Petroski took the lectern following Yu's presentation. As their director spoke, warmly and with renewed vigor, his head moved to face one side of the room and then the other as if his very soul if not his sightless eyes could reach deep within the mind and heart of each silent and seemingly worshipful member of his audience.

Murder and the sick souls of murderers all but forgotten, the conference had resumed on a high note. "Special treat," indeed. They could all return home now, assured they'd been well fed.

Aggie couldn't believe it. When she walked out of the conference room for her dorm before lunch, there was Lisa. The petite blonde squealed and reached out for a hug. Peter had chartered a plane for her, she said, which explained the speed of her arrival.

Talk about hypocrisy. Aggie hugged Lisa back.

CHAPTER 15

WEARING A PINK LINEN suit with matching pink ankle strap shoes and a pink scarf around her curls, Lisa Schwartzkopf said she was eager to hear everything. "About the murders. First things first, though. Are you sure you're okay? You don't want to see a doctor?"

Wearing her typical expression of delight with Lisa, now the evil betrayer, was not going to be easy. Unless she was ready to confront her cousin, Aggie must figure out how to don the garment of pretense.

Trembling, Aggie smiled from dark brown eyes into Lisa's blue ones. In their dorm room while Lisa unpacked, they looked each other up and down, as if they were mannequins displaying the latest fashions. Without verifying their selections, they'd done it again. Save for their typical color differentiation, Aggie's lavender linen suit matched Lisa's pink one. Aggie's purple silk blouse was twinned in Lisa's pale pink, button-down shirt. Except that Aggie wore slacks and Lisa a slim skirt.

"ESP?" said Lisa, laughing.

Late for lunch, Aggie slipped into her originally assigned chair at table four, directing Lisa to the empty place Joan had vacated when she returned to Wyoming. Aggie did the introductions. Seated across from Lisa, this arrangement put the remaining cluster members between them: the Delanos to the right of Aggie, and the Carson uncle and niece to the left. Reggie supervised the servers. Kristi, Penny said, had been commandeered by Whitehall to process investigative data on her computer. She could access NCIC from there.

"The National Crime Information Center," Aggie clarified for the table. "Among other things, like matching DNA data between known criminals and evidence collected from new crimes, they track serial numbers on guns and ballistics data."

Glancing at Lisa, Aggie caught an expression of surprise flicker across the blonde's pretty features. *So there, too, Ms Know-it-all.*

"Tell us more, Aggie," said Kurt.

Ignoring Lisa sitting there pleating and unpleating her linen napkin, Aggie continued: "Vancouver, British Columbia, is one of the few places on earth that takes DNA samples from dental work, including from skeletons. They've been drilling the teeth from ages-old skulls to crack some of their cold cases."

"Where did you pick up all that stuff?" Lisa demanded, disbelief in her voice.

"Yeah, tell us more," boomed Tom Carson. Penelope's reproachful look and shushing finger to her lips went right over her uncle's head. People from the other tables glanced over.

When Aggie glanced back, she noticed Maude Bailey with Max Houston. Their heads together, the pair whispered and giggled. Hmm, something romantic developing between them, perhaps, as Aggie noted their fingers and shoulders periodically touching. Fumbling with her roll and butter knife as a diversion, she looked again; then away, then back. Lip-reading exposed a partial exchange:

"Where can…meet?"

"Down… the lake."

"When?"

"After lunch."

"Aggie?" Lisa prompted from across the table.

Aggie was keenly aware that she often annoyed both Lisa and Randy. Somehow they couldn't appreciate that her mind, when left to drift, often produced tasty fruits, not always apparent to the obvious berry gatherer and certainly not to her logical husband and cousin. She refused to defend herself.

"Um? Oh, sorry, Tom. I heard about the NCIC somewhere, a television documentary, perhaps," she hedged, protecting Sylvia as her source.

Aggie had watched cousin Nasty, Wyoming's Secretary of State, perform the art of pretense to perfection. Like the typical politician, Nasturtium the Third could ably drive a point while bystepping the truth. At viewing a new but ugly baby, Nasty Three might gush, "Oh, what a dear, sweet, little darling." To a gawky woman in an ill-fitting dress, she'd been overheard exclaiming, "What a lovely gown." Aggie wished she was more experienced with the technique.

Just then Lisa grabbed the conversational ball to fling it into another basket. "Tell me about yourself, Penelope."

Startled, Penny blushed and ducked her head. Tom gave her a sharp poke.

Undeterred, Lisa tossed her ball in another direction. "How about you, Mr. Carson? Are you enjoying the conference?" Instead of shouting he merely nodded.

"And you two--Kurt and Don, is it?"

Battisti should hear her, Aggie thought, disgusted. If Sylvia thinks I'm good at interrogation, she ought to see Lisa in full sail.

Unlike Don, Tom, and Penny, Kurt Delano was eager to talk. While he regaled Lisa and their neighbors with examples and stories taken from Dr. P and Yu's lectures, Aggie resumed nibbling the Cobb salad.

Kurt elaborated for Lisa's benefit by sharing the purposes of the small-group afternoon sessions: to regurgitate key points from the morning lectures, exchange ideas, make recommendations between and among themselves; and pinpoint where, how, and with whom they would subsequently introduce and pursue their own blueprints for initiating "cautious, careful, incremental change."

Yeah, sure. No matter what she did, Aggie couldn't go back in time; back to the love and trust she had once taken for granted from Randy and Lisa.

"No matter how much good and meaningful information to which learners--of any age, in any circumstances--are exposed," Dr. P had said early on. "Learning does not occur until the new--or renewed--knowledge is applied. 'Application, application, application', that's the name of the game called education."

Red-mustached Don interrupted his redheaded cousin Kurt. "Another thing Dr. P said: In teaching or training, or effectuating behavioral change: 'you can lead a horse to water but you can't make him drink.'"

"Yeah," Kurt said, interrupting. "But remember what happened then."

Everybody circling their table laughed uproariously, again calling attention to their cluster. "At that point," boomed Tom, "Max Houston from Boise interrupted Dr. P to yell: 'You can, too. You can too make a horse drink. You salt his oats!'"

The room grew silent; hands attached to forks or coffee cups paused in mid-air as people ceased their own chatter and chewing to eavesdrop. Maude nudged Max, who acted like he was tempted to nibble on her earlobe.

That might be a place to start making changes--go home and nibble on Randy. Aggie couldn't see herself doing that. She giggled right out loud.

Lisa stared at her.

Salting the oats was the motivation, Dr. Petroski had repeated, adding that if you can't motivate people to learn, to change, "they're never gonna do it!"

Now how th'hell was she supposed to salt Randy's oats? Aggie had no clue where to begin.

Under Lisa's astonished eyes and ears a mighty cheer rang out. People pointed to Max Houston at table two. His cluster members grinned, praising one of their own and patting him on the back.

"Speech! speech!" somebody yelled.

"Take a bow, Max," Maude mumbled from close beside him.

From across the room, Olav Svenson winked at Aggie. She grimaced.

Ahh, the camaraderie was back. It seemed that just about everyone had forgotten there could be a murderer in their midst. Aggie's mind leapt from the good feelings to motivation for murder. She mentally summarized. Dr. P had said the motivation to change things--whether actual physical objects, or circumstances, or behaviors--had to be very strong to bring about change. Changing from a law-abiding citizen to one of society's lowest and most-hated meant that the motivation for murder had to be devastatingly real.

That could describe her, too. The sudden knowledge of betrayal had triggered in herself such murderous feelings, something similar could have unloosed the Devil in another's bosom. Could happen to any of us. That's why, she concluded, abruptly, the murderer could be any one of these otherwise nice people gathered in this room today.

These people were all professionals; every one with so much to risk if exposed. No, think again. She wasn't a professional anything, not even gainfully employed. Ahh, but neither was Mick Houston, not at the moment. Mick could have a motive, but she couldn't see him that enflamed with passion over a lost job. But what did she know. He wanted so badly to change careers, he had already met and hurdled several big obstacles: resigning his NASA position, quitting his apartment, returning to Idaho. All of these things, so sayeth Dr. P, were major life changes, even when voluntarily made. If the anticipated result didn't materialize, a person could flip out, she supposed. Mick's plan had fallen through the cracks of Jones' rejection; Jones was the sidewalk crack that broke Mick's back.

Take that reasoning a step further and apply it to the father. Suppose that Max, out of love for his son and enflamed beyond reason, did the dastardly deed. Hmm. Again, the motivation for Akunda's murder seemed clear. He had somehow discovered the truth surrounding the first murder and died for coming across that knowledge.

In another clime and under other circumstances, the murderer could be anybody; a psycho who liked to kill for killing's sake. But her companions--save for Mick and of course Lisa and herself--were all professionals, with so much at stake, so much to lose, if caught. Why risk it? How in the world could murder ever seem necessary?

CHAPTER 16

"I DON'T UNDERSTAND WHY you did it," Howard said to Harris. The Holloways sat in their newly painted green canoe, not far from shore.

Harris tied a different fly to his line. Neither brother had caught so much as a three-inch bass.

"Just because," said Harris with a malicious chuckle. "We know that Mrs. Morissey is known in the media as the President's surrogate mom, right? So I bopped her on the head as a warning."

Howie pulled up his rod. He was quitting for the day. "Makes no sense. If you meant to warn her that you're ultimately after President Davidson, where's the connection?"

Harris screwed up his face in confusion. "Uh, well. It made sense to me at the time." Then, with a giggle and a flip of his wrist, he added, "Makes me no never mind why I did it. The fun part is watching all the hullabaloo as a result. I wish we could get closer. Get a front-seat view." With clawing fingernails, Harris picked away at the green paint on the canoe. He preferred pink any day. On everything.

Sylvia approached the cousins to give Aggie an assignment. Since she and Kristi were close, Sylvia said, Aggie could probably get access to the computers without too much trouble. The search of databases to uncover background on the conferees ought to be done secretly. Otherwise, Sylvia would do it.

Aggie reluctantly introduced Officer Battisti to Lisa. If her cousin discovered she was playing detective, she'd want the whole scoop. Lisa would grab the reins to take charge of this amateur investigation. If not Randy, then

97

it was Lisa always telling Aggie what to do, as if she didn't have the sense God gave a duck; like she wouldn't come in out of the rain without one or the other telling her it was pouring buckets outside.

Standing apart, the new arrival from Wyoming listened and looked puzzled. Aggie caught Lisa straining to hear.

Armed with Sylvia's instructions and her own ideas, Aggie agreed before directing her cousin how to get to class.

"But I want to come with you. That's why Randy sent me out here. To keep tabs on you."

"<u>Randy</u> sent you here? You've talked to him since he left town?"

Lisa had the grace to briefly drop her glance before lifting her head. Her body stiffened. She looked defiant. "He said he was calling me from London."

Kristi showed Aggie the computer before leaving the dainty duo.

"Oh, boy, this should be fun," said Lisa, while picking up and opening the new journal record Aggie had begun after losing track of the first one. Lisa could read but not write Gregg shorthand. "I'll just read some of your journal before class starts."

Aggie pointed to the notebook. "Since when is murder fun?"

Lisa murmured noncommittally. "You know what I mean." She pulled up a chair beside Aggie, who had transferred from memory everything she could recall from the lost journal, plus her new suppositions. Now Lisa was privy to her private notes about Sam Jones' crude behavior, his sexual harassment of both Penny and Joan, his threats to expose Kurt's secret, and the questions she had recorded about Jones' possible relationship with Dr. P.

As Aggie scanned down screen after screen, occasionally hitting the print command to produce hard copies, Lisa read Aggie's journal, her forehead furrowed from concentration over the longhand mixed with the Gregg squiggles. Now and then she glanced up to watch Aggie's progress.

"What are you finding? Anything useful or suspicious?"

Aggie couldn't think how to resist Lisa. She sighed in resignation.

"A lot of information on Dr. P. He's obviously made a name for himself. But I knew that, already."

"What about the others you're checking on? Kurt and his cousin Don? Penelope and her uncle Tom?"

Her cousin had a good memory. Admit it, Aggie reminded herself, Lisa's input could prove helpful. Meanwhile, Aggie had to act and sound like she still loved Lisa. Picking her brain would be the method of pretense.

That settled, Aggie decided to open up, lay her cards on the table for their mutual examination. "Some records, yes. The bare facts that people have already shared."

"Jones, then. Anything on him?"

Aggie clicked on Save, and turned to Lisa. "Some. Sam and Paul served in the same Vietnam unit. Dr. P, as we know, lost his eyesight over there. He also got a medal of honor. Apparently he saved Sam's life..."

"You know that old Chinese proverb, Aggie: *Save a man's life and he belongs to you. Forever.*"

"Yeah. So what? Just because Paul gave Sam a job, Sam should be grateful. But instead, he actually resents his benefactor?"

"I see what you mean. Sounds like motivation, albeit a small one, for murder. Only turn the idea the other way around. Jones, not Dr. Petroski, is dead."

Aggie looked briefly pensive before turning back to the computer to resume her data search. "I hope there's more on Jones."

"Why?" Lisa looked puzzled. She glanced down to re-crease the crease in her skirt, then back up again. "Oh, of course; to complete your assignment, prove you're competent, eh? Or is there more to it than that? You'd like to pin something really bad, really terrible, on Jones, so you can justify his murder?"

"Why in the world would I want to do an awful thing like that?"

"Because, Aggie, confess. Joan told me what Jones did to her. She must have told you, too. Naturally you were furious with him. I'm suggesting, therefore, that now you're glad he's dead, which obviously makes you feel guilty. I ask you, dear, when is murder ever justified?"

Aggie scowled.

"Let's get back to work," said Lisa, apparently oblivious to Aggie's feelings and the aura of hate that Aggie felt had permeated her whole being. "You print what little you find, and I'll interpret it for you."

Interpret it for me, eh. Like I'm some kind of an idiot.

Aggie returned to the computer. Anything to avoid facing the woman, who, like Randy, could make her feel like a retarded child with a single sentence couched in words meant to sound helpful. It was a mystery to Aggie how they could do that--smile, lend a helping hand, while smirking with derision. People must be born with that kind of lopsided talent.

Aggie soon excused herself to make a potty stop. Alone in the stall, she bent to hold her throbbing head in her hands. What to do about Lisa?

Aggie was beginning to sympathize with the seminar murderer. She could almost understand motivation, seeing into the killer's head. Okay, sympathizing wasn't a bad thing, surely. But if she didn't stop empathizing, pretty soon she could turn into one. She remembered a quotation: *Be careful what you wish for, you might get it.* She had thought she wanted both Randy and Lisa out of her life. But what would life be like without them? No, she didn't want to get rid of the pair she loved so much. She wanted to change them. Preferably turn back the clock to before she'd caught them in bed.

CHAPTER 17

AGGIE CONCLUDED THAT SHE must try harder. If she didn't solve these murders quickly, Lisa would beat her to it. Then, out in Wyoming, Randy and her cousin would gloat, to each other and to everybody else in the family, the town and the state, and in interviews with the press. Aggie could guess how that would work. Her husband, who objected to his wife standing on her own two feet, much less gleaning the limelight, would crow with pride over his mistress. Randolph Morissey was a hypocrite.

Inside the family Randy would make it clear that if Lisa hadn't come galloping to the rescue, poor little discombobulated Aggie would be dead; butchered, for sure, as the killer's next victim.

In Kristi's office, Aggie was alone. Presumably Lisa had left for class.

Aggie returned her attention to the computer, thinking she could have used her own laptop. Exploring further, she realized that the center's various search programs were more sophisticated. Meaning what? Sam Jones, as the assistant director, had been using the computer in Kristi's absence to collect personal data on conference participants? Aggie could think of no reason, other than to blackmail people when or if Jones discovered information they would much prefer to keep secret.

Having recently pried into the Houston men's private affairs, Aggie felt briefly contrite. Yet she had no ulterior motive, she was seeking to solve these murders and return home. Well, and to bring the killer to justice, of course.

Aggie plugged in the name of Mick Houston first. Perhaps because the younger man had mentioned a religious group of some sort that had captured his loyalty. A backwoods cult, Max had called it, admitting to hiring a de-programmer and to kidnapping his son. *Rescuing* Mick, Max had insisted. Restoring his mind from the black depths of religious and political brainwashing. Briefly she thought of that Jones fellow, the one who had persuaded about six-hundred members of his cult to drink poisoned Kool-Ade and kill themselves as an alternative to giving themselves up to the authorities who were out to close down their *church*. Some cults, it appeared, meant to submit their souls to Satanic pursuits, like murder and mayhem. If this had been the case with young Mick, little wonder Max had gone after him armed with a de-programmer. Agatha hoped she never ran across such deviltry in her lifetime.

The computer coughed up a long list of items, with the data scrolling down on the screen in front of Aggie. Omigod, apparently the Wyoming church of Mick's experience wasn't merely a small flock of innocent believers. Tagged by the Federal Bureau of Investigation, the "Sin-Sick Salvationists" were suspected of being devil worshipers, and of demonstrating the more typical survivalist tactics of hoarding weapons, practicing military strategies, assigning men to security and keeping round-the-clock guards on duty, and skulking about acting suspicious of neighbors and anybody else accidentally stumbling into their conclave.

The computer cited no incidences of female participation. Perhaps it was an all-male cult. Aggie thought of the Oklahoma City bomber, of other terrorist cells, active or sleeping, several of which reportedly had their origins in the vast mountains of the Wyoming wilderness. What had the Sin-Sick Salvationist cult been plotting? The records abruptly stopped after briefly describing an FBI attack on the compound. Aggie supposed Max had already rescued his son and assigned him to de-programming by that time, which would give some indication of why the Bureau stopping tracking them. But Aggie couldn't be sure she was right, since Mick's name was not available among the group of black-listed Salvationists.

What Mick's past had to do with his present wasn't the least bit clear, either. Not unless Sam had discovered Mick's link to a cult that might—or might not—have been planning terrorist attacks somewhere in the United States or elsewhere. Canada, perhaps. Either way, armed with such ammunition, Sam Jones could have threatened to shoot down Mick's application to the center if one or both Houstons didn't pay him bribes.

Which meant that Max was also a suspect, along with his son. Just as Don, in protecting Kurt's reputation, had to be included on her list of potential killers. Thus with Agatha's computer searches, she had added two guys, not eliminated anybody.

Oh, dear. Which way to turn next. Aggie switched off the computer and rejoined the study group, pulling up a chair beside Lisa.

Aggie couldn't concentrate on the group activities. Instead, she tried to view her companions objectively, as if they were bugs under a microscope. Start with what had motivated them to apply for this program; move on to what triggered the killer instinct.

That afternoon they were assigned to role play, and to switch roles or even genders. A few people at each table stood, to pick up and carry their chairs around the big room in an effort to gain some privacy. Some people continued to stand, to posture and walk about. Others sat, facing each other or turning half-away about; depending, Aggie supposed, on whether they were portraying straightforward or embarrassing scenes. She observed and read lips, even while half-attentive to Lisa's instructions. Naturally her sugary-voiced blonde cousin was determined to take over and manage this silly assignment.

Aggie noted that Don played like he was Kurt and Kurt, Don; Penny, Tom, and Tom, Penny. Reggie played that he was the computer director and Kristi the food manager.

The double cousins stayed put in their chairs in the center of the room. Lisa played that she was married to Randy, telling Aggie that she must act like she was wife to Colonel Schwartzkopf. Disgusting, but this was Lisa's idea of fun. Lisa, playing Aggie, talked about how she would be more assertive with Randy. Heck, that was no help.

Aggie wanted to see Lisa as *Lisa, herself, with Randy.* What she was dying to ask was how and when they'd first got together. Did they always make out in her bed? How cruel. By betraying Aggie, however, the pair also betrayed Peter. Agatha wondered how Peter would feel, or what he'd do if and when he found out about his adulterous wife.

Aggie was surprised, though, when Lisa showed some perception of her feelings and the insider's view of what marriage to Randy must be like. Lisa, as Aggie, talked honestly and openly to "Randy" about how his insults and put-downs made her feel. Meaning that Lisa thought Aggie was dishonest and wishy-washy by pretending she had a good, even wonderful, marriage. This would take some thinking about.

Naw, Agatha already knew, or must always have sensed her own vacillation, if only at the subliminal level. Typically, Lisa could be sweet on top and spoiled garbage underneath. Aggie, on the other hand, merely put up a good face to others. You could hardly go around complaining about your marriage, if you couldn't think what to do about it to get hubby to change.

The cousins finished first and Lisa excused herself to go study the T. J. Jordan abstracts. She wasn't about to hang around for the post-analysis. Aggie simply sat still and quiet, watching the other players and reading their lips as best she could.

Penelope stuck out her chin and boomed while her Uncle Tom slumped, ducked his head, and simpered. When finished, they stared at each other.

"Is that what I sound like?" Tom asked her. Penny nodded.

"I look like a wimp to you?" she mumbled. Tom harumphed.

The Delanos were having a hard time of it. Aggie suspected their sexual liaison, if there was one that linked the cousins, was too private. Somebody might overhear them. Their personalities weren't all that different and if they had few conflicts between them, they probably couldn't think of anything to act out. She had hoped to overhear Jones' name and to observe how they thought they should have handled his threats while he was still alive. She worked hard at reading their lips, which wasn't easy with those double red mustaches. As far as she could determine, Jones' name didn't come up.

Reggie and Kristi's exchange, beginning with few if any underlying subtleties, quickly took a different turn. At first, like everybody, they giggled and acted embarrassed. But when Reggie played Jones and Kristi was herself, sharp words and snarling voices erupted. "I don't care what you say, *Sam*. My data records are off limits to you. I'm not giving out secured information on Reggie or any of the other personnel. I'm warning you, back off. Or I'll report your unwarranted demands to Dr. Petroski."

Aha, Agatha was right. Jones had treated the staff as badly as he had everybody else. Save for Dr. P, but no telling what went on between Sam and Paul when they'd been alone together behind closed doors. Sam might have shown Paul his obnoxious side, too, and Dr. P. simply couldn't get away from him. She knew the feeling. Sometimes there was no way out of an intimate situation short of murder or suicide.

Aggie turned away, directing her attention this time to the Bailey sisters and the father-son Houstons. At first the women interacted as a couple and the men, likewise. These partners then traded places so that Max was paired with Lucille, and Mick with Maude. That was a surprise. Aggie would have expected them to couple the other way about, Max with Maude. By now everybody must have seen them together. In private, they could already be playing patty cake. Mick and Lucille together made more sense; they were both younger, and Lucille was far prettier than her older sister. Aggie could neither eavesdrop nor read lips. She was left with one more puzzle. Of course she hadn't expected the men to confront each other over the Salvationist fiasco back in Wyoming; they'd already done that, here in the Vermont woods.

When the role plays closed and the group dismissed for the break, Aggie got a Coke and cookies, while Lisa chose green tea and celery. "Oh?" Lisa said, lifting an eyebrow and staring Aggie up and down. "You no longer watch your figure?"

Aggie bit back a retort. Had Lisa's voice been deeper, she could have passed for Randy. Her tone echoed his typical critical manner.

Lisa suggested next that they retire to their dormitory room to compare notes. "I want to hear what you gleaned from your computer searches."

If she wanted Lisa's help, Aggie supposed she should comply, but right now she felt resentful. She would prefer cutting Lisa out of the loop.

Aggie turned away from Lisa to pause at table two. She smiled and exchanged greetings, which was when she noticed Professor Bailey's open notebook. Granted, it was upside down to Aggie's view, but she couldn't believe her eyes. Shorthand! Maude, like herself and Penny, knew shorthand. Hardly anybody did nowadays, so this revelation came as a surprise. Aggie used hers in taking Randy's dictation. She wondered what purpose this skill served for the other two women. *Use it or lose it*, a difficult skill to learn, it quickly disappeared if not used regularly. Perhaps that was all their method of note taking was about. Or it was a hobby, something to pass the time during the endless meetings these women were no doubt required to attend.

After potty breaks, the cousins flopped down on their beds; Lisa's made up, Aggie's rumpled. "This reminds me of college, Aggie. Remember when we were roommates at UW in Laramie? Gee, Aggie, that was fun."

Aggie reminded the blonde that their carefree time had only lasted six weeks, until Randy had returned from Saudi Arabia. (Agatha's mom had baby-sat Joan, so Aggie could have at least one dormitory experience, no matter how brief.) But Aggie didn't feel like talking about Randy now, certainly not with Lisa.

Despite herself, Aggie remembered how funny Lisa had been during those six weeks. One night some frat boys came in and tried to steal Lisa's panties from her underwear drawer and she had caught them in the act. She'd promptly shooed them away with the backside of a broom. No doubt about it, Lisa was a take-charge woman.

Jumping up to look in the mirror, Aggie grabbed a brush and began attacking her hair as if it were eating her scalp. Diversion. She was nervous around Lisa. Leaping like a gazelle in the forest, Aggie hurled herself over the obstacle of intimate conversation. Lisa had no right to sit there talking about Randy as if he were hers, even if she had had him. Or would continue to have him until and unless Agatha found some sure way to assert her control over the disgusting pair. Force them into behaving themselves. Saying they were sorry. As if that could salve her wounds.

The only safe topic was people study. Aggie shared the Reggie-Kristi role play.

Lisa extracted bottled mineral water from her luggage and handed Aggie one. "Sounds like Reggie has something to hide."

"What I don't understand," Aggie countered, keeping her eyes downcast.

"If Kristi was so protective of her computer records in the face of Jones' demands, why was she willing to let me look into them?"

Lisa snorted derisively. "Probably imagines you're computer illiterate."

Aggie pretended to ignore her cousin. "Maybe Kristi <u>wanted</u> me to find something. And then to do something about it. Something she's afraid to do. Think about that."

Lisa shrugged, as if to imply that anything Aggie knew wasn't worth knowing. She sucked on her bottled water like a thirsty baby at the nipple. "Changing the subject, Aggie, why didn't Max and Maude pair off? They look like a couple. They act like a couple. If I, a newcomer, noticed, everybody else must have, too."

"Lisa, you're reading something sinister into every casual act or conversation. I don't understand their choice of pairing, either, but it's probably nothing."

Aggie leaned her head against the wall. She debated whether to fill Lisa in with news of the Wyoming cult and the abyss the experience had cut between father and son. Actually, she could use Lisa's input on this topic and more. Instead, Aggie wanted to close her eyes and escape into the oblivion of sleep. Without Lisa's voice rattling in her head, she could snatch a nap, finally.

With a brief knock on the door Sylvia entered. "I can't wait to hear, Aggie. Did you discover anything from your search of personnel files and data bases?"

Aggie stood from her narrow bed and went to the desk. She passed over her short stack of computer printouts. "Not much. Lots of background on Dr. Petroski, of course. I didn't get around to checking the staff. Kristi might object if she found out I was looking at her and Reggie's records."

It was clear to Agatha that if Sylvia wanted to make a name for herself by helping to crack the case, she needed more information. Officer Battisti was clearly disappointed. "Do that, Aggie. Go back and search again."

Sylvia said nothing to Lisa, although she nodded and smiled at the pretty blonde curled up like a kitten on her carefully made-up bed. "I'm back to the mines and Sergeant Thompson's put-downs. Malcolm thinks I should return to Castleton for school-guard duty. He wants me off the case. If you do find something else, something more revealing, Aggie, please let me know right away. I may not be around long." The officer departed.

Oh, dear, by withholding news of the Wyoming cult and Mick's participation, wasn't Aggie also tying Sylvia's hands? The whole point of agreeing to make computer searches was to help Officer Battisti, not hinder her further. Aggie ran out in the hall to catch up with Sylvia, but then changed her mind. The computer printouts made no mention of Mick's membership in the cult. Aggie had garnered that information herself in person. Think about the implications awhile. If the Salvationists turned out to have anything to do with this mess clear across the continent, she would fill Sylvia in later.

Lisa got off the bed and went to paw through her luggage to gather cosmetics, and then she disappeared into the bathroom. In her absence, Aggie stretched out on her bed, a soft cushion pillowing her throbbing head. She relaxed her whole body and closed her eyes for another brief session of privacy while Lisa was occupied.

Left alone, Aggie's brain shifted into high gear, to draw from her subconscious on both logical and intuitive sides. In dreamland, her mental powers dashed from right to left brain and back again, across that little brain bridge Joan said was called the corpus callosum. Swifter than lightning, connections clicked into place. Which might or might not have been accurate, depending on what she'd stored previously in either depository.

A towel wrapped around her head and another draped around her tiny body, Lisa emerged from the bathroom with a clatter, oblivious to whether her cousin might have been sleeping. A smiling Aggie lying with arms crossed behind her head greeted Lisa.

"I've been thinking, Lisa." Habits die hard and she'd spent a lifetime sharing secrets with her double cousin. Aggie could use the input, anyhow.

"And?"

"Suppose the Baileys and Houstons, all four of them, have something to hide. Look at this supposedly romantic liaison between Maude and Max. It makes no sense. He's possibly a couple of decades older, which doesn't matter. What might prove significant, however, is that initially he insulted Maude regularly. Behind her back, but barely, he called her 'Ms. Mole' or 'Ms. Wart Nose.' Suddenly they can't get enough of each other? I don't think so. A more likely pairing would put pretty Lucille and handsome Mick together, yet they steer clear of each other like one is a leper."

"I told you there might be something funny going on, there, Aggie. I'll see if I can get closer to all four of them. They don't know me." Lisa didn't give Aggie the opportunity to agree or disagree. The blonde had her own agenda. "You say Kristi feels pretty strongly about Jones' harassing Reggie."

"I think so. If body language counts. I read the passion and caring in her voice, too. Their so-called role play looked pretty darn real."

"Ah, so Kristi likes Reggie, wants to protect him."

"Seems like we're developing a long list of possible murderers."

"That's because you give credence to lukewarm motivations. The way you tell it, Don kills to save his cousin Kurt's already dubious reputation. Penny kills to protect herself from sexual innuendo. Or Kristi kills to salvage Reggie's reputation? Such *motivations*, as you call them, are too weak an excuse from whence to wreak murder."

Feeling properly chastised Aggie stared hard at her know-it-all cousin. A few hours here and already Lisa acted like an expert. Aggie pretended she hadn't understood.

"Why include Penny at all, Aggie? Looks to me she'd be more likely to wipe out her Uncle Tom if she was going to do in anybody. He's the one who insults her."

Ah, so, Lisa, you figured that out all by your lonesome. Clever girl. I put up with being berated by you and Randy, until the two of you pull the ultimate in betrayal. What an excuse for murder most foul. I do wish I could bring myself to do you in, dear girl.

"I imagine the insults have been creeping up on Penny, a spec at a time," said Agatha. "She puts up with it, and with Tom. He's her uncle, her blood-kin, after all." If that didn't clue in Lisa to her own feelings, nothing would. "Early days, Lisa, before you got here, Jones sexually attacked Penny. It was more than a mere come-on. His hands were all over her and she couldn't protect herself. That's my understanding, anyhow. If she couldn't take it, and couldn't stand Tom's blaming her for letting it happen, she could have lost it, went temporarily berserk. Remember that Jones was killed with a long hatpin stuck in his brain through the ear. Isn't that more of a weapon and a method that a woman, not a man, would use?"

"Mmm, could be." Lisa paused from drying off to lay out fresh undergarments and top clothes in hot pink.

"Lisa, every time somebody refers to the murderer as 'he', I've countered with an 'or she'. My subconscious could be poking me with the truth."

"Oh, I doubt that, Aggie." Lisa flipped a hand back and forth, as if to imply Aggie was wishy-washy, like a politician playing both sides against the middle. "You will recall, Aggie, there were two murder weapons and we've got two victims. Jones was short and so was Officer Akunda. Voila! Visualize a short person as murderer."

I already did. Didn't I just do that? "Maude's short." Aggie jolted upright, making her head throb again. She reached for the Tylenol bottle and tapped out a couple of tablets. Gulping from the bottle of water, she threw back the pills and swallowed. "Which suggests to me there are double killers for the double murders, working in collusion or coincidentally."

"Must be separate people, each one unknown to the other. Otherwise, Aggie, why kill Jones twice?"

"Unless the killer didn't think the hatpin had worked. Used a gun, next."

"Agatha Morissey, that makes no sense at all. If the killer had a gun, there's no point messing around with a hatpin, either before or after the shooting."

"The hatpin could have been a red herring." *Good grief, why must I act like a child pleading for attention?* "That would make it look like a woman did it."

Wearing pink silk panties and bra, both trimmed in white lace, Lisa poked her head in the closet behind the door to fetch new clothes. She'd changed her mind, she said, tossing the never-worn hot pink garments on the floor. She said she'd go with pale pink this time instead. Aggie could hear her fumbling around in there.

The room was shadowed in the late-afternoon light. Aggie leaned back and squinted her eyes half-way shut while Lisa puttered. At that moment the dorm door opened quietly and someone tiptoed in, a big pillow in front of him. Or her.

Aggie blinked. Was that what she was seeing or was her aching head playing tricks?

"Should I wear my light pink or the dusty rose blouse with the pink pantsuit, Aggie?" Lisa called from the closet. "No, never mind. I think I'll go with the skirt this time."

Startled, the intruder backed out.

Aggie closed her eyes briefly before reopening them. What she saw sitting on the closet shelf was Lisa's row of wigs. One wig was salt and pepper, exactly like her own natural head of hair.

Suddenly she had an idea and a full-blown plan. If, just now, there really had been an intruder, and if that stealthy approach implied deadly intent, all she had to do was get Lisa to wear the wig that matched her own hair, then go for a stroll.

The murderer, thinking Lisa was Aggie, would strike again.

Voila! Get rid of Lisa without lifting one single finger of her own!

CHAPTER 18

AGGIE COULDN'T PRAY. IF God knew the content of people's thoughts, he already understood the awful things she was thinking. Besides, she could hardly hear herself begging God to supply her with the best method of murder and the most perfect means of avoiding apprehension.

"You must call Randy, dear," Lisa insisted, while backing out of the closet with a dusky rose blouse and pink pantsuit draped over her arm.

Agatha said nothing about the stealthy intruder who'd come and gone. Nor did she reply to her cousin's bossy command.

Lisa dawdled over her cosmetics. "Why are you ignoring your husband?"

Aggie walked out the door to wander the halls before Lisa caught up.

Denied access to the smaller classrooms and also to the entire central building with its lounges and dining hall, the media continued to haunt the paths and dormitory corridors. CNN's Marci Carmichael caught the Wyoming duo leaving the dorm. The reporter snatched Mrs. Schwartzkopf by the arm, begging for a quotable quote. Lisa, the English lit major, complied: "Longfellow said: *To persevere in one's duty and to be silent is the best answer to calumny.*"

"Calumny? What's that mean?" barked the photographer.

"Slander," Lisa said with a smirk. "I would hate to speak ill of our compadres, lest I be guilty of inadvertently making a false and malicious statement."

"Lordy," Philip said. "Marci, let's find somebody else."

In the central building a television set was tuned to the news. Support staffs representing research and production departments from the broadcast and newsprint media had assembled and were already airing segments depicting the life of Dr. P and the Corner's origin and purpose. The papers also had photos, Lisa pointed out, after picking up a newspaper from one of the tables.

In the main lounge the cousins filled their mugs at the urn and headed for the back of the room. Lisa pulled Aggie down beside her on a comfortable couch against the wall.

"I don't understand why the story is getting so much attention," Lisa said. "One more murder, among many. It would be different if your Dr. Petroski were the victim. Or if he were the prime murder suspect."

"Slow news day, maybe. They've got to talk about something."

"Could be. Dr. P is a well-known, charismatic figure and Akunda's a cop."

"Black cop. I haven't tuned in or read the papers yet but sooner if not later somebody's bound to start screaming 'Racial Discrimination'!"

"Better not dismiss racial discrimination as a motive, Aggie. Suppose the killer, a white racist, actually murdered Jones as a cover-up, and Officer Akunda was all along the intended victim?"

Aggie didn't reply. She jumped up and motioned out the window. "I don't want to be stuck in here. I'm going back outdoors."

Aggie hadn't seen the CNN reporter approaching, but there was Marci again, the microphone in her hand popping up like the first jonquil of the season. This time the reporter asked what precautions she meant to take. "You could be the third murder victim, if you don't be careful."

Aggie grinned. "No comment."

"Hey, you're no official," said the pretty reporter with the bangs and pageboy cut hair. "You can't get away with that evasive tactic."

"Sure, I can. Precisely because I <u>am</u> a private citizen and have rights."

"Ah, come on, Mrs. Morissey. Give me something I can use."

Aggie pulled her arm free of Marci's grasp. Although both of these media representatives were tall, slender brunettes, Aggie couldn't label the reporter and photographer as doubles. The conference had enough twinny pairs already.

Leaving behind the reporters, the cousins took the same tree-lined path that Aggie and Sylvia had strolled the night before. Beneath the shelter of leaves that filtered out the sun, they ambled leisurely, Lisa suggesting they step up the pace. She preferred brisk power walking.

Aggie rubbed her head. "Save that for the Cheyenne parks and mall."

Lisa stopped first, to cock an ear. Then she placed a restraining hand on Aggie's arm. "Hear that?" she whispered.

Up ahead and off to the right they heard feet shuffling and muffled voices.

Aggie stepped silently and quickly into the foliage, Lisa following. A few steps later they stopped to hide behind the broad trunk of a towering pine.

In the small clearing a half-dozen yards beyond their hiding place stood Mick Houston with Lucille Bailey. Their voices low and barely decipherable, Aggie knew she would need to employ every ounce of effort to read their lips.

Head down, posture slumped, cigarette dangling from one corner of his mouth, Mick puffed and blew smoke. "Put out that cigarette," Lucille demanded.

Defiant, the apple-checked blonde tossed it over his shoulder.

"For heaven sakes, Mick." Lucille took two long strides to stomp out the smoldering butt. "Haven't you any common sense? You'll start a forest fire."

Mick shrugged. Lucille returned to face him with her continuing harangue: "I don't want your dad messing around with my sister, Mick. We left Idaho to get away from him. When Max and I broke up, he couldn't take it. Wouldn't take it. Maybe you didn't realize it or won't accept it, but Max's an obsessive-compulsive jealous S.O.B. He stalked me unmercifully, threatened me with bodily harm if I didn't come back to him. When that wouldn't work he said he'd get his revenge by hurting Maude. So we quit our jobs and moved clear across the country. Left no forwarding address and told nobody where we were going. Imagine my horror at running into the two of you here."

"So that's why my dad was so determined to get the two of us accepted into Dr. P's program. I thought he did it for me." Mick looked like a little boy, about ready to break into a sulky pout. "My dad bribed Jones to let us in. I overheard him on the phone. Didn't dawn on me that it could be any other reason than on my behalf. Sorry, Lucille, but honestly, this is all news to me. I'd been away working for NASA in Houston and only just come home. Then I was buried in the physics lab night and day, doing, uh, experiments and what not." Mick tried to back away, but Lucille held tight to the arm she clutched.

Aggie gulped. Mick had left a gap in his resume. With no mention of the time he'd spent with the Salvationists, perhaps Lucille was unaware; they hadn't met yet, or he had used his summer vacation to prowl around with the neoNazis. Mick's mind seemed to follow a meandering path—from techie to the physics lab and now to the Center for Cautious Change. She couldn't see him involved with those paramilitary, so-called religious people. The latter could be a cover for terrorist activities, but Aggie suddenly stopped supposing. Better to listen, gather factual data, than to make up stories.

From behind the tree, Lisa was staring at Aggie in disbelief. Lisa had better hearing, but Aggie was more skilled with lip reading. If either missed something, they could fill in each other's gaps later. The double cousins were used to working as a team and habits die hard. For a few moments Aggie forgot that Lisa was her worst enemy.

"Bribed Jones, you say?" Lucille grabbed both of Mick's shoulders as if to shake the truth from his unwilling lips. "With money? How much are we talking about? An info-tech consultant can't earn a lot from a state university job."

"Uh, no, not with money."

"What, then?"

"Information. Dad had something on Jones, I think. Don't ask me what, because I don't know."

"Then make it your business to find out. My God, Mick, this is serious. Because what I really need to know is, what is Max up to, now? He hasn't spoken directly to me, not once, even while pretending to talk to everybody in our group. Suddenly he's all over Maude. She's so vulnerable, Mick. With that ugly mole on her nose, how many admirers do you suppose she's had by now? She's infatuated, totally under Max's control. Your dad's a charmer when he wants to be. Surely you know that, Mick."

This time the baby-faced blonde made it. He pulled free and drew back, his big blue eyes the picture of innocence. "No, I don't know, Lucille. I know little or nothing about my dad's personal life or how he interacts with his university clients. Never mind about him and women. My mom died when I was young. He's a lusty man, Lucille. Presumably he's had his share of, uh, romance." At her look of disbelief he hurried on. "I knew you two were dating, or, uh, whatever you want to call it--an affair? Sure, I knew that. But I didn't know why you two broke up. Dad said nothing. Went right on leaving the apartment we shared every night, returning late or not at all, as usual."

"Of course 'as usual'. He was busy stalking and terrorizing me. Unlike you and Max, Maude and I didn't live together in Boise. My ex had moved out, leaving the house to me. I was all alone, except for Max peeking in the windows and pounding on my door every night."

"Egad, I'm so sorry, Lucille."

"Why should you be sorry? You didn't do anything. Max did."

"That's what I mean. I should have got out of the physics lab and my head out of the clouds. Long enough to have realized what was happening."

"Oh? And how would you have stopped him? I sure couldn't."

His hands shaking, Mick pulled from his shirt pocket a crumpled pack of Marlboros and lit up again. "Why didn't you report my dad? To Jim, his university supervisor, or to the Boise cops."

"I did tell Jim, Mick. Your dad and his boss are drinking buddies, so naturally Jim didn't believe me. He would take Max's side, wouldn't he? Good ole boys stick together, right? Apparently Max told Jim that I was a vindictive female who'd been dumped. When I went to him, Jim laughed in my face. He told me to go find another playmate. As for the police, they filed a report and forgot it; said their hands were tied unless or until I'd been physically attacked. Preferably killed! Then they'd do something." Lucille wiped her palms on her jeans. "You know the rest. The Bailey sisters left town."

Abruptly Lucille clamped her lips, turned away from Mick, and stomped off. Then she looked back, giving Aggie and Lisa a chance to quickly stoop and cower under coverage of a clump of prickly-stemmed bushes before Lucille turned and marched back to shake her fist in Mick's face.

"I aim to find out what Max's plan is, Mick. Maude is so enraptured with Max's flattering attention she won't, or can't, see reason."

CHAPTER 19

THE COUSINS REMAINED HIDDEN until both Lucille and Mick were out of sight. "I don't see what their problem has to do with these murders," Lisa said.

They walked on to park themselves on a bench at lake's edge, their eyes but not their minds on the lapping of gentle waves against the shore. Over Lake Bomoseen the late-spring breeze made ripples. Canoes and fishing boats were too far away to make out their occupants. Distant bathers could be heard splashing about and squealing in the cold water. Birds soared overhead and chirped in the trees.

Agatha leaned back, feeling peaceful. This place hardly seemed the setting for murder most malicious, nor for stalking and blackmailing. Forgetting for the moment her personal vendetta, she wished very much to see these murders solved. As for her own safety, the very notion that her life could also be in danger was too absurd to contemplate. If she could ignore her disastrous marriage for years, denying her present precarious situation came naturally.

"Their story involves Jones, too, you noticed," Aggie said. "If he could be blackmailed into accepting the Houstons, it must have been a pretty dark secret he meant to conceal." From her pocket Aggie pulled a piece of leftover breakfast toast to crumble and toss to the birds.

"Why don't you corner Dr. Petroski? Draw him out about Jones." Lisa followed Aggie's lead with crumbs of her own. "You said that he's amenable to being approached, able and willing to field all sorts of outlandish questions, whether in a formal seminar setting or after hours in his suite."

"I suppose," said Aggie. "Nobody has mentioned talking to Dr. P since the murders. Not even Sylvia. She said Whitehall let her read his notes and

114

listen to the interrogation tapes. Dr. Petroski was the first one interviewed, before retreating to stay closeted, almost constantly, behind the secured door of his own room."

"See what I mean? Could be something there that nobody's telling," said Lisa.

"Or that the police aren't willing to reveal."

"Or, they don't know what they heard. Something innocent to them might be very telling to, uh...to you, if not to me."

Lisa's betrayal shoved aside, Aggie warmed to their tennis match of bouncing propositions back and forth across the net. She stood up from the bench, eager to return to the complex and renew their quest for solutions. "Dr. P may have left clues in the answers he gave to Whitehall and Thompson, something too subtle for them to recognize. I've got to get hold of those tapes."

Back at the center they were waylaid by more of the press, with CNN's Marci and Philip at the forefront. Aggie pressed on with another "No comment."

Lisa, less swift, replied, "I don't know anything. I just got here."

In the parking lot a big bus dispelled a crowd of new arrivals, like a prehistoric beast spewing flames. Lisa poked Aggie, nudging her to take note. Led by a black minister clad in dog collar, a mob clambered onto the grassy verge. Aggie mentally identified them as black, white, the smooth-faced young, the grizzled elderly, fat, skinny, tall. More people burst out of cars, vans, pickups, trucks, SUVs and RVs. Still another bus held a band, heavy on bass and percussion. Then a group of bikers rolled in, their mounts snorting like a herd of wild Nevada Mustangs.

Armed with bullhorn the bus minister, his role obvious from his backwards collar, shouted orders. Several young men passed out placards on wooden sticks and poles.

As fast as a pack of coyote howling or a flock of geese flying, the big crowd left their vehicles behind to assemble itself into a full-blown demonstration. They marched toward the center in the middle of the compound. The band played, the preacher shouted, the protesters chanted and waved their placards.

"What on earth?" Aggie said, paralyzed in position at the edge of the car park.

"Told you so," Lisa said calmly. "They've put out the word. Akunda's murder was a racist thing. White rebellion against the uppity blacks."

"Good grief. What next?"

CHAPTER 20

NEXT CAME THE POLICE. From Rutland and Montpelier, Vermont, from Albany, New York, and points beyond. It was obvious--the cops weren't standing still at having one of their own put down. The governor, Aggie noted from lip-reading, had called up the National Guard. Police sergeants and the Guard captain quickly ordered their troops to circle the demonstrators.

The Vermont governor joined the police and other officials on the front steps of the center to try calming the crowd's clamor and their demand for news and solutions. Aggie sniffed at the sweaty odors emanating from so many people scrunched together on that warm day. Marci, Philip, and all the other media reps dashed about, frantic to capture the action, grab the choicest interviews, get an exclusive and beat their competitors.

His green paddle clutched in sweaty palms, Harris paddled faster. "Keep up, Howie, or we'll wind up going around in circles. I want a better view."

"We're too close already." Howard stopped paddling altogether, forcing Harris to quit, too. "Use the binoculars if you want to see better."

Silence fell upon them, as the brothers watched and strained to hear.

"Just as I thought," said Harris. "That's the governor's car. I wish I'd brought the high-powered rifle. I'd shoot him myself."

Startled, Howard dropped his paddle, which came loose to commence floating away. "Cripes, Harris. Help me get the paddle back." Together the brothers used their hands to frantically push at the water until Howie retrieved his green paddle with the paint chipping off and the original pink showing through. "I bet this canoe belonged to a girl," he said.

116

"Who cares? I'm talking murder, and you're mumbling about a pink paddle."

"What have you got against the governor of Vermont anyway?"

"Nothing. Nothing at all. But you said I had to start small, shoot a mayor first, then a governor, before you'd go along with my assassinating the President."

"Cripes, Harris. I thought this was all just talk."

"You got to be kidding. Didn't I hypnotize Diane out at the camp? Command her to kill Laramie's mayor?"

"Stupid exercise in futility, you ask me. All Diane did was shoot her best friend."

"That was a start. Now we're getting closer to the finish line."

"We are?"

"Sure. Our programmed killer is taking out targets right and left. Won't be long now and we'll win the Big Trophy."

"Yeah, sure, which gets us what? What's this trophy you're talking about?"

Harris hit himself in the forehead with the heel of a hand. "All this time, all this planning, I've been gearing up to make a name for myself, as the one who assassinated the president a lot of people never wanted. Isn't that worth something? I thought you were with me. What's your goal been all this time?"

"I thought you knew."

"I did too, but I guess I don't."

"To head up the Salvationists. To win souls to Jesus."

Harris looked appalled, like big brother was talking about the Devil instead of the Lord Jesus Christ. "Well, not me. I'm going after the Vermont governor myself."

"No, you're not." Howie suddenly bent over and jerked the duct tape off the hole Harris had gouged through the canoe's bottom. Water started pouring in and the canoe began to sink.

"I hope you remember how to swim," said Howard, diving into the water.

"The politicos want to grab the news coverage for themselves," Lisa said. "Watch and listen. I'll bet they play up to the cameras."

"What a mess," Aggie said quietly.

"You got that right," Sylvia said, coming up beside the cousins. The Italian officer said she'd spotted the pair from an upstairs window. Unassigned and undirected at the moment, she had slipped out the side door to sidle around the crowd. "What do you think, Aggie? Have you turned up any more clues?"

"In the last hour? Not really." Agatha had plenty of news, but had decided against talking about the Houston-Bailey conflict, or her vow to corner Dr. P.

When the authorities retreated behind locked doors and the conferees were notably missing, it soon became obvious the demonstrators had nobody to demonstrate against. Except to each other and for the benefit of the media. Blacks and whites, cops and protesters all squared off, snarling at one another like mad dogs at dog catchers.

"For cryin' out loud," Lisa finally cried. "Don't they understand it's only one, maybe two, people who've done the damage here? Murder, pure and simple. Not a war between the races or a battle with civilians facing off against the police like in some third-world country of demigods versus revolutionaries."

"Slow news day," Aggie repeated. "People need a cause, preferably something horrendous, to stir their passions."

"And those of the media."

"That, too."

Skirting the crowd, the cousins followed Sylvia. She had a key, thereby gaining entrance to the center through an unwatched door. They found themselves in the enclosed corridor connecting the dormitory to the center. Lisa mumbled to Aggie that she didn't think anybody had noticed them.

Wrong. Mick Houston was outside, too, Aggie said. Probably looking for a place to indulge his smoking habit.

"Or maybe he circled back and spotted us eavesdropping on him and Lucille. Better watch him, Agatha. He could be the perp." Indoors, Aggie assessed the situation. Reggie must be busy supervising dinner preparations. Kristi, along with a few others, viewed the commotion outdoors by peering through the half-closed slats of the mini-blinds covering the front windows. No Penny, Tom Carson, or the Delanos in sight.

Also among the absent, Aggie noted, were the Bailey and Houston pairs from group two. Not surprising, given what she now knew about them. Max and Maude could be together. Cementing their affair in his or her dormitory room. Back in the woods Lucille had stomped off, but where was she now?

Dr. Petroski, as usual since Tuesday night, was also missing. Other than his presentation following Maude's and Dr. Yu's that morning, Dr. P was conspicuous by his absence. Cowering behind his door or lying sick abed.

Ill health! Of course. Early on, Jones had shooed them off with his claims that their director's health couldn't stand up to the continual barrage of their petty questions, nor their adoration, clamoring, and hovering.

Sunday, Monday, and Tuesday, day and night, and of course that very morning--that's all they'd had of his leadership, and then, no more. Sudden silence and total withdrawal from that quarter.

Dr. P could be so utterly devastated at losing Jones that he could no longer cope or function independently. Yet when he had appeared that morning, he had willingly accepted Dr. Yu's arm for support and guidance to his chair. Their leader had resembled his former vigorous, enthusiastic, and competent self. Perhaps herein, Aggie surmised, lay the loose thread that would unravel the whole scarf of these murders.

The jangling of the ringing phone alerted those clustered beside Aggie, who motioned to Kristi. The computer operator walked over, picked up, gasped, listened, and then, eyes glazed, stared like a Zombie at Aggie.

"Agatha! Agatha Morissey!" Kristi yelled across the intervening space of no more than a couple of yards. "The President of the United States is on the phone. Personally. He wants to talk to you."

A collective gasp arose like smoke from a campfire.

"What, now?" Kristi demanded of Lisa while Aggie was occupied.

Lisa laughed. "Dominic Alexander Davidson is an old friend. Or, to take it from the media's mouth, Aggie is the President's *Surrogate Mom,* which should be big sister, by the way, as Aggie is not a lot older than Dom.

119

CHAPTER 21

WHILE AGGIE WAS ON the phone with the President, Lisa strolled to the front window to peer out at the demonstrators.

"The President called Aggie?" Maude gasped in awe, dashing past Lisa to join the crowd gathering around Mrs. M.

"What's happening?" the Delanos asked the Baileys.

"What's going on?" the Carsons demanded of the Houstons.

With all that babble Aggie couldn't hear a thing. So she did most of the talking. "Dom, it's so good to hear your voice." She paused to listen. "Yes, I'm fine.

DAD, the President's initials, as used in his various political campaigns beginning with the North Dakota race for the U.S. Senate and later for the Presidency, was an acronym well known throughout the country and world. "DAD of the country" and "DAD is here for you" were used to promote the President and his program and policies.

No getting around it. The populace generally liked DAD. He was perceived as an excellent role model, a national hero. Well-respected and accepted around the globe, the tall, slender, Abe Lincoln look-alike, complete with dark mustache and beard that matched thick wavy hair, was apparently comfortable with his position and among his advisors, cronies, and foreign dignitaries.

A popular president, with high ratings in the polls, Dom had yet to anger the special interest groups. No evidence of secret affairs, political bribes or the selling of national secrets in exchange for campaign funds; nothing to indicate that Davidson was less than sincere. The opposition could find no fodder in his personal life and history to fuel their fire. Besmirching the President's reputation had temporarily gone into the inactive file.

Except, of course, for the disgruntled outsiders; members of the political party who had not been re-elected; and also for the disillusioned youth, those energetic and restless folk who needed a target for their discontent.

Meanwhile, Dom didn't forget his old friends, even those who didn't make hefty campaign contributions or promise him huge voting blocks. As Dom had said to the media, including to Marci Carmichael of CNN, "Even presidents are people; even presidents have personal friends."

Aggie, with or without her husband, Randolph, had several times been invited to sedate formal state dinners that Davidson with First Lady Julia hosted at the White House. Julia Davidson, an educated and warm woman, played a serene and dignified First Lady role, beside her husband but politically in the background. She chaired the National Council on Environmentalism. Peter and Lisa, like the Morisseys, were no strangers to Washington, at both the White House and the Pentagon. Colonel Schwartzkopf was a military advisor, Randolph Morissey a geological and petroleum consultant.

"Dom," Aggie said into the phone. "You and Julia are in danger every moment of your lives. I'll be all right. Trust me."

"There's no question about trusting you, Aggie. It's the bad guys I don't trust." Listening to him, Aggie smiled. Sometimes the President still sounded like the young lad she'd first known--"bad guys," indeed.

Their exchange was no more (and no less) significant than usual--good friends reaching out to one another across the continent with compassion and caring. Dom asked her to keep in touch, let him know what was happening. For all their closeness, Aggie couldn't imagine interrupting the President with his many important issues and his very busy schedule to tell him she was okay, or to remind him that she came from a long line of survivors. Nevertheless, she agreed to be careful, like promising candy to a child.

Dom changed tactics. "I plan to drop by Lake Bomoseen to see you, Aggie. We'll have to make it quick, as Julia and I are on our way to Milwaukee to speak to the brewers. But Julia made sure they put a bottle of Dom Perignon to cool on Air Force One. We've never missed celebrating our birthdays together, Aggie, and I'm not skipping this one."

"Whatever you wish, Mr. President."

Hanging up the phone, Aggie was immediately bombarded.

"What was that all about?"

"Why'd he call you?"

"What'd the President want?"

"Has the White House heard about the riot already?"

"Riot?" Disdaining to answer, Aggie all but skipped across the room to stare with Lisa out the window.

Behind them Reggie was having a tough time corralling the kitchen staff and servers to insist they complete their duties. They didn't want to miss anything. En masse, everybody gathered around the two little ladies, seemingly anxious to protect them—from what, she wondered, besides each other. Then she awakened as if from a daze.

Put a couple of unrelated things together, like the demonstration outside and the President's call inside--and you got a whole conspiracy. Some of her companions might wonder if this protest business was merely a ruse, that it had political underpinnings, or was part of some great international plot of intrigue. They might suspect foreign terrorists and hidden bombs about to explode.

Together the cousins listened to the postulated theories and queries: "Terrorists?"

"Drug deal gone bad?"

"I'll bet Jones owed big bucks to the syndicate."

"Yeah, Jones got taken out and Akunda just happened to be in the way." "And our Aggie is their next target because she found out?"

Ignoring the babble, Aggie was enthralled by what she saw outdoors. She had to get outdoors immediately. Hauling Lisa by the arm, she turned away from the window to push determinedly through the bystanders.

"What's happening now?"

"What'd the President say?"

"Where's Aggie going?"

Tuning into their clamoring voices, Aggie smiled sweetly. "We're going outside to join the protesters."

CHAPTER 22

"THIS PROTEST DEMONSTRATION IS truly remarkable," Lisa exclaimed, clutching at Aggie's arm to hold her back.

Agatha disagreed, but bit her tongue to keep silent. It seemed clear that all this thunderous activity must be mob psychology prompting the mass hysteria.

At first the movement was gradual, and then swift, as people appeared to change quickly from individuals to one bulging body storming speedily toward some grand finale. Afterwards, Aggie would compare the demonstration-turned-riot to a small dam leak, followed by a great tidal wave, completed by the smoothing calmness of a new lake forming, expanding, and re-establishing itself.

It began with two warring factions--the protesters led by the black Reverend Leopold Paxton, facing cops and National Guardsmen; there were no women among the latter. The cousins slipped out a side door to watch in awe from behind a cluster of evergreen trees and bushes.

Bullhorn and pistol lowered, the reverend on his side and Sylvia Battisti on hers walked slowly, cautiously, toward one another. They could have represented an Indian nation and a U.S. Cavalry unit, waving white flags and coming together to negotiate a treaty. The reverend and the officer conferred quietly and briefly. Then, together, they climbed the steps leading to the small landing outside the center's front door. From this vantage point, a position of authority, Reverend Paxton raised his head and his eyes, though still open, to utter a few short eloquent words of prayer. His strong bass voice--bare, without benefit of bullhorn--resonated over the heads of the mob.

"Oh, Lord, bless us this day. Bathe us with your loving grace, and guide us to seek unity and harmony. Together, let us mourn our lost brother. Amen."

Swiftly, before the moment of silence and awe was lost, Leopold and Sylvia looked at one another. They smiled, clasped hands, and began to sing.

That's all it took to turn around the crowd, from battling, suspicious enemies to a unified choir comprised of individual and civilized human beings. Those who didn't know the words or thought they couldn't carry a tune hummed: *Amazing Grace, Whispering Hope*, and, finally, *We Shall Overcome*.

The circling band of cops and guardsmen became individuals, too, mingling with the protesters who at first hesitantly and then wholeheartedly welcomed the defense team into their midst. They too clasped hands or entwined arms so that with the last song they were all swaying back and forth.

The media went wild. Reporters scribbled or yelled into their cell phones or mini-dictating machines. Still cameras clicked and flashes flashed, videocams hummed, and reporters and photographers alike stumbled over the cables snaking along beneath their feet.

"One man <u>can</u> make a difference," yelled a CBS man into his phone.

"One woman, too, don't forget," corrected an ABC woman at his elbow.

"The Power of Prayer," proclaimed a *Christian Science* reporter to a Jehovah's Witness from *The Tower*.

It was Marci, though, who focused on Aggie and Lisa. "Aggie, Aggie! Over here." With Philip close on her heels, Marci ran toward the double cousins. "What'd he say? The President. What'd you tell him?" In her excitement and determination to be first with this late-breaking story, Marci forgot to pose the standard reporter's question of *How did you feel*?

This time Aggie refrained from taking the detour she preferred traveling or the "No comment" response. She decided to be up front for once. Well, if only partially; the rest of her conversation with the President was personal and private.

"Dom, the President, is an old friend, Marci. He just wanted to be assured of my continuing good health and safety."

The attractive brunette was clearly disappointed. Marci protested, with an "That's all?" The photographer fidgeted behind her.

When asked how she knew about the President's call, Marci confessed that a kitchen helper had slipped out a side door for a cigarette and had inadvertently bumped into the reporter. Marci grinned. "Off the record, Aggie. Are you taking any specific precautions? Have the police arranged for security, for your protection?"

"I can't see them doing that." Aggie rubbed her head.

Lisa poked the reporter to get attention. "Maybe Aggie's not worried, but I am. What do you propose, Marci?"

"Get a body guard, for heaven sakes."

"Why? What do you know or suspect that leads you to believe I need protection?"

"Look, Aggie, Officer Battisti's been talking to me. She thinks you're in danger."

"But, why? From what or whom?"

"Because you know too much."

Aggie started to protest with a *Who, me?* but was stopped in mid-breath by a nudge from Lisa. Guess she was supposed to shut up.

Shortly the huge outdoor crowd broke up, to return to their vehicles and hit the road. For home or wherever they could make another splash.

Indoors, a collective sigh released the conferees from their temporary paralysis staring out the windows. Reggie announced that dinner was delayed. Give us an hour, he said. The others dispersed to freshen themselves for the evening or to recap the late afternoon events. For many, that meant retrieving cell phones to call family and friends—give them the inside scoop and give themselves a boost up the ladder of those in the know while they were at it.

One major problem inhibited their goal—somebody had stolen all the phones.

In their room Aggie wailed: "But Lisa, what do we know that we don't know we know?" She drew from her large carryall the stack of computer printouts she'd retained for herself. Battisti had her own set.

Aggie cautioned Lisa to guard the papers carefully and not to gossip. According to Kristi, Jones had collected the material--sometimes sensitive, often private--building an extensive background file on every seminar applicant.

"Let's pour through these things, Lisa. We've missed something."

"Plenty of *somethings*, no doubt. Agatha, there are too many partners running around. It's hard to keep track of all of them."

"Not really. There are only two pairs who look alike: the redheaded, red-mustached Delano cousins from our group, and the apple-cheeked, baby-faced blondes from the other table--the Houstons, father and son."

"I know, but..."

"What's troubling you?"

"Everybody is paired. Seems to me you've concentrated so much attention on tables two and four that you don't know anything about the people at one and three."

"A number of them left before you got here. You're right, though. I know little or nothing about the remainder. You can watch them."

Lisa pouted, before changing the subject. "If you don't call Randy, I'm going to. Your husband deserves to hear from your own lips that you're safe."

Lisa's remark didn't go down well. Aggie could feel herself choking with anger. She turned her back. Retreating to the bathroom, she needed to regain her composure. If Lisa wanted to call Randy, let her. The pair of lovers probably missed each other. Aggie splashed cold water on her flushed face.

Emerging, she divided the printouts, and the pair curled up on their separate beds to read the dossiers silently. A mutter erupted, then Lisa sighed.

"Listen to this, Aggie. Here's a guy, Joe, who was orphaned as a boy. Both his parents were killed in a car wreck. Drunken driver. How sad."

"You could introduce him to Penelope. She too was orphaned and her parents too are dead. Died when their house burned down. Penny was over at Tom Carson's, enjoying a sleep-over with his daughter, her cousin. Tom and his wife raised her."

"So? I don't see any significance about that."

"Look at Penny's situation from her side. Could be she's been suffering a case of the guilts ever since. She lived, but her parents didn't. Had she been home, she'd have died too. That's typical, I believe. To feel guilty about escaping when your loved ones don't."

Aggie expected her cousin to protest. Lisa often showed her disregard for Aggie's field, calling her occasional pronouncements *all that psychobabble stuff.*

This time Aggie got an arched eyebrow. Lisa countered with, "Or maybe Penny's resentment of Tom is nothing more than teenage rebellion, and the girl hasn't quite grown up yet."

Aggie was raring to pick a fight, but not over lukewarm theories. She could scratch Lisa's eyes out. Two females fighting over one man, her Randy. Better to go along on the issues that didn't matter. Or that she supposed didn't.

"Could be. Lisa, my eyes are tired. Let's save all this for later."

The ringing telephone awakened Aggie with a start. If it was Randy, she didn't want to speak to him.

"Hi, doll. I miss you," said the Wisconsin grandpa. "Miss me?"

Good grief. "You hardly know me. I'm a married woman, you know."

"Then your husband's a lucky guy. 'Cuz you're one cute, sexy little lady."

"Who was that?" Lisa demanded, suspicion written on her face. "While the cat's away, the mouse will play, is that it? Don't tell me you're having an affair with one of these guys."

Okay, I won't tell you. Takes one to know one.

Dinner was delicious but quiet. People were exhausted from all the emotional energy they'd expended. Reggie outdid himself with cold vichyssoise, Caesar salad, pork roast, peas, French bread, and baked Alaska. After that, the wait people served fruit, cheese, and nuts, followed by coffee and brandies. Nobody wanted to party. No invitations to gather in Dr. P's suite were forthcoming.

Late in the night Aggie awakened to the sound of Lisa's soft voice whispering sweetly. To Randy? Aggie turned her back and covered up her head, feigning sleep. In reality, she felt flushed. She could choke with such hate infusing and spreading throughout her whole being.

Long after a full moon arose over the sleeping masses, a tiny wisp of smoke lifted its head from the little clearing deep in the woods to look around, search for buddies, and join them in what would soon grow into a great conflagration. Forest fire!

CHAPTER 23

AT FOUR O'CLOCK IN the morning, Aggie got up to pee. Upon returning, she discovered Lisa awake, too, her head off the pillow and leaning on an elbow.

"Aggie, Randy is sick. I called home last night. Talked to Peter. He said Randy's in the hospital."

"What? Sick from what?"

"Food poisoning. Something he ate."

Aggie couldn't take in such news. Her first thought: *Hubby ate that spoiled food from my refrigerator.* She'd killed him, after all. "Ohmigod!"

She realized then that Lisa couldn't have been sweet-talking Randy. Last night it was Peter on the other end of the line. She crawled back in bed.

"Hey, kiddo. Aren't you going to call home?"

"Uh, oh yeah. That would be a good idea." Drat, Aggie hoped she didn't sound unconcerned. Truth was, she was as nervous as a cat on the Cracker Barrel veranda with a bunch of senior citizens rocking back and forth. Pulling on a robe and her fuzzy bunny-rabbit slippers, she walked across the room to the desk and sat down, her back to Lisa. First she dialed Joan. No answer. Then she tapped out the numbers for her home phone. Perhaps she'd catch Clara. By now the family maid should be home from visiting her sick sister.

"No answer anywhere," Aggie said, heaving a sigh she hoped didn't sound like relief. She wasn't sure she could handle the truth about Randy's condition.

"For cryin' out loud, Agatha," said Lisa, clearly exasperated. She got off her bed to pace. "Call the hospital. Get the news from the horse's mouth."

Short of breath, fingers trembling, Aggie picked up the phone again.

"No use," she said, replacing the instrument. "Phone's dead." Aggie then tried to call out with Lisa's cellular phone, a phone that had escaped confiscating. Same result.

Finally Lisa stopped badgering her and returned to bed. Aggie tried to sleep.

Lisa sat up again. "Aggie, I've been meaning to ask you. Did you ever find your diamond engagement ring?"

Stupid woman. If I'd found it, wouldn't I be wearing it? "No, Lisa."

Aggie fell into a troubled sleep. Silence once again reigned in their room.

The Memorial Day weekend would officially open the season, with the arrival of the summer people from New York and elsewhere throughout New England. By then their camps, meaning large and small dwellings, would be open, with plenty of people around to notice anything amiss. In mid-May, however, there were few folks milling about in the area other than the conferees. Most of them, like Aggie, slept on, dreaming dreams and innocently expecting tomorrow's sun to rise.

First a cloud hovered over the woods. Then the flames hungrily licked their way from bush to bush and through the grasses, slithering up the tightly wedded trunks to feed on their tops and then to leap from tree to tree and bush to bush.

At last the flames shot into the sky, the conflagration crackling like a Fourth of July display of giant-size fireworks. Great clouds of smoke billowed overhead. Caught and spread by the wind like gossip between cousin Nasty Two and her vast congregation of rumor mongers, the fire that began with a tiny, unsquashed, still-burning cigarette, soon gained massive proportions.

In the small village of Castleton five miles away, an insomniac out for a smoke of his own noticed first. Leaning on a post on the back porch. He sniffed the air, wrinkled his nose, and gasped. Then he came unwound, but not before mashing hard on his own discarded butt.

He yelled at his Missus to get up. "Fire!" he hollered. "Call the mayor. Alert the volunteers," of which Bud was one. "I'm outta here."

Still dressed, Bud hastily donned protective gear and raced out to his old green truck. He would stop only to pick up other volunteers, who were experienced at fighting fires, but mostly small fires--backyard brush or smoldering garages from careless weekend workshop hobbyists.

Bud's wife Lois knew what to do. She and the other wives and daughters, sisters and nieces, the elderly and semi-disabled, the neighbors and friends would move into gear as rapidly as their able-bodied menfolk. Their jobs: making and hauling great urns of coffee, tea, and drinking water to the backside location; fielding calls by walkie-talkie and cell phone and relaying directions and requests for assistance by phone, e-mail, and fax; gathering more gear. Generally the women provided support as the backup team. Most of the physically fit men and some of the townships' younger, more venturous women willingly responded to the fire-fighting emergencies.

Between repeated, worried glances at the smoke-filled sky, Lois fretted that this time the volunteers could make no more than a tiny impact. "Might as well pee in the ocean, for all the difference they're going to make."

"Shu-ah," said her neighbor, in a true Vermont accent, all the while loading her own van with stocks of edibles from her freezer.

In the home of the Castleton mayor, whose overnight guest was Vermont's governor, the two men hadn't yet recovered from the riot out at Dr. Petroski's facility. All was quiet as the grave; except for their wives, both of whom snored. Such noise! Which may have been what awakened the men.

On the phone to the mayor's wife, Lois yelled "Fire, fire! Forest fire out at Lake Bomoseen!"

Aggie, Lisa, and most of the other conferees slept on. Their batteries removed, Lisa's hearing aids, one for each ear, lay on the bureau deep in their own untroubled slumber. These inanimate objects, so necessary to the hearing of so many people, didn't, after all, jump into duty. They could hardly replace their own batteries to make themselves operable, and then dash across the room to jump onto Lisa's bed to find their home in ears that were otherwise as deaf as Aggie's. All of the double cousins were hearing impaired; had been, since birth, a gift from Grandpa Auld.

The exception to the dormitory slumberers numbered but three sleepless souls: Dr. P, plus one more man and one woman; among whom could be counted the murderer--singular or plural.

One among this trio covertly tiptoed down the hall to stand outside Aggie's room to pause. One ear pressed against the door to listen. A hand in a pocket clutched a weapon. The other hand stealthily twisted the doorknob. A fit of coughing, footsteps, a door opening and closing. The startled creeper paused, cocked head, and waited impatiently.

Then the noise from a couple of dozen fearful folk broke loose like hell itself.

Voices yelled. Footsteps thundered. People screamed, clutching hastily donned robes or shawls. They ran barefooted or in slippers or in sneakers with untied shoelaces.

They bumped into one another. They fell down and clambered back up. Wailing and moaning and a few shrieked questions filled the air.

"What's happening?"

"Where are we going?"

"Who's in charge?"

Then, "Fire!"

"Fire?"

"Where? The dorm or the center?"

"Do we stay put or get out?"

The three insomniacs mingled with the others. Two of them had forgotten to get out of street clothes into sleeping attire. Too late to return to his and her rooms to rectify the mistake, thoughts scrambled through an array of possible excuses. Had to be believable.

Bringing up the rear, Aggie and Lisa trailed behind two street-dressed people. "Out late or up early?" Aggie teased.

"Oh, uh, up early," said the woman, blushing.

"Yeah, that's right," echoed the man. "Up early."

Aha, another romance ablossoming.

Now they were herded by Reggie through the covered walkway connecting the dorm to the center. With Dr. P on Reggie's arm, the director, clad in pajamas and robe, looked like death warmed over; gray, disheveled, haggard. The poor man looked his age, totally handicapped by his infirmity. No longer their competent, able leader, the industrial psychologist of international repute looked solely dependent on Reggie's leading him around and telling him what to do.

Reggie planted Dr. P in a chair against the wall as if he were a fragile orchid seedling. Their leader slumped beneath one of the glowing lanterns. The staff including Kristi had located, lit, and set about an array of candles and kerosene lanterns, supposedly to dispel the gloom of the early-morning hour.

Penny sidled up to Aggie. "I'm scared," she whispered.

Aggie circled the girl's shoulders with a sheltering arm. "We'll be rescued. Soon, I hope. But I know the feeling, dear. Come sit beside me."

"It's not only the fire. My Uncle Tom hurt my feelings." She didn't say how or why, and Aggie didn't want to ask why hurt feelings could be frightening.

They sat down at table four. With Penny's tears drying, her head bent over the handkerchief she wadded into a ball, Aggie whispered to Lisa, "What on earth?"

"What, what?"

"What could have happened to Dr. P to make him lose all his confidence and charisma so quickly? You didn't get to meet him early on when he was filled with fire and vigor. Now, look. He's nothing but rag and bone, a shadow of his real self."

"Maybe this is his real self, Agatha. What you guys saw could have been the façade he donned while on stage. Back in the wings he might typically crumble."

"You make it sound like he's a puppet, and Sam Jones was pulling his strings. Or that Sam served as the prompter in this drama--the prop and the buffer. Dr. P seemed real enough, Lisa. Especially during our late-night sessions sprawled on the floor at his feet. Then he was as natural as nature, as the wind and sky and earth and water."

"And fire," Lisa added, as if to complete the analogy. "Fire! There's a forest fire raging out there, Aggie, and here you are fretting about your Dr. P. I don't see you that concerned about Randy, either. You'd better try calling him again."

"I did. Phone lines are out."

"Use your cell phone."

"It needs charging." Agatha didn't look at Lisa's face. She knew what she'd read there—disgust that Aggie hadn't brought her charger or thought to charge up her cell phone before they left their dorm room.

Reggie left their director's side to move forward and front. "Attention, everybody," he called. "Don't panic, but I've got bad news."

With the fire raging all around them, they were effectively cut off from the outside world. That was the reason for the candles and lanterns, he said. "No electricity, and the phone and cable lines are down. No satellite or cable connections, so no battery-operated radios or TVs..."

"No computers!" wailed Kristi. Max mumbled something but he didn't look upset. Aggie spotted him hiding a grin behind the coffee mug raised to his lips.

"Cell phones?" Lucille asked, pulling hers out from under the tablecloth.

Reggie shook his head. "I already said we're surrounded by the fire, with smoke billowing overhead. So no signals." He sounded exasperated. Too many things too rapidly bombarding the poor lad from all directions. He was losing his cool.

Aggie understood. Out in Wyoming where lots of ranches were nestled in the meadows and surrounded by the towering mountains of the Rockies, some ranchers couldn't reach the outside either. Satellite television, yes; cell phone access, no.

"That's the least of our problems," Reggie continued. As a native, he knew the routine, he said. The local volunteer fire department would be called in. Experienced forest firefighters would rapidly descend from all over New England perhaps from Appalachia and the Rockies as well.

"Jumpin' Jehosaphat," said Olaf, sounding excited but appearing undisturbed, as he looked across the room to wink at Aggie.

"Question is," Reggie said. "Can they get here and do their job in time?"

"Time for what?" Carson boomed from the far side of Lisa.

"Don't act dumb, Tom. In time to save us," Penelope said, leaning across Lisa to jerk on her uncle's robe. She sounded more assertive now. Aggie wondered what had brought on the change of mood, almost a total flip of personality, like turning the taps from hot to cold water.

"I don't believe our cell phones won't work," said Mick Houston. "I'm going to go check." He disappeared, to the great relief of the half-dozen milling about near the physicist, who smiled, winked, or otherwise wore their emotions right there on their faces for everybody to read.

When Mick returned, his own face showed a road map of frown lines. "You're not going to believe this," he shouted at the assemblage. "My phone is gone, and so is Max's. When I talked to Reggie and Kristi, their phones have also gone missing. It's like everybody's cell phones just got up and walked off."

"That's easy to figure out," said Penny calmly. "I saw a big pile of them on the floor behind the pulpit in the chapel. Somebody stole them and hid· them from you'all."

"What on earth?" exclaimed Lisa, finger to her lips.

"Why didn't you scoop them up and bring them back here?" roared Tom.

"None of my business."

Ignoring the hubbub around them, Aggie said to Lisa, "Forget our missing phones. Mine wasn't working anyhow. What we need here is Ned Fleetfoot." The clan invariably used both names when talking about their second cousin, the son of Nasty Three, Wyoming's Secretary of State. Nasturtium's ex-husband was full-blooded Arapaho off the Wind River Indian Reservation, where he'd worked their casino.

"That's right! He was a professional firefighter before returning to Cheyenne to manage that Laundromat."

CHAPTER 24

OUT IN WYOMING THEY got the news over breakfast--seven o'clock mountain daylight savings time. Colonel Schwartzkopf tuned in CNN.

Six-six and big all over, Peter missed his wife. He was glad that Lisa and Aggie would be returning soon. Agatha should be at her husband's bedside.

Just then Marci Carmichael, one of Peter's favorite field reporters, came on the screen. "Where yesterday the Vermont Corner for Cautious Change was the site of a major demonstration and protest over the murder of an African-American police officer, today is another raging scene. This time, a forest fire has the Corner's occupants completely surrounded, totally cut off from the outside world, and virtually held captive. With us today..." she continued, pointing the microphone in the face of a balding, apple-shaped little man with red-veined nose like Rudolph the red-nosed reindeer.

Peter and Lisa's daughter, Beth, came in the kitchen from her big house next door. "Dad? When's mom coming home?"

"Shh. Grab a cup of tea and pull up a chair, hon. Your mom and Aggie are in the news again." Peter, Lisa, Beth and her husband Brad were as close as silverware in the fork and spoon drawer.

Tiny blond Beth, seemingly a clone of her mother in the looks department, gasped, shuddered, and sat down, forgetting the tea. "Please protect them and keep them safe." She whispered the prayer with her daddy as witness.

On screen, Marci and her photographer were, in turn, being questioned by Castleton's red-nosed, apple-bellied mayor, who demanded to know how the CNN pair came to be first on the scene, arriving ahead of the rest of the press by a whole fifteen minutes. Marci admitted, with a smirk for the camera, that she and Phil had booked a room at a nearby bed and breakfast.

"Just lucky, I guess," Phil muttered.

"When the riot, uh, demonstration reached closure," Marci told the Castleton mayor, "everybody else pulled out. We decided to hang around. I, uh, we thought there might be more to come. A story isn't finished--in my opinion--until the perps are arrested, tried, and convicted, and the case is closed."

It was a long impromptu account from the reporter more accustomed to the other end of a broadcasted interview. Marci took a quick breath and aimed the microphone at Sylvia shuffling her feet at the mayor's side. "What's it look like, Officer Battisti? And do you think the forest fire will flush out the serial killer?"

Sylvia gasped. This was the first public mention of a serial killer. Undaunted, Marci continued, addressing the viewing audience. Among which, out in Wyoming, Colonel Peter and daughter Beth sat with eyes glued to the set.

"Tell us your feelings, Officer," Marci pleaded, pulling Sylvia by the arm to put them both in focus. "Do you think the murderer is still there, along with the others at Dr. Petroski's facility? Any chance you're about to make an arrest?"

"Um, you'll have to ask Detective Whitehall those questions, ma'am."

Undeterred, Marci whipped up another batch of questions, like beating a bowl of pancake batter. "Let's skip over the past murders for now. What's your educated guess about the fire's impact on the killer's next move?"

"How would I know?"

Peter laughed. Out in Wyoming, the Colonel as amateur chef had stuck his experimental egg-ham-cheese-onion-green chili casserole into the oven to bake. The aroma suffused the Schwartzkopf kitchen. Putting on hot-pad mittens, he rose from the table to check on his creation.

"That cop's sure working hard to avoid Marci, but the CNN reporter won't let this fish get away. Marci's good, damn good," Peter said.

With both hands shaking, Beth lifted to her mouth the cup of fragrant cinnamon-apple herbal tea her father had poured for her. "Dad, you're taking this too lightly. Mom and Aggie are in mortal danger. Don't you care?"

"Of course, sweet thing. But I've known those two a good long time. They'll be okay, I swear it, on your great-great-great-great-grandmother Rose's grave. And the dynamic duo will also solve the double murders in the process. Mark my words."

"Yes, daddy, I'll try to be calm, but it's so hard." Beth sipped, and fell silent.

On the screen Marci was having better luck with the fire topic than with the murders. The Castleton cop agreed to speak. "The fire is spreading fast throughout the surrounding woods that extend for miles," Battisti said. "Don't know how long it'll take to contain it. Could take days. Weeks, maybe. We're going to lose a lot of timber. Buildings--houses, lake camps, businesses, you name it, We've called for evacuation. However, the people trapped inside Dr. Petroski's place are in real danger."

Now Colonel Schwartzkopf opened his eyes wide.

At this point Philip focused the lens of the CNN videocam toward the street, which was also Highway 4 leading into Rutland. A line of vehicles streamed into, through, and beyond the village of Castleton.

"Firefighter units from the Catskills and Pocono mountains, also from the Appalachians, are already arriving," said Sylvia. "But that might not be enough. If not, we'll call for experienced smoke jumpers from the Rockies."

"What about the Corner's occupants, though?" Marci demanded. "Won't they get burned to a crisp before they can be rescued?"

"Good grief!" Beth gasped. "Must she choose such horribly graphic words?"

Standing in front of the kitchen's central island, gloved potholders in hand, Peter stared hard at the screen, as if by his will alone he could get Marci to recant her words. The hot casserole in his hands all but forgotten, his jaw dropped, his eyes stared intently at Marci coming to them from two-thirds of a continent away.

"You've got to do something, daddy!"

"I will. I'm going to, Beth. Right now!" Peter's grim expression, clenched teeth, and jutting jaw signaled, as it always did--to his staff, to Pentagon and White House officials, to the enemy, or to the family (nuclear or extended)-- that he was in control. Exit daddy, husband, cousin, and chef; enter Colonel Schwartzkopf at Command Center.

Peter set down the casserole. He removed his mitten potholders.

The Colonel picked up the phone and placed a series of calls.

CHAPTER 25

THE WHOLE REAL STORY was both less, and more, dramatic. Less, because they weren't as threatened by the fire as the media implied. More, because the madness of murder and a murderer, singular or plural, still on the loose within the complex, was an ongoing threat.

Dr. P's Corner was not as threatened by the forest fire as the press believed or suggested, for several reasons. First, the main building was surrounded on three sides by paved parking lots, with the dormitory on the fourth. Second, the roofs were covered with old-fashioned fire-resistant slate shingles; this was, after all, Vermont--land of slate, marble, and maple syrup. Still, the center's occupants found themselves in a dangerous situation, with no way out.

Close to the fire, yet removed by the distance of two cabins, the Holloway brothers hovered in angry disagreement.

"I say we forget this silly business and return to Wyoming and my flock of Salvationists," said Howie. "I'm sick of Vermont and tired of vacationing."

Furious, Harris hurled a china plate across the kitchen at big brother. Howie ducked and simultaneously pulled the missile out of the air. Unlike a Frisbee he'd most likely toss back, he calmly set the plate on the table.

"Forget your fury and your mission, Harris. It's time to evacuate before we're caught by the fire and can't get out."

"I don't care. I want to see how my plan plays out. I've been working on it at least as long as the nine-eleven terrorist schemers must have done."

"You can't. No way can you get close enough to discover whether your post-hypnotic suggestions have taken root."

"We can see the aftermath."

"Better to catch it on the news."

"No!" Harris stomped his foot like a spoiled child denied ice cream.

"Yes, Harris, I insist. If we don't clear out, we'll be the only ones left at Lake Bomoseen except for Dr. Petroski's conference participants. Think about it. The cops and the media will expect to interview us. Your target will spot us. You, if not me, too, will be identified as the schemer behind the scenes."

Howie turned his back and Harris stuck out his tongue at big brother.

Meanwhile, out in Wyoming, Colonel Schwartzkopf called the White House. He demanded access to the President. After identifying himself, he was put through immediately. Dominic Alexander Davidson promptly agreed, without argument, to all that Peter proposed.

Ned Fleetfoot, too, complied with the Colonel's demands, locking the Laundromat and posting a sign: "Closed until further notice." In his room behind the washers and dryers and customer service area, Ned gathered his fire-fighting gear and clothes. He left the premises and drove at high speed out to F. E. Warren Air Force Base west of Cheyenne to join Colonel Schwartzkopf.

In their room Agatha and Lisa again poured over the printouts obtained from searching personnel files. Kristi had passed the time awaiting evacuation by adding another stack to their cache, this one containing credit and military records. They had to do something with their time besides gnaw fingernails.

Actually, it felt good to again be working in tandem with Lisa. They had spent their lives as twinnies, playing and working, dreaming up projects and carrying them to fruition, from political fundraisers to clan parties. Aggie didn't see why Lisa had to go and spoil it all by playing the adulteress.

Shortly they were called back into the central building, where everyone was supposed to take shelter. In the great room and lounge, the dining hall and all of the small seminar rooms, the blinds were closed, the drapes drawn. Keep at bay, if possible, the persistent demands of the smoke and heat attempting to gain entrance and overwhelm the inhabitants. Early on and under Reggie's direction, the staff along with a few volunteers had climbed to the attic to sandbag and wet down the bags hauled up there; a "dike" as it were, between the hot, slate-shingled roof above and the ceiling below.

People shuffled restlessly from one spot and room to another. Some slumped tiredly on straight chairs in the dining room and couches in the lounge.

Sergeant Malcolm Thompson was the only outsider among them. Assigned to remain with the conference group, he too was now an unwilling captive. He strolled or stalked among them, alternatively issuing commands and looking lost and discomfited.

Under the current danger, Aggie nearly forgot about her husband, languishing out home in his hospital bed. Yet the status of his health kept bubbling up from the stew pot in her muddled mind that she'd thought could be left alone to simmer on its own.

Excusing herself, Agatha headed for the chapel. She must bring herself to pray. She would pray for the return of Randy's good health (if mental illness was his problem), and pray that she had it in her to forgive him. She would pray that she could give up this feeling of hatred she harbored toward both Randy and Lisa and move on with her life. On her knees in the quiet room, back lit with dim lighting, she bowed her head and closed her eyes. She pleaded with the Lord to give her the strength to endure. She promised God that following their rescue from the fire, she would examine her motives and desires. She wanted so badly for things to be back the way they were, when Randy was faithful, or she supposed he was, and for Lisa to love her, not fall for Aggie's husband.

Returning to the main room, Aggie vacillated between clinging close to Lisa and mingling. As tired and frightened as everybody else, she realized they all needed action or they would fall apart. The notion seemed to materialize out of nowhere: *To stay sane, to control your destiny, you must first control yourself.*

Turning to Lisa, Aggie said they must resume their quest for a solution to the murders. "Nerves are frayed and emotions close to the surface," she said. "Let's keep a sharp eye and ear at the ready, Lisa."

"You're guessing somebody will break under all this pressure."

"One or several. Doesn't necessarily imply that when that happens, those who lose control are killers."

"No. In fact, the murderer, realizing that possibility, might be more cautious than anybody else."

The cousins decided to separate. Lisa wandered about in the main room, while Aggie relocated on a couch in the lounge. Across from her sat Lucille Bailey and Mick Houston, huddling and conferring in low tones. Aggie polished her glasses and set them back on her nose. Her vision was crystal clear. No risk that she'd see double, as with the double vision that had attacked her out in Wyoming.

Under pretense of reading the latest novel by C. J. Box off her Kindle, a popular digital reader, Aggie actually stared at Mick Houston and Lucille Bailey. Lip-readers do not concentrate on mouths alone, she had told Randy more than once. Facial expressions, including eyes and muscles, plus the movement of jaw and cheek, all contribute to the message. Put them together and you can produce a delicious recipe with its own special flavors. This time the ingredients for the dish came from Mick and Lucille's words.

Aggie felt like a spy with a secret microphone hidden near the pair. Both of these attractive young people were articulate, and they could enunciate well. No problem following their conversation.

"Mick, I know it was you who set the woods on fire. You and your damn cigarettes."

He began to cry. The tears gathered and spilled over, though he made no sound. "I know, I know. Should I confess? I'm so sorry, so very very sorry. What will they do to me?" Houston covered his face with both hands.

"There, there, Mick." Lucille leaned close; rubbed his shoulder, patted his back. "Maybe I was too hasty jumping to conclusions. The Delano cousins are also smokers. I've smelled tobacco on their breaths and from their hair and clothes. Could have been Kurt or Don, I suppose."

Mick glanced up, relief written across his face. "What about Max? Is my dad still bothering you?"

She jerked away. "Why do you ask?"

"Are you kidding? After all you told me about his stalking and terrorizing you before you left Boise, I'd have thought he'd resume giving you a bad time the minute you're back in the same company. Uh, you know what I mean--all of us together here."

"We aren't 'together', as you put it," she snapped. "You know he's after Maude, now. Although I can't imagine who'd want my ugly sister. Unless he plans to do her harm. As, uh, revenge against me."

"That's right. I remember. You said that when my dad's threats to hurt you did no good--that you refused to capitulate to his demands--Max said he'd go after your sister. Omigod! What if he does?"

Lucille looked uncomfortable. She glared around the room as if to check whether her wart-nosed sister or Mick's father was within earshot. "Never mind, Mick. I'll take care of Max."

When the pair of them glanced her way, Aggie realized she had let the Kindle drop to her lap. Couldn't hide behind that ruse. She closed her eyes.

That did no good at all. Visions of Randy gasping his last breath swam across the screen of her brain. Opening her eyes, Aggie gasped. The room was cloudy with smoke seeping in through the cracks. She and her once beloved husband might end up meeting their Creator simultaneously.

CHAPTER 26

"AGGIE, I THINK YOUR Dr. P did it," Lisa said. She plopped down on the couch.

Agatha opened her eyes and sat up straight.

"What? Dr. Petroski? You can't be serious."

"A lot of signs point in his direction." Lisa passed over a mug of coffee.

The double cousins had grabbed their large carryall bags when evacuating the dormitory. Lisa as usual carried with her "everything but the kitchen sink." By contrast, Aggie's bag often held wads of clean but crumpled Kleenex and empty plastic bags ready to fill with scraps of food--to eat sometime later or to feed birds and other small creatures. Plus she carried the usual female paraphernalia of makeup, emery boards, notebook, pen, and keys. And two packages of orange-flavored tic tacs.

This time each of their bags also carried one-half each of the computer printouts. They had noticed the personnel files were much less complete than the dossiers prepared on each conference participant that presumably Sam Jones had assembled.

"What did Dr. Petroski think he needed with so much background? I'm wondering if your wonderful Dr. P meant to blackmail some of you."

"Sounds more like Jones."

Lisa asked Aggie to watch her bag while she made a run for the restroom. Aggie nodded, but promptly forgot, because at that moment she spilled coffee down the front of her lavender silk blouse, and had to rush off herself to dampen paper towels.

"Now, what, love?" Lisa washed her hands and watched Aggie. "Oh, let me do it. I've got spot remover in my bag." Lisa looked around. "Where's my bag? You didn't watch it? Or bring it with you?"

"Sorry."

When they returned to the lounge, both carryalls sat where they'd left them. Beige and tan, the look-alike bags appeared untouched. Except that they were interchanged, which Lisa discovered while pawing through Kleenex and plastic sacks. "I've got your bag and you've got mine. Only, know what? My printouts are gone. How about yours?"

Which was when they discovered that both halves, the complete set of printouts, were missing. "Just like my journal," Aggie fumed. "Now, really, Lisa, how could you think poor old Dr. P was capable of doing this? He's blind. And look there. He's still slumped beneath the lantern, half out of consciousness."

"I suppose." Lisa plunged through her bag after the spot remover and then went to work on Agatha's blouse. "How about Penelope, then? You said she uses Gregg shorthand. If she stole your journal, she'd be able to read it. I don't know of anybody else who can do that, not in this modern day and age."

"Warty Maude, maybe."

"Okay, I'll concede the point, two people out of forty, or however many people this conference started out with, including the staff members." Lisa continued to scrub at Aggie, using such a rough stroke her cousin could feel it on her tender skin beneath the thin blouse.

She squirmed beneath Lisa's administrations. The blouse, like all the garments Lisa attacked, would come out fine. Aggie wished the solution to these crimes was that easy. Or that she could decipher the cause behind Randy and Lisa's betrayal.

"No, Agatha. I've changed my mind. Couldn't be Penelope. She's too small and weak. She could hardly heft the hatpin, much less a gun."

"Lisa, we're small, too, but hardly weak."

"Look at the facts, Aggie. I don't know about you, but I'm dismissing the Delanos. They're caught up in each other, and sweet and innocent, too, almost like newborn babes." (Aggie rolled her eyes, at nobody in particular.) "No, I can't see either of them as the murderer. Forget Reggie, too. No motivation that we've uncovered, and he's been run ragged under all this pressure trying to feed us. He hasn't had time to dash about killing people."

"The Houstons?" Aggie countered. "We still don't know how or whether Max actually blackmailed Jones to get them admitted to this seminar. What information could he have employed? What big bad secret about either Jones or Petroski did Max know?" What Agatha was thinking, but didn't say, was that Mick was the one with the secret. She had no clue about how Mick's stay with the Salvationists fit into the center's puzzle.

"There, dear. Your blouse is good as new." Lisa replaced the spot remover and carefully rearranged her bag. She also checked to see if anything else was missing.

"Back to Maude," Lisa continued. "I see no motive there. In my opinion we should dismiss her, too. But what about Kristi? We haven't discovered why she was so upset with Jones for wanting access to her computer records. He must have been the one, after all, who prepared all those extensive dossiers on the conference participants. Sounds like he planned to blackmail anybody who was susceptible. Or why bother?"

"By susceptible, you mean people who could easily be blackmailed because they had some big bad secret to hide." She had no answers. "Let's circulate. I need to get up and move around."

"While you're at it, go sit with Dr. Petroski. Ask him some pertinent questions."

"Like what? I hate to invade his privacy."

"Ask him about anything that puzzles you. Interrogate the man, Aggie. Pose direct questions, dear. For instance, what blackmail ploy did Max use to get the Houstons accepted into this program? Try to find out why Jones countermanded Dr. Petroski's verbal offer to employ Mick as a consultant with the Corner. If what Max said out in the clearing when we eavesdropped is true, then Paul had already offered Mick the job. There must have been some lapse of time before Sam intervened, because Mick had time to resign from his NASA position and give up his apartment."

Aggie wriggled in her chair. She didn't want to do this. But suddenly Aggie realized she had another question for Dr. Petroski, one that had mystified her from the beginning: why was her name on the roster of conferees even before Joan had filled out the application? Aggie's daughter had told her mom that she was expected, and if Aggie didn't show, Joan wouldn't be allowed to enroll, either.

"Wait, wait," Lisa added. "Before you go, I want to verify some things with you."

"Like what?"

"Try to remember what was in those dossiers, Aggie. Off the computer printouts that were stolen from us. For instance, I remember exactly when Dr. Petroski was born and where, because the date and place are so memorable: Pearl Harbor Day, December 7, 1941; in the tiny town of Auld, Nebraska. Auld, get it? Like our maternal grandparents."

"Goodness gracious, Lisa."

"What, what?"

"That's the exact same day and place of Sam Jones birth."

When the cousins had first divided the computer printouts to study and ponder, Aggie took the first half of the alphabet and Lisa the last. Thus Aggie's lost records included files on the Baileys, Carsons, Delanos, Sam Jones, and the Houstons, while Lisa had the remainder, including Paul Petroski.

"Okay, I'm ready if you are. Lisa, you circulate, and get some news about the fire, while I take on the venerable Dr. P." Aggie gulped air, as if readying herself to dive into deep waters, which is exactly how she felt. She didn't want to challenge their leader. She, not him, might drown.

In the dining room where Lisa wandered, the anxious and exhausted occupants had seemingly consumed endless cups of coffee. The big urn was empty and Reggie or anybody else among the few kitchen employees who had been caught out here in the fire had as yet to assume the duty. Possibly disgusted with all the pointless questions he could not answer, Officer Malcolm Thompson was short with everybody. He tossed out the dregs of what must be his sixth or seventh mug, he told Aggie, and left the room. Kurt and Don Delano held hands under cover of the white linen table cloth on the far side of the room. Agatha smiled.

Kristi was off somewhere, too, probably in her office. In passing Agatha, Lisa whispered another command. Aggie should ask permission to use the computer again. She could produce yet another set of printouts.

"No, I can't, Lisa. No electricity; no computers, remember."

Tom Carson vacillated like a bargain shopper over piles of discounts, booming complaints one minute and assurances the next. No sign of Penelope; in the kitchen, perhaps. Some of them had volunteered for staff support, since Reggie seemed ready to fall apart. Better to peel potatoes and wash dishes, set and clear tables, than to sit around attempting to twitter away their frustrations and fright.

Everybody else complained that somebody should have found their phones by now. Even if they couldn't get a signal to outside, at least they would feel better with the familiar toy in their hands. Losing a phone was like wandering around half-naked. After Reggie had visited the chapel, following Penelope's admission that she had spotted the pile of cell phones there, he returned empty-handed. "Somebody beat me to them. No phones, and no clues where they went."

Now Aggie reminded Lisa that the missing phones was not an omen but an outright warning. "Whoever took them wants to see us held captive. Out of touch with the world. Unable to call for help."

"You're thinking that the killer purposely set the forest fire? Wants to see all of us burnt to a crisp? That he's holding us hostage? Aggie dear, don't think like a ghoul."

"He. Or she."

"'She'? I doubt it."

"Why not?"

"I can see a woman mad enough to kill a man, but not to commit mass murder by burning up a crowd of innocents."

Lisa had a point.

Lisa and Aggie left the dining room to recheck the lounge, opting for the foyer where a love-seat size sofa sat near the entrance and the bank of pay phones. Except, as typical the world over, no doubt, most of them had been removed. No point, what with the popularity of the cells. The cousins couldn't see through the heavy oak double doors at the front and the telephones were either missing or inoperable, so they were stranded.

"You haven't tackled Dr. Petroski yet, I see."

"People coming and going are too close to him. I don't want to be overheard."

"Trying to get up your courage, too, eh."

"Okay, tell me, Lisa. What signs suggest to you that Dr. P is the killer?"

Lisa withdrew a small spiral-bound notebook from her bag to flip through the pages. "Hold the thought, please, of his and Jones' simultaneous birth date and birth place. Now, listen to this: Paul and Sam served together in the same unit in Vietnam, where Paul saved Sam's life."

Aggie nodded. "So what?" This was an exercise in futility. Lisa's point was common knowledge.

"The by-then blind Petroski gets not one but several university degrees. Without Sam. Then for years your Dr. P works--again, alone--as a corporate consultant." Lisa paused to look up. "No record that Jones ever went to college. Sam's personnel records indicate he held a series of low-paying jobs: gas-station attendant, waiter, cook's assistant. He collected unemployment checks in California. Suddenly he turns up in Vermont as the Rutland postmaster. Rutland, mind you, next door to Castleton, Lake Bomoseen, and your Dr. P's Corner for Cautious Change here in New England.

"A job with the postal service, Aggie, requires that you pass a civil service test and produce references and recommendations. Put your thinking cap on, my dear. From collecting garbage, Sam leaps into the responsible position of handling mail, supervising employees, preparing government reports? I don't think so. Jones would need to produce a record of experience, of integrity and organizational abilities. Get real."

Agatha couldn't help it, instead of biting her tongue to keep silent, she felt more like fighting back—doubling her fist and socking her double cousin on the end of her little perky nose. Why did Lisa have to be so condescending? Or had she always been like this, and Aggie hadn't noticed, or had constantly made excuses for the little blonde bombshell? Maybe she should try taking on a new stance, hitting half-way between the two extremes: "Get real yourself, dearie," she said, with an effort at sounding confident.

Startled, Lisa reared back. Making an exaggerated gesture, she reached into her shirt pocket for her glass case, removed her glasses, and slowly tucked each ear piece over each separate little shell-like ear. Then she proceeded to stare at Cousin Agatha over the top of the rims. "Come again?"

"You said 'get real.' I just said 'get real' too. Right back at you."

"Good grief, my dear. Sounds to me like you've gone half-daft."

Egad, no matter what she tried, Agatha couldn't win. Dealing with Lisa meant coming off sounding half-daft, half or more of the time, exactly the way Lisa put it. Or how Randy would do it, too.

Agatha vowed to put this scene, and every other one just like it, behind her. Think about something else. Any time a person thought mostly about herself was a time when you went all catty-wampus wibbly-wobbly inside your head. Better to think about others. Or other things. Like taxes and death. Yeah, sure, death. Fire and brimstone. Murder and mayhem.

Aggie stared at the painting on the wall opposite, another among artist T. J. Jordan's abstracts. The startlingly vivid colors of blood red, harvest gold, eggplant purple, and obsidian zigzagged across a black background. The title, *Dark Heart,* appealed to Aggie just now. Somebody in the crowd had just such a heart filled with just such terrible dark intent.

"Aggie? Agatha? Where's your mind off to, now?"

Aggie shrugged, dragging herself back to the puzzle "Yes, dear. I have no thoughts on the matter, except to suggest coincidence. Somebody knew Sam, and spoke on his behalf. That's how he got the job in the Rutland Post Office. Oh! Oh, dear."

"'Oh' is right. Petroski. Soon thereafter, Sam leaves the postal service in Rutland to join his old wartime buddy, Paul. The 'old friend' he hasn't seen or possibly even talked to in three decades. The man who was born on the exact same day. That's too much 'coincidence' for me."

"I can agree with that much but, again, so what? How do you jump from a renewed acquaintance to Dr. Petroski as murderer? Keeping in mind, of course, that the man is blind. How could he know he was killing the right person? Or that nobody was looking?"

"Forget the physical details for now. Think motivation, instead. Which leads me again to blackmail. Yes, blackmail, kiddo. All the signs point to it. Sam prepared all those dossiers in preparation for blackmailing conference participants. This could be an old scene with him; something he does with every seminar. Who knows how many people he'd already been blackmailing? Could be Penny or Maude or Kristi, this time."

"You're vacillating between a woman and Paul Petroski as the killer?"

Lisa plunged on, ignoring her cousin's question. "Sam blackmailing Paul--could be something that goes all the way back to Vietnam. Sam makes Paul recommend him for the postmaster job in Rutland and then, later, into hiring him here as Paul's assistant director. Petroski takes it for awhile, even comes to lean on Sam. Only now Dr. P's aging, his infirmities are beginning to get to him. Petroski acknowledges his physical dependence on Jones, but also recognizes that Sam is getting worse. Jones wants more and more authority and resents Petroski's fame and his following of faithful admirers. Sam plots to make money from blackmailing participants; if blackmail worked with Paul, why not with others? For money. Petroski finally admits that he's hired a thug; a rude, crude misfit. Paul snaps. He kills Sam in a murderous rage..."

Caught up in Lisa's graphic description, Aggie dived into the deep waters of these suppositions. "And then with his terrible remorse, Dr. P fell into this funk. Changed overnight."

"You got it. That's the way I've got it analyzed."

"Lisa, your premise still doesn't account for Akunda's death. Nor Paul Petroski's blindness."

"Okay, so Dr. P gambled. Or he killed Sam when they were alone together in Paul's room and then he shoved Jones out in the hall."

"Officer Akunda?"

"The cop was getting too close. Petroski had to take him out, too."

"You're forgetting Dr. P's disability again."

"No, I'm not. Blind, he couldn't be sure Sam was dead. That's why Paul used two different murder weapons. How about that? As for Akunda, you can solve that one. You can't expect me to fly back here to Vermont and solve both murders for you. You do the other one."

Good grief. A favored expression among the entire Auld-Vicente clan. Agatha decided to give Lisa the benefit of the doubt, whatever that worn-out saying meant. She told Lisa her theories would take some mulling over. She leaned her head against the wall and closed her eyes, effectively shutting Lisa out.

Lisa rolled her eyes, clearly she wasn't buying Agatha's attitude. Lisa challenged Aggie to stop postponing her assignment. She re-issued her command: "Go talk to your very precious Dr. P." Two could play at this game of sarcasm and exaggeration.

Aggie said she would. However, they were interrupted. A shout followed by an echoing wave resounded from the dining room, "Max's been shot!"

CHAPTER 27

THE ASSISTANT COOK HAD discovered Max's body, bleeding from a shot in the head, when she went to the big walk-in freezer off the kitchen. Nobody came forward at Thompson's demand for information. Nobody admitted to knowledge of what Houston was doing in there, when he'd arrived, or who might have trailed him.

Following the ensuing hubbub--with Officer Thompson running around like a headless hen, and lunch delayed by a frazzled Reggie, and mole-nosed Maude Bailey sobbing her heart out--Penelope Carson began to pray. She planted herself smack in the middle of the dining room with eyes squeezed tight shut, hands folded worshipfully in front of her nearly flat bosom, and body shaking. In a tremulous, high-pitched voice, the distraught young woman, weaving and wailing, tipping forward and backward and sometimes sideways, exhorted at and pleaded with the unseen Deity to guide and comfort them in their sorrow and despair.

Like strangers packed compactly into a small elevator, one and all responded to the proscribed etiquette. Heads bowed, eyes closed, lips moved in private and individual supplication.

Sorrow and despair? Somebody was neither sorrowful nor despairing, Aggie mused.

Couldn't be Dr. P. Of course not, never could have been. Perky Lisa was acting the complete idiot to even propose such a proposition. Exiled with the rest of them from the dormitory where his permanent suite stood at the head of the first-floor corridor, dear Doctor Petroski had sat huddled for hours in one chair or another--in the dining room beneath the lantern and later in Reggie's kitchen. Reggie told Aggie he didn't know what to do with or about

148

the fragile old man, and nobody else had any ideas. Not even Kristi. Dr. P suffered from whatever had caused the dramatic switch that made of their once dynamic leader a pitiable skeleton, a shell of a man to be avoided. Agatha guessed that nobody knew what to make of it.

Kristi, whose computer job gave her something in common with Penelope, rushed forward. Throwing an arm lightly across the girl's shoulders, Kristi led the whimpering wisp across the room toward Aggie.

"Can you look after her?" Kristi pleaded. "I've got to get back to the office. Officer Thompson has me culling the lists of past conference participants. With no computer, I've got to check the paper files. Don't ask me why."

Anything, Aggie supposed, to keep the staff occupied. With his directives, Thompson made it appear he was onto something. She wished it had been Sylvia, not Malcolm, who'd been caught inside the ring of fire with them when the woods exploded in its full force of fury.

What were Battisti and Whitehall doing in the interim? Aggie could imagine Castleton's mayor and Vermont's governor wringing their hands and dodging the press, like Marci and Philip. The CNN pair would be reporting and interviewing endlessly, that was a given. Without sleep, possibly with little or no food or water. Coffee, sure; they'd be consuming mugs and mugs of the stuff. Hyper, that described everybody. Use of the technology wiped out, including television and telephones, she could only imagine the stress level rising until it grew to tidal wave size.

"Poor Joan," Aggie said to Lisa across the whimpering Penny, who, with all that huddling up into herself, could have passed for a ball of yarn. "Joan was so eager to attend this conference and there she is, stuck out in Wyoming."

"Good grief, Aggie. We're the ones who're stuck. Joan's out in the open, free and safe." Lisa glanced meaningfully at Penelope, whose eyes were squeezed shut. "Now's your chance, Aggie. With Dr. P in the kitchen, go talk to him. I'll watch Penelope."

If Penny squirmed or peeped out of one eye, the cousins didn't notice.

"Okay," said Aggie, getting up to cross the room. She dreaded intruding on Paul Petroski's grief, or whatever ailed him.

She glanced over her shoulder at Penny. What was Max Houston to Penny, she wondered, that the girl should carry on so over his death?

Left with Lisa, Penny continued to slump--no longer crying, praying, or saying a word. Shrugging off Lisa's touch, her attempt at comforting, the girl just sat there, folded up tight as a morning glory beneath the mid-day sun to sink deeper inside herself.

Aggie geared up to approach Dr. Petroski. She wished she hadn't promised Lisa she'd do this. She might have been keeping an appointment with the dentist to have an impacted wisdom tooth removed.

Maybe she'd wait until later. Postpone the dentist's drill. Think up some excuse for Lisa that might sound plausible.

Out in Wyoming, Colonel Schwartzkopf had refused to acknowledge either detours or postponements. With authoritative demeanor, he brushed them aside. While Lisa longed to be home with Peter, her husband was at that moment zooming across the continent to her rescue. In a two-seater, lightweight superjet, the F-16A Fighting Falcon flying at 1,320 miles per hour, or Mach 2.05, put Peter and Ned Fleetfoot in Albany, New York, less than ninety minutes after leaving Cheyenne. Wearing full firefighter's gear, Ned was strapped in behind Schwartzkopf.

Thanks to the President's intervention, a Super Cobra helicopter awaited the pair at the Albany Airport next door to Vermont; specifically, Castleton and Lake Bomoseen and Dr. Petroski's small campus complex known as the New England Center. During Vietnam, Peter had flown the Hueys, the UH-4 Helicopter, which were able to put soldiers on the ground in forward places, haul and deliver supplies, and meanwhile provide added firepower from their machine guns to protect the men they were sent to evacuate. Later the Hueys were replaced with the Cheyenne, but it didn't last beyond the seventies, as it in turn was replaced with the Cobra, and then by the Super Cobra, which flies at a-hundred-sixty miles per hour.

Secret though the Colonel's maneuverings were meant to be, the press--in the form of a lone reporter--nevertheless was alerted. Carl Crosby, from an obscure weekly down in Arkansas, the Carsons' home state, finally got a ho-hum okay to make the trip. Armed with a piddly expense voucher (he planned to sleep in the back seat of the no-doubt dented car he'd reserved from Rent-a-Wreck), Carl--the mid-tall, mid-girth, mid-twenties reporter, mid-way through a journalism degree from a middling-reputation college--was discouraged and disgusted.

Last on the Vermont Corner's murder scene, probably. Nobody of worth left to interview who hadn't already been interviewed to death. The key players locked away now inside the circle of flames. Everybody knew what a forest fire looked like. With Carl's cheapo, low-budget camera, he'd get to film nothing earth-shattering to send home. Just a bunch of flaming trees billowing smoke clouds; with black and white film, no less.

Crosby crossed the tarmac from his plane, a slow-flying propeller model the editor had booked for him, his posture slumped, his feet dragging. His grand goal of getting into that great world of big-time journalism fading with the setting sun, Carl cursed.

"Damn S.O.B. of an editor. Too late, too late." What the hell could he report that hadn't already been covered and endlessly regurgitated?

Lifting his eyes to the heavens as if to plead for divine intervention, and then back to the tarmac, Carl spotted the Super Cobra revving its engine (but not yet twirling its whirly-bird blades). At that moment, dropping from the sky like an eagle zooming out of the stratosphere to snatch an edible goodie from its nest, Schwartzkopf's Fighting Falcon swooped in and landed near the Cobra.

Out jumped Colonel Schwartzkopf from the pilot's seat and, from behind, the half-Arapaho son of Nasty Three, Wyoming's Secretary of State, dressed in full firefighter's garb. Carl Crosby from Arkansas gaped as the two men paused to hug some dignitary before racing to the Cobra, hopping in, and setting the rotors whirling. They took off, headed east.

"What the hell?" Crosby gasped.

Black-haired, black-eyed Mark Prescott (nee, Mario Pesci), presidential aide and right-hand man, couldn't resist. Stepping away from the clump of scowling security men looking suspiciously in every direction--to fulfill their role in protecting Dominic Alexander Davidson, President of the United States of America--Prescott joined Crosby.

Mark Prescott didn't care whether Crosby was the disheveled bumpkin he appeared to be or an Eurasian terrorist. Looked like Mario Pesci (Prescott, that is) had an appreciative listener.

"What you're privy to, here, youngster (Mark enjoyed playing the condescending role), is the opening act of a great drama. The President and entourage," Mark jerked a thumb back over his shoulder toward the First Lady, Julia Davidson, the tall blonde standing with the President's executive secretary, Rose Washington Lincoln, both of whom were surrounded by various other aides, assistants, associates, and security staff. "are en route to the forest fire in Vermont.

"Colonel Schwartzkopf will drop firefighter Ned Fleetfoot from Wyoming straight into the central zone. You know," Mark clarified, as if the bumpkin had no access to the unending TV coverage nor any understanding of what he saw if he did. "Over that-a-way, in Vermont."

Out popped Carl's videocam. This scene was too good for just black and white film in his newspaper's still camera. Crosby caught the Super Cobra lifting off and the Falcon camped nearby. Then, with long-range attachment (it was his very own very expensive video camera), Carl zoomed in on the President.

Prescott gaped, speechless at last.

"How do you feel about this?" Crosby asked, poking a mic in Mark's face.

"Uh, why, happy, I guess. I mean, uh, glad to be part of the scene. But, uh, maybe I'd better check with the President, get permission for you to use all this in your, uh, what? Where? Some little local TV station?"

Behind Mark, the President and First Lady laughed. Well acquainted with Mark's tendency for self-aggrandizement, they suspected what he'd been doing--telling tales out of school.

Carl Crosby, junior reporter from Arkansas, ran on eager feet toward the President, and even while guns were drawn and security men took the shooter's stance, Carl continued racing forward. Dom quickly yelled a warning: "Stop, halt! My God, man, come ahead, but cautiously, lest you be ventilated with a hail of bullets."

Down went the pistols and revolvers, relaxed came the stance.

"You want an interview with your President? Young man, surely you know that 'DAD is here for <u>You</u>'!"

Harris finally conceded. Howie was right, the brothers should get the hell off Lake Bomoseen. Harris, however, left alone. The pastor of the Sin-Sick Salvationists floated, face-down, in the middle of the lake. When he'd pulled the plug on the canoe, he didn't know that Harris had taken private swimming lessons on the QT. Harris, but not Howie Holloway, could swim.

CHAPTER 28

"LUNCH IS READY," REGGIE announced. He nearly got knocked over as the group, exhibiting the first stage of mob formulation, rushed toward and past him.

In the kitchen, edging toward Dr. P and stiffening the spine of her resolve, Aggie turned away. Ah, saved by the food manager! She had a good excuse for Lisa about why she hadn't interviewed their leader.

Acting as one body, yet with little or no eye contact between and among, as if one's neighbor could be the vicious killer, everybody milled around. Uncertain whether to sit at their first or second assigned tables or somewhere else, they mingled, bumped into each other, drew sharply away.

Shambling listlessly between the Wyomingites, Penelope was at last speaking again. "Let me sit by you, Aggie, please."

Agatha wouldn't have been the least little bit surprised to hear the girl add the appendage, "Pretty please with sugar on it," to her plea. Aggie no longer thought of Penelope as a woman; she was too childish acting. How could she manage the Arkansas government department's computer center with this kind of demeanor? Like Dr. P, Penny was rapidly disintegrating. Was she actually that afraid, discombobulated? Or was her entire repertoire of personality presentations nothing but a ruse, a bit of play-acting?

"Of course, dear." Under Aggie and Lisa's arm-holding and back-patting guidance, the trio of women sat at the no-number table against the far wall. The duo's glance indicated consensus. Aggie wanted a panoramic view of the assemblage. Backs to the wall, sitting with Penelope between them, Aggie also sought to convey to Penny a sense of security. She would defend the cowering girl from a marauding army, if it came to that.

153

Silly business. Why was Penny so frightened? She feared another verbal attack from her Uncle Tom? So what? Aggie lived with this sort of behavior day in and day out. Normally, she was used to it. Surely the child was, too. The poor dear obviously needed to develop a backbone, some assertiveness, learn how to stand up to Carson; and, also, to the likes of Jones and his ilk.

Carson suddenly loomed over them, scowling and snarling. "Where've you been, Penelope? I've been looking all over for you."

Why didn't the child tell him? Penny had been with Aggie and Lisa for at least the past half-hour. Or, had she? No, that wasn't right. At one point Penny had excused herself to use the facilities. Everybody, with their frayed nerves and all that coffee, had worn a path to the restrooms.

Penelope slumped further into a tiny knot, a mere shadow of humanity. Aggie saw Lisa clamp tight her lips. She knew her once beloved cousin well. Lisa could tell off Carson; do it for poor Penny. Before Aggie or Lisa could launch a counter attack, though, Penny pushed back her chair and raced across the room. She twisted the knob and slammed the door behind her. Shrugging, Tom had the grace to blush. He stammered an apology and left their table.

With Penny gone, Lisa took the vacated seat next to Aggie.

"Okay, what'd Dr. P say?"

"Uh, I didn't get to talk to him."

"What? Why not?"

"I got interrupted. Reggie called lunch and Max got himself murdered."

After giving her a funny look, Lisa sat quietly, looking properly chastised for one brief moment before switching to stare round at their companions. "Look over there at the next table," Lisa murmured. "Looks like Maude is coming unraveled." Soft sobs growing in intensity emanated from table two. "Read their lips, Aggie."

Mick and Maude had their heads together.

"Lucille killed him, Mick. I'm sure of it," Maude whispered. "She was so jealous when Max and I got together. Lucille never got over it when he dumped her, you know."

"What are you saying? I thought it was the other way around."

Maude stared over the big mole on the tip of her nose that made her appear cross-eyed. She gasped before wiping her eyes. "Surely you know better than that. Max must have told you the whole sordid story. Your own father?"

"We weren't all that close," Mick muttered lamely. "I was preoccupied all hours in, uh, well, probably in the physics lab…"

"Yes, but surely…"

"So, tell me. Give me the facts, the true story."

"Lucille's got a compulsive obsessive-possessive personality. She drove her husband off; and, I mean, off. He left in the dead of night. He told me he was heading for Mexico, where he was sure she'd never find him. He knew she was a predator. As for me, her sister? She hated it, really hated it, when I made friends, female or male. When she and Max got together, I finally got a breather, thought I'd get some space at last. But Lucille treated Max the same way she treated me and her first husband. She was jealous of everybody, me, his students, his colleagues. He couldn't even look at, much less talk to anybody, but what she was all over him; clawing him, screaming, making a nuisance of herself, making scenes in public. Max told me he was at the end of his rope, didn't know how to break it off, get rid of her."

"I can't believe this. Dad said nothing to me. He did seem to change, though. Now that you mention it. I wondered about that, what could be wrong, what made him look so drawn, so haggard. I figured he was worried about me." At that point Mick surprised Aggie all to pieces. He opened up and told Lucille about the Sin-Sick Salvationists. Which surely meant there was nothing sinister going on there.

"Dad pretended to join the cult, but his real purpose was to rescue me. I overheard our associate pastor, fellow by the name of Harris Holloway, tell his brother he intended to use hypnotism on selected members; those, apparently, who appeared the most amenable to post-hypnotic suggestions."

"On Max, you mean?"

"Right. By then I'd discovered Harris had doctored dad's tea with a concoction comprised of one part arsenic to two parts foxglove."

"Omigod, Mick. One or the other should have killed Max. Both are deadly poisons."

"Not in such small quantities. A pinch of each, though, was all it took to screw up our heads."

"Yours, too?"

"I think so."

Aggie glanced away from keeping her eyes pinned on Maude and Mick. To Lisa, she mouthed, "Tell you later." Keeping what they'd said to herself, Aggie couldn't believe Maude's story; exactly the opposite from Lucille's. Nor that Mick would admit to membership in the Salvationist cult. And then to actually reveal their method of control.

At that point Mick pulled an even bigger surprise. Reaching into the front closet near Aggie, he pulled out a rifle and waved it around the room. What on earth was the fellow up to? Aggie could only surmise that Mick was acting on a *post-hypnotic suggestion,* as he'd called the orders issued by the cult leaders.

"Listen up, everybody. I've had military training and I know how to use this thing. Whoever hid our cell phones better 'fess up. Give 'em back. Or

I'll shoot some of you dead between the eyes." Mick pulled the trigger and plaster fell from the ceiling. Another shot and the crystal chandelier came crashing to the floor.

People gasped, some paralyzed, others running for cover. Penny sat immobile, and so did Dr. P., both of them seemingly oblivious to both people and surroundings.

As for Mick, the poor lad was deranged. He had flipped out over his dad's murder. How could Mick not see the absurdity of his command, Aggie wondered. If the killer wasn't going to admit to murders, why would he—or she—confess to hiding cell phones?

Out of the corner of her eye, Aggie noticed the Delanos slipping up on Mick. One on each side, Don and Kurt quickly wrestled the rifle from Mick. The younger Houston burst into tears and sank to his knees. "I'm sorry. So sorry."

Aggie pushed between folk to reach Mick first. She rubbed his shoulders, wiped his cheeks with her handkerchief, whispered in his ear. "I've heard about the Salvationists, Mick. It was your dad who managed your escape, right?"

He nodded. "Yes, but they weren't all bad. Only the extremists wanted to make war on America. That's when I decided to clear out. Even before dad arrived."

"Okay, I guess I can buy that. But why did you go crazy right now?"

"Go crazy? What are you talking about?" Mick appeared truly stunned, like he had no awareness of losing his cool, of shooting up the center.

"I think you need help, Mick," Aggie said.

"You're nuts." Mick got up off his knees and stood to tower over Aggie.

She backed off. Returning to Lisa, Aggie told her to keep an eye on Mick. "I don't trust him not to come completely unglued again. Like that Jones fellow who laced his followers' Kool-Ade with poison, the Holloways apparently controlled their people, too. Moreover, I believe their hypnosis worked at least partially with Mick Houston.

"Oh, for heaven's sake, Agatha. Your imagination has taken another wild leap into the stratosphere."

"Okay, Miss Smarty Pants. How do you account for Mick's strange behavior?"

Ignoring the question to zero in on the label, Lisa leaped up to confront her cousin. "Why the name calling, Aggie? What's wrong with you?"

Aggie stood to face down Lisa, nose to nose. "You! You're what's wrong, Lisa. Bedding my Randy! How dare you!"

"What?" Lisa's little hands flew from her blond curls to cover her mouth. "Get real. When was this supposed to have happened, anyhow?"

Aggie named the day and the specific time.

"Don't be absurd. At that very moment Peter and I were hosting a cocktail party out at the base."

"F. E. Warren Air Base?"

"Where else, silly."

Aggie couldn't think straight. She plopped down on her bottom to think.

Gradually order was restored. The Delanos swept up glass and dumped it in the trash, while Maude kicked the plaster against the wall, as if it didn't matter. People returned and resumed their places around the tables. Mick emerged from the men's room and Lucille from the ladies'. Immediately Tom and Reggie took charge of Mick, hauling him off to the side where a big round post stood in the middle of the room separating serving from seating and dining areas. Deftly whipping out a rope from his hip pocket, Reggie motioned to Tom and the two of them tied up the Houston chap. Aggie cringed.

But then Agatha's brain, as if ripped open by the killer's hatpin, zoomed clear across the country to her beloved home in Wyoming. She tried hard to call up the scene she had seemingly memorized to remember for all time— Lisa's blond head disappearing down the back stairs while Randy zipped across the hall wearing nothing but towel on his way between bedroom and bath.

Stunned, Aggie leaned back, deep in thought. How could she have been so wrong about Lisa and Randy? Of course now she knew the woman with her husband couldn't have been her favorite cousin. But that didn't mean Randy was innocent.

"Where are the servers? Everybody must be starving," Lisa said. The crowd was growing as restless as hungry kindergartners left without lunch.

Lisa reminded Aggie she was supposed to be lip-reading the exchange between Mick Houston and Maude Bailey. "Since he laid the gun down, they've resumed talking as though nothing untoward ever happened."

Agatha looked at the post where Mick was tied, with Maude scooted up close in her chair. Neither one appeared the least bit dismayed that his movements were inhibited by all those knots tied in the heavy rope. They just went on whispering like it was any normal day in any normal place.

Dutifully Aggie followed Lisa's orders, she kept her eyes on the couple's lips.

"So then what happened?" Mick demanded of Maude. Both of them continued to act like nothing untoward had ever happened. Talk about denial.

Aggie, too, was suffering from a bad case of denial. But right now she had jobs to do—reading lips and following up on Dr. P. Deal with her personal feelings and Lisa's news later. Like, if Randy hadn't been bedding Lisa, then who was doing it in her bed?

"Mick, listen to me. I want to tell you the honest truth. Max and I formed a secret partnership. We plotted out in Boise. Implemented our plan, and succeeded. Until this damn relationship conference threw us all back together again."

Maude wiped her tears and after a few moments of silence squared her big broad shoulders, big as a football player padded to the nines. "Lucille and I left the state. Got jobs in West Virginia. Then Sam Jones brings us all back together again. He must have had a vicious sense of humor, as well as access via computer hacking to all our whereabouts. It wasn't enough to blackmail Max and you about joining the Salvationists, Sam had to enlist Lucille and me into the picture here. The membership of Dr. P's conference was totally mapped out, Mick. It had to be Sam Jones who did it. Who else would care, or bother?" With tear-filled eyes, Maude stared cross-eyed around the room.

Aggie gasped. She'd been right all along. The invitation issued to the Houstons from Idaho and the Baileys from West Virginia was no accident. And neither was hers and Joan's appearance at the conference. But why them? What did she and Joan ever have to do with Sam Jones? Or Dr. P either, for that matter.

Penelope returned to squeeze between the double cousins. Lisa sighed in resignation before demanding that Aggie share what she'd gleaned from lip-reading.

Agatha figured she wasn't the only one wreathing from their confrontation. Rather than talking it out, Lisa veered off to renew discussion of the murders.

Aggie could appreciate the non-personal topic. She complied by briefly catching Lisa up to date. Penelope inadvertently listened in.

Over the top of Penny's bowed head, Lisa next directed Aggie's attention to the cop. "Officer Thompson has no backup, no resources," she said fitfully, her frustration showing at being left out of Mick and Maude's secrets. "How can he corral everybody, keep track of them, much less initiate a proper investigation?"

Penelope raised her eyes to stare briefly back and forth at the double cousins. "That's an awful story," Penny said. "I thought Max was the bad guy. But it's Maude."

Aggie stared at the girl, wondering whether she was supposed to read something into Penny's remark.

"Do you suppose," said Lisa, ignoring Penny and getting no more than a nod from Aggie, "that Thompson feels like the nincompoop he resembles? So much pointless running about from one spot to another, issuing orders, reversing them, demanding alibis? Why question some people and not others?"

"Thompson will probably get around to the three of us pretty soon."

Again Penny lifted her glance, startled as a deer flushed out of the woods by a hunter. She gasped and blushed before dropping her head again to resume her comatose-like stare.

Although Reggie had convened them for lunch, there was no evidence that food was on the way. Perhaps the officer had directed Reggie to make the announcement simply as a means of getting everybody seated, in one place.

The fire raging beyond the building all but forgotten, the fear of death by horrible burning was replaced by the lesser rage of involuntary incarceration and the suspicions that reigned as king within these walls. The others were not alone. Aggie and Lisa continued to speak along innocuous lines.

"I wonder what's for lunch," Lisa mused.

Stomach growling, mouth watering, Aggie wished the servers would appear.

Sustenance. They all needed to be fed and watered before they collapsed or panicked. They could rise up as one, a great frightened frustrated tidal wave to wash over and drown the poor policeman.

"Somebody's got to do something!" Lisa said over the babble and outrage of their neighbors. "Thompson's lost it. Somebody go see about our lunch."

"Yes," agreed Olaf, materializing in front of them, and pointing a finger at Aggie. "I admit it, Aggie. I had dreams of the two of us getting together until you insisted on being true to your husband. But jumpin' Jehosaphat, I've had my eye on you all week. You're a born leader, doll. If you can't lead this group back to sanity, nobody can."

That's all it took, somebody to believe in her again. As effortlessly as sailing off the high diving board, Aggie leaped to her feet. "Thanks, Olaf, I needed that," she whispered, before turning to take charge.

Banging a spoon against a half-filled glass of water, Aggie called for order. With grim determination, steely stare, and an authoritative tone, she swiftly captured attention.

"We're all reasonable adults, and you are professional people. Let's start acting like it. Let's reformulate ourselves into our original clusters and let's start talking to one another--calmly and quietly. Among ourselves. Let's start by making lists."

"Meanwhile, what are you going to do?" Lisa whispered, when Aggie finished.

"I'm going to do what I promised you I was going to do. Go talk to Dr. P."

Lisa tugged on Aggie's shirt. "What about Mick Houston?"

"What about him?"

"You said he was in a state of denial. Didn't appear to recall waving that rifle around or shooting up the place."

"Not my business."

"Aggie!"

Aggie jerked free. "I mean it, Lisa. We've a series of murders to help solve, besides facing a fire that's about to burn us all up. We don't have time for a man who's sick with grief over his dad's death and half-crazed from a cult's prior brain-washing. He's safe for the moment, and with him tied to the post, we're all safe from him. Just in case he's the serial killer, I mean."

"But, Agatha," Lisa insisted, continuing to tug at her cousin's shirt tail. "What if the crowd here turns into a mob? You know, threatens to lynch the poor Houston chap?"

"Keep an eye out, Lisa," Aggie ordered. "You make sure they don't. But, just in case they do dream up a lynching plan, you come get me."

CHAPTER 29

Dr. P was no help to anybody. Reggie had reseated their leader at the head table, but Dr. Petroski, like Penny, merely shrugged into himself. He was like a lump of clay that people kept rearranging. Officer Malcolm Thompson scowled at Aggie, before visibly relaxing.

Now Penny was missing. And so was her uncle.

With everybody generally occupied, Aggie was free to get away. She desperately needed to pause, to think. She was sick of worrying about other people; time to assess her own situation.

She detoured to the ladies room to splash cold water on her face, park herself on the couch and close her eyes. What if this was to be her last day on earth? What if she would never need to face Randy? Or, what if she did?

If God could forgive, why not her, a mere mortal? Still, God forgave people who repented. Lisa hadn't confessed to having an affair with Randy. On the contrary, she'd had an unbreakable alibi for the time frame. Back to the basic question: if it wasn't Lisa Aggie had seen with Randy, then who was it?

Okay, babe, try this on for size, Aggie said, talking to herself: *get out of this predicament in Vermont, go home, confront Randy, and start standing up for yourself.*

Eyes closed, she might have been transported to the feet of Dr. P and his discussion of marital relationships. One fellow had been complaining that his wife never did what he wanted her to. Dr. Petroski's reply, Aggie now realized, could apply equally to either sex. He had told the young man that "Women are human beings, too, remember. Your wife is not just a piece of clay for you to mold, for you to clone yourself into. A woman comes from her own family, with her own set of family genes and DNA, with her own culture and habits and ways of doing things and thinking. Women are not put on this earth merely to drive men crazy, you know." At this point Dr. P chuckled and everybody had laughed.

So that's how you merged in a marriage—not thinking alike every minute; rather, appreciating similarities while respecting differences. *Act, don't react,* she reminded herself, from another of Dr. P's lectures. *Be quiet when you're hurt, think a few moments, long enough to count to ten, before popping off. If you cannot think like your partner, from his perspective, at least give him the right to his views. Then ACT, as a responsible adult, not a hurt child.*

Aggie's mind reeled. Her eyes popped open. "Thank you, Jesus!" she squeaked, aloud and alone. Sincerity, not irreverence; surely the Lord could read her heart.

So what's your conclusion from all that, Agatha, my dear? Randy is a human being, with a right to his own opinions? Humph.

So what? Did she plan to change herself for him? Perhaps a few things. Those she could not, she must accept in herself before she could expect him to. Meanwhile, she might also try to take him for what he was--a cranky old coot, to be sure, but he was hers. And by golly, if she loved him, why not fight for him? Whoever the other woman was, at least she wasn't Lisa. Lisa and Aggie could still be best friends. Thank God for that.

Aggie opened her eyes to recall where she was and what she'd promised Lisa she'd be doing--interview Dr. P first. Then check to see what everybody else was doing.

Kurt and Don spotted Aggie emerging from the ladies' room. Approaching, one on each side, the redheads looked at her expectantly, as if she had the answers to all their questions, the solutions to all their problems. They drew her over to their table.

"What should we be doing Aggie?" Don Delano said. "While you were gone, we've just been sitting here; chewing our fingertips to the bone, as it were." Kurt nudged his cousin. "Oh, yes, Kurt wants me to ask you what the sergeant intends to do with us."

Having taken charge momentarily, she had become their heroine. They expected more out of her. Everybody needed tender loving care, and they'd unofficially appointed Agatha Morissey as the caregiver. Humph. She supposed she could pretend this was a charity committee she chaired. Get herself up and doing things. Whatever she could dream up. For now. Try to help solve problems, get them out of this scrape. Well, since she was no firefighter, putting out forest fires was impossible. If they were all going to die, they might as well go out together, being nice, that would be something.

And if they could solve these murders, pinpoint the serial killer, that would be something else.

She bit the bullet. "Kristi, if you don't mind, you serve as recorder for table four. Don, Kurt, share with Kristi what you've seen and heard; anything unusual, out of the ordinary, from the conversations and behaviors of our fellow conferees. Then brainstorm awhile, before specifying, outlining, and recording."

"Let it all hang out, right?" said Kurt, leaning forward and perking up. "This procedure is right up my alley. We convene in subcommittee meetings at the state department of education all the time to do exactly this kind of thing."

"Right on," echoed the other Delano.

"You bet," agreed Kristi. "We do the same sort of thing here at Dr. P's Corner."

Aha, she'd accidentally hit on it, a technique familiar to these professionals. Which gave Aggie another idea.

"You're right. First, before you begin, though--Kurt, Don, Kristi, each of you take one of the other tables and describe the brainstorming technique that's familiar to you. Oh, hey," she interrupted herself. "While you're working with the other tables, ask them to save their notes. Then Kristi can enter the results in enumerated format on the computer. As soon as it's up and running again."

"Ooh, what if we burn up first?" Kristi protested.

The cluster four trio in front of Aggie glanced apprehensively at one another, as if to confirm Kristi's fears. Acknowledging the moment, Don shrugged, poked Kurt, and nodded to Kristi. "Forget the fire. Nothing we can do about what's happening outside. Let's worry about what we can do inside."

Aggie's suggestion apparently worthwhile, the trio, as one body, switched expressions from anxiety to anticipation. She had given them something useful to do. Aggie wondered if it really could be this easy to inject new vigor into them, like blood into nearly destroyed, collapsed veins.

"When Detective Whitehall returns, I'll turn over our notes to him. Right, Aggie?" said Kristi, rising from her chair.

The Delanos also stood. "Wait," Don said, raising a hand to halt their departure. "First, Kristi, you'll let us read the data, won't you? Then cluster four can try to unravel this mess ahead of everybody else, including the cops."

Kurt looked dubious, nervous. He rested a hand on Don's arm, his eyes full of pleading. "What if, uh, there's something, er, bad about us, Mrs. M? Don and me, I mean. Can we get Kristi to delete that stuff first?"

"Come off it, you two," Kristi said. "The two innocent lambs among us? What's anybody likely to say that could possibly embarrass the charming Delanos?"

"Never mind." Aggie shooed them away, like a gardener upset with bunnies nibbling the carrots. "Be off with you. We'll tackle minor problems as they occur."

Aggie's idea might have had merit, but it didn't reach fruition or even bud. Too little, too late. Because just then Penelope burst into the room wearing a full-length billowing gown of white gauze. Eyes blazing, body trembling, arms stretching high and wide, she twirled about in all directions. Then she shouted, "We must pray!"

Astounded, everybody stopped talking, sipping coffee, and shuffling their feet to freeze and stare. Where was the timid, wispy waif everybody knew? Devoured by and replaced with this avenging angel?

Standing in the center of the room, hands now folded in the prayer gesture, Penelope neither lowered her head nor closed her eyes. With eyes wide open she stared at the ceiling. In a voice loud and shrill, she exhorted her God for intervention, pleading for the forgiveness of sins too dastardly to define.

Abruptly Penelope ceased whirling to address and encompass her stunned audience. "We're all going to die if we don't act. Now! Everybody! We've got to lift our voices in mighty prayer and anthems unto the Lord. Plea, beg for deliverance from our destiny--death by fire!"

Lucille, who'd entered on Penny's heels, looked like she didn't know what to do—spit or go blind. Aggie tried to define what she saw on Lucille's face-- dismay? fear? No, panic was the best label Aggie could pin on the Bailey woman. Lucille turned toward the exit.

Too late.

Penelope caught Lucille by the arm, tugging at her, pushing her forward into center position. "Lucille, you lead us. Oh, sinner, pray for forgiveness, pray, pray pray!"

Like the Biblical Lot's wife, changed in the blink of an eye from flesh to a pillar of salt, Lucille stood silent and still, her face washed of all color.

Undaunted, Penelope shoved together the group that now numbered four from table four, who by then had also reached the middle of the big room. Apparently strong and able again, Penny hauled and pushed these four central figures, lifting their immobile limbs to attach at the waists, each to the other.

"Come now, everybody, up on your feet and get moving. We're marching, and let's sing it, *Marching to Zion.*" With that, Penelope shoved Lucille ahead of her, clasping the Bailey woman around the waist. Reaching back, she fastened Kurt's robot-like hands to her own two sides.

Ah, a line of dance. Aggie hopped up to join the group. Behind her, Olaf snatched her by the waist. "If I can't have you, doll, at least I can touch."

Now that she was no longer frightened of his stalking her, Aggie could appreciate how nice it was to be found desirable. She glanced over her shoulder to smile at the distinguished former professor of art.

Penelope's clear, high, and amazingly resonant voice rang above the throng with the words of the old hymn, now sung in Dr. P's face. Dr. Petroski suddenly came out of the funk he'd sunk into for days; actually, a mere few hours earlier. Eyes no longer glazed, body no longer slumped, Dr. P stood straight. Smiling, with no words spoken, their former leader passed around the head table to attach himself to Penelope.

Surprisingly (or perhaps not), everybody gave silent consent to follow Penny's example by their mass exodus from their own tables to jump up and willingly participate. Soon the rafters resonated with voices as the long line of humans physically attached to one other snaked about the room and between and among the tables.

Just as suddenly, nature too complied. Thunder crashed and lightning flashed.

The wind shifted.

The heavens opened.

The heavy rains fell.

CHAPTER 30

"I'M EXHAUSTED," MUTTERED LISA to Aggie at the big front window where people gathered to watch the rain falling in great sheets. The two giant beasts of nature battled bitterly, each determined to win: rain versus fire.

"Me, too. My kingdom for a nap."

Lunch was served, finally: peanut butter sandwiches with honey, canned vegetable soup, and milk to drink. Aggie couldn't wait to hear Lisa's news, although she didn't want to admit she hadn't as yet tackled Dr. P. She whispered, "Did you get a look at the shorthand in Maude's notebook?"

"Later," Lisa mouthed, nodding at the table.

"Yuck," Kurt murmured to the group as he spooned the lukewarm soup.

"Ick," growled Mick to Maude at table two over his sandwich. Aggie was lip-reading, but caught nothing significant. Lunch hadn't been worth waiting for. Reggie 's food preparations were no longer up to par.

"I wonder what's the matter with Reggie?" Kristi said. "I'm going to go check on him." In her haste to leave, she spilled her soup. The abandoned sandwich, with only one bite missing and growing soggy in the spilt soup, looked as forlorn as an orphan left out in the rain.

"What's with Kristi and Reggie?" Lisa asked the table.

Don and Kurt grinned. "Don't you know? They just got engaged."

"What?" Aggie couldn't believe that with all their sleuthing, she and Lisa had missed most of this blossoming romance. "How, uh, when did that happen?"

Both eager to speak, the Delanos sang their tale in alternating duet style:

"They've been in love for months."

"Reggie wanted to get married, Kristi resisted."

"Reggie was afraid he'd lose his job because madman Jones was jealous of the kid's efficiency and creativity."

"That's what Kristi told us, anyhow."

"Of course Reggie did have something to hide."

"He had a juvenile record of shoplifting."

"Which is supposed to be secret; a sealed record."

"Reggie was working at the post office and pilfered some stamps..."

"No big deal, because he paid them back; also paid his debt to society with community-service hours. Point is, Jones was the one who caught Reggie; threatened he'd get even, someday. So that's what Sam was holding over Reggie's head. Jones planned to fire Reggie and wanted some scoop off Kristi's personnel files..."

"She said she vowed to 'fight him to the death'. I know, sounds ominous after the fact, but it was just an expression. I'd swear it, wouldn't you, Don?"

"You bet." Don turned to Aggie and Lisa with a knowing grin. "While you're listing suspects, I think you can safely scratch Kristi's and Reggie's names off your list."

"Yeah," Kurt said, bobbing his head up and down like an engine's pistons. "With the fire, and everything else going on, Kristi told us she finally realized life is too short. She doesn't need to stay single to 'find herself'. She and Reggie'll do it together."

"They'll go to Delaware, their home state, as soon as we get away, and Dr. P gives them time off together. Small wedding in her local chapel. If we don't burn up."

Aggie was thrilled. Romance, amidst all the trauma. With such exciting news, she nearly missed hearing Lisa describe Maude's notebook.

Signaling need for a potty break, Aggie and Lisa went off to the restroom. "Are you ready to tell me about the Baileys and the Houstons?"

Aggie summarized.

"I'm thinking seriously about Lucille and the fracas over Max. We don't really know which sister was telling the truth. When we overheard Lucille and Mick in the clearing, he seemed so eager to get a smoke I'm not sure he was all that tuned in. Later, when Maude was telling Mick the same story, though in reverse, Mick didn't seem to question that, either."

"Ah, I'm following you. Whichever sister is lying could be the one with the psychosis and also be the murderer. Only we're back to square one with the same old question: why take out Jones and Akunda, if Max was all along the intended victim?"

Suddenly Aggie felt up to tackling Paul. "I'm going to talk to Dr. P now."

"Well, about time." Lisa gave her cousin a shove out the door.

When Aggie joined him, Paul Petroski said he relished peanut butter and honey. He sat alone at the head table, and told her to pull up a chair. When he reached for his sandwich and missed, she pushed it over to him.

Aggie didn't bother with more chitchat, she simply jumped right in. "Dr. Petroski, my name is Agatha Morissey from Wyoming. I would like to ask you some questions; rather personal, I'll admit."

"Of course, my dear. Yes, I remember you, from our informal chitchats in my suite early in the week. Your husband Randolph is in the oil business; that right? And as of this moment he's in Turkmenistan? I'm sure he must be worried about your safety here in my program; what with the murders and now this fire."

What a memory. How'd he do that? While appearing half-out and then totally beyond awareness, inside his head he'd been reviewing his notes? Never mind. Gulping, Aggie scooted her chair closer to his and turned her head away from the crowd. Who knew, somebody else in the room might also read lips.

"You said you have some personal questions. Fire away, my dear. I have nothing to hide."

She'd thought she was ready to launch her crucial questions, like firing missiles from Colonel Schwartzkopf's Blackhawk, but Dr. P's charisma was getting to her. She wished she could run and hide; anything to avoid prying. Committed, now, Aggie blundered in, like a barefooted, stringy-haired, unwashed flower child into the grand ballroom at the Waldorf-Astoria.

"Uh, while working at the computer, uh, Kristi's computer, we--that is, my cousin Lisa and I--happened to call up your personnel files. I owe you an apology, Dr. Petroski, I know it was a terrible intrusion of privacy, but there it was--your birth date and birthplace, and, uh..."

Paul smiled while he finished chewing a bite of sandwich. Then he grinned, his deep-set blue eyes twinkling. Oh dear, he'd caught her out.

"And of course you 'just happened' to have also accessed Sam Jones' personnel records, too, right?"

Agatha gasped. She might as well have been Dennis the Menace with his frog ready to poke down Mr. Wilson's neck. Caught in the act!

"Never mind, my dear. I know what you and your cousin, the new arrival from Wyoming, have been doing. Trying to solve Sam's murder. Good for you. For both of you. No need to apologize. I could hear your gasp and sense your body tension. It's all right. I appreciate your efforts."

"You must miss Sam Jones a lot."

"Yes, and no. He was a big pain in the butt, that's for sure. But I owed him something."

"From back when you served in Vietnam together?"

"Oh, way before that. We're twins. Fraternal, not identical. Actually, we had two different fathers. Unfortunately, our mother was promiscuous--she had two men, within an hour of each other. She confessed her story before she died. Sam, however, never forgave our mother. He took his own father's name, ran around telling everybody he was the bastard son. It wasn't hard to figure out which father was which; I looked like mine, and Sam looked like his. Sam didn't have to go around calling himself a bastard, but he did. Ran off when he was fourteen. The family didn't know his whereabouts until I ran into him in 'Nam. Then he disappeared again. Popped up here much later and wanted a job. I didn't have anything at the time, but I was so delighted to see him again, I helped him get hired in the post office over at Rutland. Before long my assistant director here quit and I offered Sam the job. End of story. Are you satisfied, dear?"

"No, not quite." Aggie caught her breath. "That's an amazing tale, though."

"What's troubling you? You said my reply doesn't close things for you."

"Jones was obnoxious. Now he's dead. So he must have been something more than just a pain in the behind to somebody else. Was he blackmailing anybody, do you know? And, Dr. Petroski, with all due respect, did Sam blackmail you to get your job recommendation and then the job here with you?"

Dr. P did a surprising thing, then. He threw back his head and roared with laughter. "Yes, of course he blackmailed me. Or he thought he had. Claimed he was going to 'tell the world' that our mother was a slut. He was right. She was. Besides, she's long dead, now. Overdose. That's no secret, though. I've told a lot of people. When the time is right or it's appropriate, like when a client is bellyaching that things aren't his or her fault, he had a bad parent or poor upbringing. Then I tell them about my mama. She paid for her sins. What's that got to do with me? That's what I tell people, that I--like them, like everybody--am responsible for myself. So, you see, Sam's threat was no threat at all. Didn't 'make me no never mind', as they say."

Aggie felt like a limp sail on a calm day. "Bu-but, then, why, who?"

"Who killed him? I thought you might have discovered that by now. I'd hoped you had, or soon would. I'm tired of all this commotion, these people. Guess it's time for me to retire. Forget the consulting business. Go nap in a hammock, like Dennis' neighbor, Mr. Wilson." Dr. P smiled but looked decades older than his age. He had taken Jones' death hard.

"I can guess what you're thinking, Aggie. That I'm too young to retire.

Well, I'm not old at all in years, but in life. I had a bad fall recently, hurt my back. It gives me a lot of pain. And then I think my brain is plumb worn out; carrying around so much information in my head."

"Oh, dear. How did you hurt your back, or is that a secret?"

Petroski grinned again. "You'll love this, Aggie. It fits right in with your opinion of Sam. He threw me down the stairs."

"What? Don't you, uh, hold a grudge? Didn't you hate him for that?"

"Pointless to hate a dead man, isn't it?"

Her mind whirled and twirled again. Paul's confession put him right back on Lisa's list. Had he told her about Sam shoving him because he figured she'd find out, anyhow?

"You didn't answer my question, Dr. P. Do you know for sure or did you suspect that Sam was blackmailing your clients? Or, that he planned to in the future?"

"Yes, of course. I thought that was obvious." Dr. P took another big bite of peanut butter and honey sandwich. He sat there munching slowly, as if to delay the inevitable. Aggie waited; not patiently, just silently.

Dr. Petroski laughed. "Max Houston from Boise turned the tables on poor Sam, though. Came up with his own blackmail scheme. Max was so mad that Jones had countermanded my job offer to his son that he was determined to counter-countermand Jones. Max is--uh, was--an info-techy, you know; a hacker. It wasn't hard for him to uncover and compile Sam's whole shoddy history. Max contacted Kristi and she downloaded Houston's file--the entire record of Sam's criminal background. His history of petty thefts and his bigger con games--mostly blackmail. I guess you didn't get into that; Kristi promised me she'd keep that part of Sam's record secure. Anyhow, Max blackmailed Sam and, grudgingly, Sam admitted the Houston pair as members of the conference. End of that story."

"Not quite. I overheard Lucille say her and Maude's invitation was contrived. That the sisters were set up. Do you know anything about that?"

"Sure. So was your invitation. By the grant givers, the Holloway Foundation. Don't ask me why, though, because I don't know. Harris Holloway, the assistant to the founder of the Salvationists, simply said he was doing you and the Bailey sisters a favor by insisting that your names be included on the invitation list."

"In deep thought Aggie shook her head. Since the blind man couldn't see her, Paul nudged her arm. "Any more questions?"

"Dr. Petroski, your explanation still doesn't explain why Sam's dead. Nor Max Houston, either."

Paul sighed. "Don't I know it. I've been in such a sunken funk, not because I miss Sam. But because I feel like such a failure. I'd planned to see if I could persuade him to submit to counseling and therapy. Probably would have failed at that, too. Anyhow, my head's spinning in trying to figure out what the hell is happening."

Unknown to Aggie, and to everybody else except Reggie, who was up on the roof checking the slate shingles at the time, another drama was about to unfold. Reggie gasped in awe as he spotted the Super Cobra helicopter hovering high above.

Out hopped a parachuter wearing firefighter gear. The chopper set down in the parking lot out back, behind the big bay doors. Right afterwards, a big metal box dropped, also by parachute.

While Reggie stared, the firefighter raced to unbuckle the crate and extract equipment. Nearby trees smoldered. The heat was horrendous. Hauling the contraption, the firefighter hurried to the doors in pursuit of protection from the encroaching blaze.

Reggie yelled, but his croaking voice went unheard in that thunderous roar of the fire that fought to resist death by extinction from the rain. Rapidly descending down the wooden ladder up which he'd climbed, Reggie stepped off at the bottom just as the middle rungs caught fire; a leap of flame, escaping the onslaught of rain, found its target. Luckily, the central complex building was constructed of brick and fieldstone, resistant to fire. Not all of the window or door frames were so fortunate. The newer replacements were made of metal, the remaining old-fashioned ones were not. They too felt the lick of persistent flames.

Unknown to Reggie, and also to Ned Fleetfoot, the firefighter, more theatrics were unfolding in Castleton, not far removed. The President with First Lady Julia and entourage, including Carl Crosby, the neophyte reporter from Arkansas who was now tucked within the exclusive inner circle, and Julia's compassion, waited with the mayors of Castleton and Rutland, the governor of Vermont, Detective Whitehall, and Officer Sylvia Battisti. Everybody was anxious for news.

"Good news, I trust," the President said to Julia and Carl. "Colonel Schwartzkopf should have dropped Ned Fleetfoot by now. Ned has a walkie-talkie."

"We'll be able to set up communications with the insiders," Sylvia said.

"I can't imagine what happened to Sergeant Thompson's field phone," Detective Whitehall complained.

"How do you feel about all this, Mr. President?" Marci asked, armed with her microphone and buffeted by Philip the photographer.

Dominic smiled indulgently. "I 'feel' hopeful, how do you think?"

"Any words for your Arkansas supporters, Mr. President?" Carl Crosby said.

"Sure. We'll have this situation under control in no time, folks; no need for alarm," Dom replied without blinking, stuttering, mumbling or fumbling his words.

Beating Marci and Phil in greeting the Colonel, Carl hoped to once again scoop CNN and all the other big-time media reps. His editor down in Arkansas was ecstatic. So too was the Little Rock press and the Arkansas state governor. Crosby's discovery and early report from Albany was the first in the nation to reveal that the President was present and the U.S. Air Force was involved in the attempted rescue of the conferees trapped in the eye of the forest fire.

Blowing up dust and dirt, Peter landed his whirly bird nearby. He stopped the rotors, switched off the engine, and ran to join Dominic and his party.

All these things were unknown to the insiders, save for Reggie, who was busy administering soothing balm to his blistered hands, and eye wash to his stinging eyes. The rest of the conference participants were about to be hit with another sock to the belly.

"Tom's been shot!"

"Carson's dead!"

"What the bloody hell!" roared Officer Thompson.

Penelope sobbed. The double cousins comforted the little blonde, Aggie clasping the trembling girl in her arms and Lisa going pat-pat.

Outdoors, Ned Fleetfoot sprayed foam on the blazing bushes and smoking wooden window frames. No time to make his presence known indoors; he had to work fast and efficiently.

Malcolm again ordered everybody to convene in the dining room. Almost immediately Lucille and Penelope asked to use the facilities.

Officer Thompson said he was going to take roll, see who else was missing; collect alibis, interrogate, make notes. Reading Malcolm's lips as he muttered to Dr. P, Aggie noted his cliches. He intended to get this show on the road, run up the flag and see who saluted, break the cookie and see how it crumbled, throw out the shoe and see who it fit. Time to shine. You bet.

172

Lisa, seated next to Aggie, appeared quite agitated. "I've got a confession to make," she said. "In case we die, I think you should know."

I don't want to hear this. Aggie took a deep breath.

"I can't believe my housekeeper couldn't find your engagement ring, Aggie. She's a whiz. She said that she and Randy searched high and low, all over your house. I'm so sorry, dear. I shouldn't have sent her over there to prowl among your private things. Please forgive me."

This was the big confession? "What are you talking about?" Aggie snapped, trying to sound like an adult, not a hurt child. Aggie stared hard at Lisa, before glancing down at her ringless left hand. "Susan went to my house to look for my ring?"

"I wasn't talking about Susan, dear. I meant my former housekeeper. You remember Mary Alice. You used to say that she and I looked so much alike, we could have been doubles."

"Mary Alice and Randy? Not Susan, the African-American?"

"Right. Mary and Randy both searched the house for your diamond ring."

Right into my bed! Aggie thought, but didn't say.

"Never mind, darling. I'll help you look when we get home. If we do."

Suddenly a great light dawned, suffusing Aggie's whole being. It was the rebirth of love for her dear double cousin. Aggie threw her arms around Lisa.

Aggie hovered behind the potted palm in the corridor. Lucille's behavior made Aggie nervous, and she meant to follow the Bailey woman. Discover, perhaps, whether Lucille was the compulsive-obsessive sister and not Maude. Lucille disappeared into the ladies' room and shortly thereafter in floated Penelope, looking like a ghost in her gauzy dress. Aggie whipped off her leather belt to wrap tightly around a fist.

She shoved the tub filled with dirt and a potted fake palm in front of her, straight into the restroom. The two women gaped. One of them stared at Aggie from eyes glittering with hate. The other looked so frightened she might have seen a mouse skittering by.

Or a hatpin.

Her belt still wrapped around her hand, Aggie kept right on shoving the tub. Until she was peeking between the fronds straight into the eyes of the killer. A hand, holding the deadly hatpin, shot toward her.

Aggie shifted and shoved. The hatpin went flying across the room. Lucille tripped and slipped on the wet floor, still damp from the janitor's cleaning.

Penelope collapsed in a heap beneath the palm tree. Aggie fell on top of the two women.

But not for long. Belt whipped free, Aggie flung it around the killer's neck and, in two quick movements, swift as the Greek god Mercury, she tightened one end at the neck and secured the other to the palm tree. Then Aggie hopped away. She nodded at the innocent woman, who promptly jumped up to plop down on the killer's feet and sock her in the belly. Aggie stamped her two little feet on the killer's wrists and stared down into a face mottled with rage.

"So, confess, already," Aggie demanded. "Why'd you kill all these people?"

EPILOGUE

NED FLEETFOOT'S HEROISM QUENCHED the fire's most dangerous advance. The fire wasn't out, though injured by its worst enemy--rain. The fire would spread by fits and starts to cover a half-million acres.

The lad who was half-Arapaho and half-Nasty Three knew his business. Ned Fleetfoot got just about everybody to safety, after leading them through the clearing that appeared as a meandering path from the center through the still smoldering trees to the road leading into Castleton.

Half-way through the forest the serial killer broke free from her wrist bindings and dashed into the woods. Alert, Aggie ran after the woman to again attack. Like an offensive end on the UW Cowboy football team.

Down they both went. With Officer Thompson right behind.

While he recuffed the woman, hands behind her this time, Aggie started to get up. Instead she flipped over on her back, right into a burning bush.

Her hair caught on fire.

Burned right down to the scalp before Thompson could beat it out.

"How did you feel when you captured the serial killer?" CNN's Marci asked later, with Philip frantically filming. And then, not totally without feeling, "How do you feel, period? Does your head hurt?"

Not only had Aggie burnt her hair and scalp but she had also singed off her eyebrows and lashes. Following plenty of ministrations--medical from professionals, personal and emotional from family and friends--Aggie was ready to talk.

Instead of answering Marci's questions, though, Aggie stared off into space a bit before looking around at the assemblage. She grinned. "Did you know it was criminologist Robert Ressler, a former FBI agent, who directed the agency's first research program of violent criminal offenders, who coined the term *serial killer*?"

"Good grief," said Lisa.

"What made you suspect her?" demanded Detective Whitehall, ignoring Aggie's condition and her addled jabber.

The detective turned to Marci. "Guess I shouldn't have been surprised. When I called Cheyenne to check on Mrs. Morissey's background, I talked to a Walt Fletcher with the Cheyenne PD. That's when I heard how she'd caught an escaped convict single-handed. Moreover, she foiled a pair of robbers after that."

Sometimes Aggie wished she couldn't read lips. This was embarrassing.

Whitehall turned back to her. "We're all waiting to hear, my dear. What clued you in to her?"

"A number of small things," Aggie demurred. "And one big thing. I believe she's manic-depressive; bi-polar." The psych-soc major didn't name her field or describe how she had recognized symptoms suggesting psychotic and sociopathic behavior.

"Like what little things?" Carl Crosby from Arkansas whispered in her ear.

Julia Davidson had described the youngster's naivete and bumbling to her old friend, Aggie, who could certainly empathize with a bumbler. So Aggie didn't ignore the naïve reporter from Arkansas; instead, she produced straight answers directed at Crosby.

"Body language, rapid personality switches--hot versus cold, shy versus aggressive," Aggie murmured. "She was invariably missing when the murders took place. Sometimes only for minutes. She kept her gun at the ready, taped beneath a toilet tank in the ladies room. And then there was the shorthand, which she could both read and write."

Lisa was sheltered within her husband's bear-like embrace. She could have been a lemon he wanted to squeeze for making lemonade.

Gathered in the cozy living room of the Castleton mayor, with his wife serving cookies and milk, the group continued to question Aggie while she recapped. On one side of the room sat the President of the United States with his First Lady, the mayors of Castleton and Rutland, and the governor of Vermont; with, of course, the secret service people hovering nearby and all around the outside of the neat white cottage complete with picket fence and roses. On Aggie's other side ranged her family: the Schwartzkopfs, Lisa and Colonel Peter, and Ned Fleetfoot. In front of her stood Whitehall, Thompson, and yes, Sylvia, who'd gotten in on the finale, despite Malcolm's efforts to ban the rookie cop. Behind the police stood Carl Crosby and Marci with Philip, though the photographer wasn't allowed to film.

"Why kill so many people? Why Max Houston, for cryin out loud?" posed Lisa, still holding hands with Peter on their end of the chintz-covered couch.

Aggie shrugged from her perch on a big brown leather ottoman. "Why not? A sociopath is deranged. Penny could have overheard Lucille ranting about how Max abused and terrified her; all a lie, of course. It was just the reverse. Lucille confessed to me when I confronted her with our evidence from lip-reading and eavesdropping. For awhile Lisa and I imagined that Lucille's personality disorder made her a likely suspect."

"Maude, too," Lisa added.

"Go ahead, Lisa," Aggie deferred to her cousin. "About the shorthand."

"We figured whoever stole Aggie's journal had to know shorthand. Both Penny and Maude, but nobody else, fit that category. Or so we thought, at first. Actually, Aggie thought it was Gregg shorthand when she spotted Maude's open notebook. Trying to read upside down was what threw her off. Maude often mixes Chinese characters in with her longhand. The fact that it wasn't Gregg shorthand eliminated Maude."

Aggie resumed. "Taking out Tom Carson and Sam Jones was more to the point. They'd both harassed Penelope. Tom's abuse was even worse than Sam's, as he'd sexually molested the poor girl during her childhood while she lived with him and his family. Tom blackmailed his niece into submission with the threat that he'd reveal her initial crime; that she started the fire to purposefully kill her parents…"

"Did she?" asked the President.

Aggie shrugged. "That, we may never know. After a lifetime of Tom blaming her, Penny may not know herself whether she did it on purpose or not at all."

"Penelope talked to you?" Thompson demanded, gawking.

Aggie nodded, but did not elaborate.

"The reason, probably, that Agatha was never killed," Lisa said, "was that Penny actually liked our Aggie. So her attempts to do away with our beloved cousin were pretty half-hearted."

"Like hitting Aggie over the head in the forest?" suggested the President.

"I suppose," Aggie replied. "Though I'm not sure, and we'll probably never know the answer to that, either. I mean, just because Penny's the obvious culprit doesn't mean she was indeed the perp."

"The hatpin was sure enough a red herring, right?" Sylvia asked Aggie, who nodded.

"What about Mishka?" demanded Whitehall.

"Akunda? Hah!" Aggie snorted. "The protestors were correct this time. Penny really did despise blacks; 'darkies,' she called them."

Gasps and mutterings followed. Carl and Marci scribbled furiously. Philip, lost without his videocam, squirmed.

"I don't get it," Thompson grumbled. "How and when did Penelope tell you all this? She was handcuffed to me continuously after leaving the center."

"Some of it in the restroom. The remainder was in the barely coherent note she passed to me. She must have anticipated capture. I believe that serial killers subconsciously seek surcease from their pain and evil doings."

"Aggie was always kind to her," Lisa interceded, as if that should explain it.

"She always is," said Peter.

"That's our Aggie," said Ned Fleetfoot.

"But you were also an intended victim," said Carl Crosby. As he told Aggie, he was embarrassed that a fellow Arkansan had turned out to be the killer. Yet another part of him told him to be proud that he was there at the finish line.

"True, but isn't that also typical of the manic-depressive? Up one minute and down the next. Penelope was pale, frightened, wispy; shortly thereafter she was leading us in prayer, hymns, and dance. She probably couldn't make up her mind whether to kill me. If she'd had her wits together, all of a piece, then yes I'd be dead. But she didn't, so forget it."

"Sounds to me like biting the hand that feeds you," the President said. Julia Davidson nudged her husband and pointed to his upper lip. Dominic Alexander's mustache was dotted with droplets of milk and crumbs from cookies.

Aggie smiled. Sometimes the President still looked like her young, gangly Dom.

At that moment the closet door in the hall burst open and a male figure flew across the foyer and into the room, straight onto the lap of the President. Strong hands reached to claw at Davidson's throat.

"Not my Dom!" screeched Aggie. "Nosireebob!" She stuck out her foot, catching the perp in the groin.

"Eeeeeeee," squawked Harris Holloway.

Crumpled on the floor at Aggie's feet, the stranger with the pink paint coloring the underside of his fingernails mumbled his plan, as if he were bound and determined to finally broadcast it across the land: "I hypnotized Penny and told her to kill the President when he visited you. She wasn't supposed to kill all those other people."

The pair of secret service men standing guard at the front door quickly descended to haul Holloway up by the scruff of his collar.

"What about Mick?" Aggie said, hanging on to Harris' pant leg. She was going to get answers to her questions even if she got thrown into the paddy wagon with him. In Aggie's mind, this was the jerk who'd been pulling the strings behind the players.

"Mick Houston was an FBI plant," Harris muttered. "But I hypnotized him anyway. And then I hypnotized his dad when Max Houston invaded us."

"Didn't work, though, did it," Aggie snarled.

"Part-way," Harris said, smirking at her as they dragged him from the room.

Returning to the others, but with her mind awhirl, Aggie promptly knocked over her glass to splatter milk across the knife-sharp crease in Colonel Schwartzkopf's Air Force uniform. "Oh, dear. Peter, I owe you an apology."

Lisa, armed with big carryall bag and her spot remover, left with Aggie for the bathroom. While Lisa scrubbed, Aggie stood on dainty feet in her bra.

"Aggie, what about Lucille Bailey? She was in the restroom with you and Penny. How did she react?"

Aggie smiled. "Lisa, that might be the one good thing that came out of all this. Lucille was so appalled that we had suspected her. She demanded to know why, of course. When I tried to explain--later, after she got Thompson to take charge of Penny--she had a fit. Maude joined us and confirmed our image of the pretty Bailey sister. Lucille agreed to see a therapist. At least she admitted she needs help."

"For all your bumbling, dear, you do manage to do some things right."

"I must call Joan. She'll be frantic."

"And Joan can tell Nasty Two. After that, you don't need to call anybody." Nasty Two was the Clan Gossip. Lisa passed over her cell phone.

"Mom!" squealed Joan from Wyoming. "Oh, thank God, you're all right. Lisa, too? Ned and Peter?"

"Of course, dear."

"But we heard you caught on fire! We've been so frightened."

"Yes, dear, but a cop beat it out. Burned my hair, though."

"Just?"

"And eyebrows. Eyelashes singed too. Hurts some. But I'll heal."

"What happened to your hair?"

"Gone, dear. Oh well, I can always wear a wig until it grows back."

"I simply can't think straight," whimpered Joan after a pause.

Finally Joan resumed. "Naturally I want to hear all the news; every little thing. Don't you dare leave anything out. First, though, tell me. Did you make any resolutions from your week with Dr. P and while enrolled at the Corner for Cautious Change?"

"Funny you should ask, Joan. Yes, I did. I'm going to take one small step at a time to bring your dad around. First, by telling him how his insults and jibes make me feel."

"Thank God, mom. Now you know why I wanted you to enroll."

"Why, you little snippet! And here all the time I thought there was no 'hidden agenda' with you. That what I saw was what I got."

"Hah. You're not the only one who can fudge the truth and play games."

When Aggie called Randy, his response was typical. He complained of a stomach ache.

"Darling, I hope you didn't eat from those old dishes in the refrigerator."

"Don't be silly. Picked up a bug while abroad." Then he added the usual: "Hey, I'll be expecting some of your delicious fresh-baked bread and apple pie. Better yet, I can hardly wait for some sack time with my beloved wife."

She'd already opened her mouth to start initiating her plan: to tell him how she felt about his insults, suggest they see a marriage counselor, invite feedback. Wait a minute, she didn't have to do everything at once. One small cautious step at a time, that was Dr. P's recommendation.

First things first. Pay attention to Randy. She thought about what he'd just said.

Had she heard correctly? Her husband had called her beloved?